Lov & Punishment

'A fast-moving, funny, poignant novel about love, loss, revenge and punishment.'—*Herald Sun*

'... well worth picking up ... whatever effect it has on you, it can't fail to make you laugh.'—*Good Reading*

'A quirky, painfully honest yet hysterically funny account of one woman's journey towards relationship closure.'—*New Idea*

'... her timing is impeccable.'—*Sydney Morning Herald*

'A fast, poignant and funny novel about life, love and a shiny, sharp pair of scissors from Australia's favourite comedienne, Wendy Harmer.'—*Western Advocate*

'*Love & Punishment* is easy-going chick-lit of the superior kind.'
—*Sunday Magazine*

'Fun rules here, and in the Hollywood ending, so does the fairytale.'—*Sunday Telegraph*

'... a welcome addition to the growing list of chick-lit with an Australian accent.'—*Bookseller & Publisher*

WENDY HARMER is Australia's best-known comedienne. She is a mother of two, veteran of countless international comedy festivals and hosted 2DayFM's top-rating Breakfast Show for 11 years. Wendy is also the author of three books for adults, including the best-selling *Farewell My Ovaries* (Allen & Unwin 2005) and *Love and Punishment* (Allen & Unwin 2006) as well as two plays, a series of children's book about Pearlie, an urban park fairy, and the libretto for *Lake Lost*, a production by Baz Luhrmann for Opera Australia. Wendy has hosted, written and appeared in a wide variety of TV shows including ABC's *The Big Gig* and *In Harmer's Way*. She has also hosted the Nine Network television Logies and has been a regular newspaper and magazine contributor, writing columns for *Australian Women's Weekly* and the *Sydney Morning Herald*'s *Good Weekend* magazine. Wendy is currently working on her new television series *STUFF* which will be broadcast on ABC national television in early 2008.

Love & Punishment

Wendy Harmer

ALLEN&UNWIN

Lyrics on p. 17 are from 'Without You' words and music by Peter Ham and
Thomas Evans © Apple Music Ltd. admin. by Essex Music Australia Pty Ltd.
All rights reserved. International copyright secured. Reprinted with permission;
p. 68 'Sunday Morning Coming Down' by Kris Kristofferson © 1969 Combine
Music Corp. For Australia and New Zealand: EMI Songs Australia Pty Limited
(ABN 85 000 063 267) PO Box 35, Pyrmont, NSW 2009, Australia.
International copyright secured. All rights reserved. Used by permission.

This edition published in 2008

First published in 2006

Copyright © Wendy Harmer 2006

All rights reserved. No part of this book may be reproduced or transmitted in
any form or by any means, electronic or mechanical, including photocopying,
recording or by any information storage and retrieval system, without prior
permission in writing from the publisher. The *Australian Copyright Act 1968*
(the Act) allows a maximum of one chapter or 10 per cent of this book,
whichever is the greater, to be photocopied by any educational institution for
its educational purposes provided that the educational institution (or body that
administers it) has given a remuneration notice to Copyright Agency Limited
(CAL) under the Act.

Allen & Unwin
83 Alexander Street
Crows Nest NSW 2065
Australia
Phone: (61 2) 8425 0100
Fax: (61 2) 9906 2218
Email: info@allenandunwin.com
Web: www.allenandunwin.com

National Library of Australia
Cataloguing-in-Publication entry:

Harmer, Wendy.
   Love and punishment.

   ISBN 978 1 74175 174 1 (pbk.).

   I. Title.

A823.3

Set in 11.5/18 pt Sabon by Bookhouse, Sydney
Printed in Australia by McPherson's Printing Group

10 9 8 7 6 5 4 3 2 1

For Dale, Michael, Paul, Bruce, Louis,
Amanda and Tennyson Street

One

'Now, Francie, I want you to look in this mirror and tell me what you love about yourself. I want you to think of all the good qualities you have and all your talents. Tell me why *you love you*.'

Francie took the hand mirror and looked into it long and hard. She saw the blonde streaked hair with its track of dirty brown roots, the dull grey eyes and puffy eyelids rimmed with red, the trail of watery snot and the flaked, dry lips. It was not, as they say, a good look.

I hate you. You are an utter loser. A fat lump of nothing. Give up. Go home. Disappear from the face of the earth, evaporate into thin air. Just do everyone a favour and fucking die. You will not be missed . . . by anyone . . . ever.

Francie dropped the mirror into her lap and reached for the box of tissues. She howled again and this time the sobs were so deep and resonant it seemed as if they echoed off the sides of a bottomless, dark canyon where her heart should have been.

'OK then, we've obviously got a bit of work to do,' said Faith brightly.

A bit of work? Now there was an understatement, thought Francie grimly. This was more of a demolition job. Knock me down and start again. The foundations are rotten to the core and the house built on top should be condemned. Call tenders. Back up the trucks. Bring in the wrecking ball.

Faith leaned forward and brushed a strand of hair from Francie's damp forehead. 'I think we have some issues here. Fear of abandonment, co-dependence, lack of self-love . . .'

'No, no . . .' Francie snivelled. She looked up from her lap and into Faith's kind cow eyes. 'You just don't get it! It's not that *I* don't love me. It's that *Nick* doesn't love me!

'And as for "a fear of abandonment"? It's not a fear. It actually happened!

'And all this co-dependence crap? Of course I depended on him! If I hadn't depended on him you'd be telling me I had "commitment problems".'

'You're very smart, Francie.' Faith sat back in her red velvet thinking chair and twiddled the row of amethyst rings on her plump fingers.

Too bloody smart for you.

'But you have to ask yourself, if you are so smart, why are you sitting here tonight and paying money for my advice?'

And that, Francie had to admit, was a very, very good question. In fact, there was a simple reason why Francis Sheila McKenzie was sitting in the blue velvet confession chair in the front room of Faith and John-Pierre Treloar, Relationship

Counsellors. Francie's friends had all told her that if she didn't get professional help they would hire a hit man to kill her.

'You have to reach out, Francie. Dip into that well of friendship and love that's there for you when times are tough,' someone had said when Francie finally crept from her bed blinking into the sun like a half-blind opossum emerging from its mother's pouch.

So she'd done that. She'd dipped and dipped and dipped again, until now the well was almost dry and she was scraping through the muddy residue of goodwill with her bare hands. Now even her own mother was screening Francie's telephone calls. No-one could bear to hear the story again. Of how six months ago her lover of five years, Nick Jamieson, had dumped . . . Dumped? Was that a good enough word? How about betrayed, rejected, discarded, abandoned, dismissed, unloaded, jettisoned, disposed of, dispensed with? Let's just say he had left Francie for another woman.

And here was the clincher. This 'other woman' was OLDER than Francie. Eleven years older. What an absolute joke! There were any amount of witty and bitchy remarks to be made if she had been eleven years YOUNGER than Francie. Francie knew them all. She'd rehearsed them in her head.

'He's a child, Francie. You were always too grown up for him emotionally.'

'It's all about his dick. It's physical. It's gotta be. It'll wear off.'

'Men . . . they just don't want the intellectual challenge of women their own age!'

3

If Nick had run off with a twenty-one year old, Francie would have been automatically declared the winner. But this woman was forty-three! Middle-aged! That made her fourteen years older than Nick! Almost a decade and a half older! This left Francie with the obvious conclusion that it was *her* everyone was making witty and bitchy remarks about. *She* was the one who was emotionally stunted, intellectually challenged and bad in bed.

Every way Francie looked at it, she was the loser. And if you wanted icing on this monstrous, towering, ten-tiered loser cake, here it was: this other woman was also FAMOUS! Famous in the worst way possible—she had the enduring respect of her peers and the general public. Her name was a byword for credibility and integrity throughout the land. It was enough to push you right over the edge.

Poppy Sommerville-Smith was an actress, *Daahling!* Not one of those television or cinema lightweights—though of course she'd taken the odd character role in a dramatic mini-series or art-house movie—but a real *stage* actress. A '*marvellously gifted, intelligent, intuitive*' actress. Shakespeare, Molière, Brecht . . . all that.

When you saw her fine-boned face on a theatrical poster— the luminous dark eyes and the gracious, cultivated curve of her mouth—you just knew the show would be an *eagerly anticipated, first-rate, landmark production!*

And then she was billed with Francie's leading man. Nick and ~~Poppy~~ (Francie couldn't say their names in the same sentence)! Nick and this rat-faced, predatory, dried-up, desiccated old hag, had met during a production of Chekhov's *The Seagull* by the Melbourne Theatre Company. The play should have been called *The Pterodactyl* as far as Francie was concerned. And the bitter irony of it was that in the play they had taken the roles of Madame Arcadina and Konstantin. Mother and son! And what charming little incestuous tableaux had been played out backstage in their adjoining dressing rooms?

If Ms Sommerville-Smith had merely been prettier than Francie, she could have handled it. If all it had taken was hairdressing, dieting, teeth-whitening or yoga at some luxury spa, Francie could have done that. But there was no luxury spa where one could go to become *gifted, intelligent and intuitive.*

If it had taken some kind of cosmetic procedure like having Botox or collagen or silicone injected or implanted, Francie could have done that too. But unfortunately, Francie felt what she needed wasn't some bovine extract or fish toxin or man-made substance. It couldn't be bought in a glass vial. It was *charisma*! That certain something, X-factor, star quality which Francie didn't have and felt she would never, ever acquire as long as she lived.

Not that Francie didn't have her own creative talents as a cook, home decorator and writer. And not that Francie was unattractive. She was actually very nice looking. Her face was a perfect oval and her features were absolutely symmetrical. Dove grey eyes were expertly placed on either side of a nose which was just the right size. Her top and bottom lips were balanced in an almost mathematical equation and her mouth was in exact proportion to the rest of her face. Her skin was a nicely chosen fair shade and even her freckles seemed to have been art-directed to smatter over the bridge of her nose in a pleasing arrangement. She was of regular height and shape.

In fact, if you were a child drawing a pretty lady, this is how you would have made her, right down to the fair hair flicking up at her shoulders. And that's how Francie thought of herself— as a line drawing on a piece of paper. Neatly coloured in. She was unfinished, insubstantial. She was a cartoon compared with the prize-winning portrait of Poppy Sommerville-Smith. And in the end she had been screwed up and thrown in the bin. She was not being hard on herself, she reasoned, just realistic.

How had this happened? Where? Why? When? Nick had said over and over that nothing had happened. Well, not until his relationship with Francie was over. And when was that? Er . . . that was a bit tricky to pin down . . . Exactly.

'It didn't go past a few kisses,' Nick confessed after one particularly acrimonious session with Francie. 'We mostly just sat and talked about what to do about our problem.'

Our Problem? This, of course, had been Francie. And how does a woman you have slept with for five years, who wants to have kids with you, who has helped support you financially and adores the ground you walk on, end up being a *problem*?

And how does this same woman end up being *our* problem? Meaning a problem shared with someone you've only known for three months and, apparently, have only kissed? And why didn't Francie see any of this coming? None of it made any sense. So, that's why Francie was sitting here tonight in the blue velvet confession chair in front of Faith Treloar. She was looking for answers and was prepared to pay good money to find them.

Faith kept on quietly handing Francie tissues as she sat and sobbed. When at last she came up for air Faith spoke calmly with a reassuring hand on Francie's knee: 'Let me tell you what we are going to do here in this room together. We are going to do some, what we like to call, *grief-work*. We are going to understand your loss, resolve it and move on. How does that sound?'

Impossible. That's how it sounded. Faith searched Francie's face for signs of acceptance or a shred of courage. There were none.

'Do you think there's any chance he'll come back?' she whispered.

'No, I don't,' said Faith. 'I think you have to face it. He's gone.'

Francie had such a broken, sad, hopeless look about her that, honestly, if she was an animal you would have taken a shotgun and put her out of her misery. And at that very moment Francie would have thought you were doing her a favour by blowing off her head.

Two

From: Jennyk@uhu.com
To: ssingle@SunPress.com
Subject: Help!

Dear Francie,

My boyfriend Steve and I broke up last year. We have already had 'one last bonk'. Now he wants another one. Can you have more than one? How many can you have before you're actually back together again?

Jennyk

Of course, Francie was exactly the wrong person to be asking for advice on this question. She really wasn't a well woman. But it so happened that her *Seriously Single* column in the *Sunday Press* liftout section, *P.S.*, was one of the most popular features of Melbourne's top-selling weekend newspaper.

After the break-up, Francie had taken three days off when she lost the ability to stand upright. But then she'd had to come back to work. In most cases going back to work and 'keeping your mind busy' would be a good thing. Especially if you worked handing out tickets to lovers illegally parked, or maybe in the tax department. Or in an abattoir. But Francie's job meant that every day she sat in the office wading through dozens of emails from battered and bewildered ex lovers from all over the country. This should have made her feel that she was not alone. Instead it made her feel as if she was yet another victim of a nation-wide epidemic of despair.

It would be fair to ask how someone who was thirty-two years old was still writing a column for a liftout in a Sunday newspaper. But that would be making the assumption that every journalist had ambitions to be a foreign correspondent or the editor of a prestigious magazine. Francie didn't. She'd seen enough award-winning journalists up close to know it wasn't what she wanted. She'd seen them at election time staggering into the office late at night dragging suitbags and laptops. Watched as their faces pitched forward in despair when they saw their cubicles had sprouted a dense foliage of urgent yellow Post-it notes in their absence.

She'd heard them arguing over the phone about why they couldn't leave the office to pick up the kids from day care, take the car in for a service or make it to the restaurant before dessert. 'Just start without me,' was a phrase she had heard her colleagues say so often that she wondered how they'd managed to have kids in the first place. She vowed never, ever to utter these words herself. She would always be there, on time, for her own life.

Francie had had her chances to fly. She'd even left the *Daily Press* for two years to take up a position as a feature writer on a new lifestyle magazine. For a year she'd produced not much more than bright, enthusiastic paragraphs about scatter cushions, scented candles and designer appliances. She'd helped out with photo shoots of perfect interiors in some of the nation's finest homes. She'd fetched and carried teapots, trivets and trinkets to be artfully placed by perfectly polished stylists. Francie felt as if she was a chipped earthenware plate on a table set with fine bone china.

After twenty editions of *Here and Now* it was suddenly *been and gone*, and she had absolutely nothing to show for it except one hundred and fifty free cookbooks and a vanity unit crammed with sample-sized jars of body lotion and sea salt scrubs. Oh . . . and there had been an eighteen-month relationship with a carpenter from an infotainment television show. She suspected he'd used the same excuses with her that he used with his clients: 'I'll be there next Tuesday, if it isn't raining.'

In the end he'd left her for the skinny whippet blonde who presented the wall-stencilling segment. They'd published a best-selling book of handmade children's furniture featuring recycled wood and decorative bio-paint finishes.

Francie was glad to get a job back at the *Press*. The *Sunday Press* to be exact. She was 'a good little writer with a lively turn of phrase' according to the managing editor. While she wasn't going to the parliamentary press gallery any time soon, that was fine too. She hadn't realised how much she'd missed the atmosphere of a newspaper office, where the thunderclouds of breaking news rolled over the vast open plain of desks and cliff faces of glass. Francie watched with endless fascination as journalists, editors and subeditors were stirred to frenzied activity by the approaching storm fronts of world events.

She smiled to herself to see her female colleagues at the *Press* scurry past her corner desk with rubber bands in their hair, leather scraped off the heels of their shoes, buttons missing and paperclips holding sunnies together. It was a relief to be back where crimes against fashion didn't rate a second glance. She'd almost copped an on-the-spot fine for wearing a floral scrunchie at *Here and Now*.

Francie had an affection for *P.S.*—the weekly ten-page liftout on Melbourne's arts and entertainment scene of which she was deputy editor. There were contributions from various arts reviewers and columnists to be edited and the odd feature story to write, and she enjoyed free access to every nightclub, music and arts venue in town. But she had a suspicion that she should have been feeling more. Where was her ambition? Her drive to succeed? It was something she could barely admit, even to herself, that without a relationship, there didn't seem to be much point to it all.

Five years ago everyone had been partying like it was 1999 . . . which it was. But where was the man to guide *her* around the dance floor? With the New Millennium on offer, supposedly revealing a fresh horizon of boundless opportunity, what she really wanted was a nice boyfriend. It was hardly the sort of aspiration which was likely to make it into print: 'What I'm looking forward to in the New Millennium is someone to kiss me on the back of the neck and bring me a glass of water in the middle of the night.' *Francis McKenzie, 26, journalist.*

And then she had met Nick. It was on a chilly July night at the opening of the Melbourne Film Festival. Within six months she had waved goodbye to her mother and brother in the family home in the outer eastern suburb of Blackburn and set up house with him in a little worker's cottage in the back streets of inner city Richmond.

The years at work had then flown by in a distracted haze as Francie lived for the holidays and weekends she spent with Nick. They shopped for furniture, painted walls and hung pictures together. Francie learned to cook. She and Nick planted a garden. And when she stood and regarded her creation—from the cast-iron front fence threaded with white tea roses, to the wooden back fence and its trellis of jasmine—Francie had a sense of pride and achievement she had never quite found in her day job.

Francie had been surprised when she was given the new *Seriously Single* column by the then *P.S.* editor. Giving Francie— who regarded herself as an almost 'smug married'—the job of writing a column for sad singles had seemed like a joke. But she'd made a success of it, despite the fact that before her own break-up she had been dipping into a ragbag of well-worn platitudes to answer readers. Fragments of half-remembered stuff which had happened to her when she was a teenager, second-hand stories from friends and snippets out of self-help books.

She couldn't really take her readers seriously back then. You can't find a man? Look harder. Your boyfriend had a one-night stand with another woman? Dump him. All the men you meet are wrong? Too picky. Your boyfriend's left you? Buy a new hat. But now! Now she was an expert on being single and her replies to the lovelorn had that unmistakeable ring of authenticity. There was an air of desperation and a hard core of bitterness which made readers recognise her at once as a kindred spirit.

So . . . to the matter at hand. Should 'Jennyk' go back to Steve for another 'last' bonk? Once she would simply have replied 'no way' and moved on to the next inquiry. But now, Francie thought differently. She knew that if she had one more chance to lie next to Nick, she would take it, no matter what the consequences.

The thought of never smelling his chest again, of never hearing him murmur 'I love you so much' on his last breath before he slid into sleep. Never being able to wake early just to see his face in perfect peace on the pillow beside her. The way his top lip formed a glorious cupid's bow that she wanted to kiss into wakefulness so that when he opened his caramel brown eyes, the first thing they would see was her. The thought of never being able to do any of this again tightened a band of grief across Francie's chest.

Francie wanted to reply to Jennyk: 'Seduce him into bed any way you can. Drug him if you have to. Tie him up and sit on him. Throw away your birth control and get pregnant. Make him marry you. Live "happily ever after".'

Instead she typed:

Dearest Jennyk,

I know (hell, do I know) that when you feel lonely and sad you want to turn to the person who is the greatest source of joy in your life. But, tragically, Steve is not that person anymore. OK . . . one last bonk is understandable, but two is regrettable and three is unforgivable. (Are you two in love or just lazy?)

You have to kick your Steve habit—and fast. Leave him out of your romantic (and sexual) fantasies. Think about anyone BUT Steve . . . George W Bush should do the trick.

But, since I know it's inevitable that you will go back one more time, TRY NOT TO DO IT AGAIN! One day I hope you will stop bashing yourself up.

PS I can come over and hit you in the head with a rock if you want the same sensation.

She hit 'save' on her computer screen.

If only Francie had the chance for 'another last time'. But the one night she had with Nick PP (Post Poppy) had been an embarrassing fiasco. She had managed to get him into bed at least, and have sex (sort of), but the aftermath had been bloody.

The plan had been simple enough. It was four weeks since Nick had moved out. *The Seagull* had finished its run and Francie thought that once he saw Madame Arcadina (aka Madame Predator) away from the footlights he would come to his senses. She knew Nick was infatuated with her but, after all, actors had infatuations with their leading ladies all the time. They wore off. If you discounted Paul Newman and Joanne Woodward . . . Will Smith and Jada Pinkett Smith . . . Tom Hanks and Rita Wilson—aaargh! Think about Tom and Nicole instead!

She had rung him on a Friday afternoon to ask him to come over to the house in Richmond that Sunday night to collect some cardboard boxes of clothes and CDs. He had agreed. Her hands were trembling as she hung up the phone and her mind raced with a thousand scenarios. The one she settled on— stupidly, idiotically (looking back)—was that he was coming home for good.

The Saturday had been spent in a frenzy of preparation. Francie had already lost four kilos from her amazing new weight loss plan of substituting alcohol for food, so the size-ten jeans were dragged out from the bottom of the cupboard. The morning had been spent in the groovy boutiques of Chapel Street looking for a top to go with them. Nothing sparkly or obvious, but something which showed off her newly svelte midriff. She settled on a beaded singlet in a fetching shade of heliotrope. Which rhymed with 'hope'. A moody blue-violet which she knew set off her fair hair and grey eyes.

The afternoon was spent with her hairdresser. She didn't want a radical new look, which, after you had been dumped, was always a neon sign of desperate transformation. As if you weren't trying to cheer yourself up so much as get into a witness protection program. She just wanted her hair a touch blonder, brighter and more optimistic.

On the Sunday afternoon she had taken a long bath. Exfoliated, moisturised, painted nails and shaved legs and underarms. Again, nothing obvious, just tried to compose a picture of herself at her lovable best: the Francie who Nick had come home to after a long day in rehearsal and been inspired to say, 'Look at you, you beautiful thing! Come here now and kiss me.'

As the shadows grew long over the little house, Francie had paced from room to room. She'd watched stylists art-direct perfect, beckoning, welcoming interiors. She knew it was all in the detail. The small touches which registered in the subconscious and made you long for home. Surely Nick would see them too. The way the old wooden floorboards in the kitchen shone a soft toffee brown under the single bulb and its tortoiseshell shade. The way the red velvet piping on the old Art Deco armchairs invited you to trace their contours with your fingers. The way the mantelpiece they'd painted a soft rose picked up the same shade in the pink and cream floor rug. She remembered them both standing back and holding hands as they admired their artistry. With a brilliant piece of lovesick logic she figured that while Nick might have left her, he surely wouldn't want to leave this house!

But there were still so many decisions to be made. Should she put on some music? Dave Matthews. Their favourite, 'The Christmas Song'? It was the song they played over and over when they spent 'Happy Holidays' in New York in the snow. No. He'd know straight away it was a set-up. She realised she was humming 'White Christmas'.

A bottle of wine? Champagne? That would imply there was something to celebrate. Maybe he'd bring a bottle with him. If she saw it in his hand she'd know.

Should she cook? Roast lamb, his favourite? But that would have the whiff of seduction about it even more than the music. Would cooking for him show she was a victim? Waiting for him to carve? Or just that happy domestic life went on without him? He'd see through that too. No-one cooks roast lamb just for themselves.

She should open a bag of potato chips. That would be a casual gesture. Leave them in the bag or put them in a bowl? STOP DOING THIS!

I can't live . . . if living is without you! Aaargh! An ACTUAL Bridget Jones moment! Save me!

Candles? Too obvious. Maybe she would burn the candles an hour earlier and leave the scent of ylang-ylang hanging in the air. How long would ylang-ylang hang in the air anyway? And then she couldn't get ylang-ylang out of her head. Ylang-ylang, ylang-ylang, ylang-ylang! If she hadn't been so distracted, so dumb, so pathetically, hopelessly needy, she would have recognised the sound of a warning bell.

In the end she elected to go with k.d. lang, the potato chips (in the bag) and a glass of white wine. She burned one vanilla-scented candle, turned on the lamps in the lounge room and curled up in an armchair with a magazine. This is how she would be discovered. Peaceful and content. Cool, contained. Single, singular. It would look entirely casual to the untrained eye. Although a forensic expert inspecting this crime scene at a later date would have noted the fridge stocked with beer, the scrubbed bathroom and clean sheets, and deduce that someone was definitely expecting something more than a casual visit.

By the time Nick arrived two hours late at 9 pm, the candle had burned down leaving an acrid smell in the air. She'd turned off the stereo, thrown her magazine at the wall and was well on the way to being drunk. This was unsurprising since she had eaten only three pieces of sushi and two potato chips all weekend and had consumed almost a bottle of chardonnay since six. Her careful art direction was coming unglued.

When, finally, Nick pushed open the front door and walked into the lounge room, Francie barely managed to restrain herself from running into his arms. Her grief at the loss of him was perfectly understandable. It was as if one half of her own body had been hacked off with an axe. And now here he was, as familiar to her as her own arms and legs. She would have liked to attach him like some flesh-coloured prosthesis so she could start walking again.

He looked as handsome as he ever did. Tall and lanky with his shiny black hair longer than she remembered, and falling down over his eyes. He looked good in anything he wore. Tonight it was jeans over boots, a scruffy red T-shirt and an old denim jacket.

His shuffling, awkward movements and lack of eye contact kept her at a distance. They both could sense there was an empty space between them which one of them had to have the courage to broach.

You could have guessed the place where their strangulated small talk turned into one of the most passionate moments Francie and Nick would ever experience in their lives. It was in the bedroom. She was going through the wardrobe to find Nick's favourite brown suede jacket. He was sitting behind her on the bed. Their bed, for five years. She knew he was looking at the Degas print on the wall they had brought back from their visit to Paris.

He finally said, in a strange, sad whisper, 'Francie. What's happened to us?'

She turned and replied, 'I don't know. I'm scared. I miss you so much.'

And then he reached out to her and pulled her down on the bed. They clung to each other so tightly it was as if they were on the edge of a precipice. In front of them was a drop of a thousand feet into blackness.

Nick cried as he kissed her. He traced his tongue over her flat stomach and expressed amazement at her new sharp hipbones. He cried as he buried his face in her breasts, her hair, between her legs. Francie cried too. She only remembered it later, because while she was with him it felt as if her rational mind had gone and she was just a dead thing which was being coaxed back to life by the smell and touch of the divine. Then he was inside her and she wrapped her legs around him. Francie felt she was about to have a full-on Mills & Boon 'oneness with the infinite' moment when reality whacked her hard across the side of the head.

'Have you got any condoms?' Nick had stopped moving and was looking down at her in the half-light coming from the open doorway.

And then Francie blew it. It was as if she had seen the edge of the cliff and suddenly decided to hurl herself off.

'Don't stop, Nick. Let's keep going. Let's have a baby.'

In the deathly silence after Nick had pulled himself out of her and rolled over onto his back, Francie sensed she was falling, falling, falling. His next words signalled that she had hit rock bottom.

'No. I don't want a baby with you, Francie. Is this some kind of trap? Because if it is . . .' Nick sat up, 'it's fucking tragic.'

Then he was pulling on his jeans and finding his boots. Francie could say nothing. She turned her face into the pillow and opened her mouth to howl in agony but not one sound came out. She could hear him hauling on his jacket. She knew Nick was angry.

'I knew I shouldn't have come here. I tell you something, if I am ever going to have a child, it won't be because I've been seduced into it. It will be something I do consciously with someone I'm in love with.'

As soon as he said those words Francie knew she would never forget them until the moment she died. Although that moment might come in the next few seconds.

She knew Nick was standing above her now, looking down at her bare back. She must have looked so pathetic lying there that he was moved to pity. He sat down on the side of the bed next to her, sighed and spoke deliberately.

'I'm sorry. I shouldn't have said it like that. I do love you. Obviously. That's why I see you and end up in bed with you. But I don't want to be in a relationship with you anymore. I don't want to be with anyone. I thought I'd explained all that.'

Francie could feel her shame and humiliation solidify into blind rage.

'You—have—not—explained—anything—to—me,' she said into the pillow.

Then she rolled over, pulled the sheet to her chin and sat up. She struggled to control her voice as angry tears stung her eyes.

'You told me you wanted to end this. You told me you were leaving. You said you wanted to be by yourself. And that's it, Nick. That has been the only explanation I have ever had from you.'

Nick stood up and walked to the bedroom door. He turned to her.

'I have tried to explain to you, but you won't listen . . .'

Francie dragged the sheet from the bed, wrapped it around her bare body and followed him. She was whining, pleading. She couldn't help herself.

'I *am listening*! Why don't you love me anymore? Is it because of her? When did you stop loving me? Do you love her now? How did it happen? Why didn't you give me a chance? Why was I the last to know? YOU HAVEN'T TOLD ME ANYTHING!'

Nick was now standing by the front door. His hands were thrust deep into his jacket pockets and he was inspecting his scuffed black boots. Francie screamed at him, knowing that half the street would be able to hear her. She couldn't give a shit.

'AND WHAT? WHAT AM I SUPPOSED TO DO NOW? HOW AM I SUPPOSED TO UNDERSTAND ALL THIS WHEN YOU WON'T TALK TO ME? TALK TO ME!'

Nick opened the front door and the cool air of the evening rushed inside. Francie leaned against the wall in the hallway and pressed her hot, wet face into the plaster.

'I can tell you one thing for sure. I want you to know that if we had had a baby, I never would have left you.'

And with that Nick had walked out the door.

Now, Francie sat at her desk in the office asking herself, for the millionth time, what he'd meant by that. Did he mean that they *should* have had a baby? No, he couldn't have meant that because she'd brought it up with him before and he always said he wasn't ready. She guessed what he'd meant was, that if he had been a father he would never have abandoned his child. That meant he would have stayed in a loveless relationship with her for the sake of the children. And that, ladies and gentlemen, was supposed to demonstrate to Francie that he was a good, moral man. Only it didn't.

Barely a week after that humiliating night, Francie was sitting by the window on a tram in St Kilda Road when she saw them walking hand in hand outside the Arts Centre. She watched as they paused to kiss. She had stumbled off at the next stop and been sick in the grass just next to Melbourne's famous floral clock.

Francie looked at the clock on her desk now and at her calendar. The time was 3 pm, the date was 19 November 2004.

It was exactly six months since Nick had walked out. She read the thought for the day: 'The best and most beautiful things in the world cannot be seen, nor touched . . . but are felt in the heart,' *Helen Keller (1880–1968)*. Well, that was true. She hadn't seen Nick for six weeks and hadn't touched him for longer, but, in her heart, he was at his beautiful best. Stop this! Stop thinking about him like this!

The worst part of it was that Francie was a writer. She was supposed to be good with words, but whenever she thought about her life now, the best script she could come up with was a soap opera with a soundtrack by Enya. If Francie could have composed her own 'Thought for the Day' it would have consisted of just one word—*Why?* It would be a great merchandising opportunity—a desk calendar for the brokenhearted. Only trouble was, the first six months would seem like yesterday. And the next six months would stretch into infinity.

Francie sighed and had finally managed to drag her mind back to the screen in front of her when a familiar fog of Chanel Christalle perfume settled over the desk.

'So, you all set for the big move tomorrow?' Gabby Di Martino pushed Francie's in-tray aside and found herself a perch. She tossed her long, tawny hair and crossed her long, tanned legs.

Gabby was the newly appointed editor of the paper's weekly *P.S.* section. It was the job Francie might reasonably have been expected to get when her previous boss left to have a baby, but she'd been passed over. Maybe someone in management had seen Francie was just going through the motions of late. Noted the pile of sodden tissues beside her keyboard and registered *emotionally unstable*.

'It's not anything personal, you understand,' the managing editor had told Francie. The disembodied voice echoed from way, way down one end of a mahogany desk that was big enough to accommodate a space shuttle landing. Francie was down the other end. A small, blonde sandbag which had lost most of its contents.

'*Ms Di Martino is a talented and capable journalist and we at the* Sunday Press *are thrilled to have such an experienced staffer keen to take up the reins on* P.S.'

The dark wooden doors had closed behind Francie and left her standing in the corridor to piece together the story.

Gabby Di Martino had unexpectedly landed back in town from Sydney. Francie wondered if she had compromising photographs of someone on the fourth floor in a zippered compartment of her butter yellow Dior handbag. A minion at ground zero would have to be sacrificed to make way for her. The minion would be Francie, who by now was accustomed to being everyone's favourite doormat. She didn't mind. In fact she thought she'd be better suited to compiling the obituaries page. Or maybe even that obscure paragraph of the *Sunday Press* titled 'Late Changes to Television'.

The entire third floor had been mesmerised watching Gabby move her gilt-edged mouse mat and plug-in make-up mirror into her office. More information came to hand as the days went by. Impeccable sources had it that her sudden arrival in Melbourne had indeed been precipitated by a ruinous love affair with a certain publishing executive. She had come down south to cool her high heels and wait for the old bastard to negotiate a settlement with his vengeful wife.

This explained why Gabby, at the age of thirty-five and looking every inch the glamorous media princess, had been banished to the far-flung reaches of the *Press* empire. She should have been editing a glossy magazine from an office with a grandstand view of Sydney Harbour. Instead she was in Melbourne looking out at the arse-end of a five-storey car park. From what Francie could see, Gabby seemed to be taking it reasonably well. There was the sense she was just passing through. Someone would appear with a getaway limo and spring her out of this dump any day now.

So Francie was still deputy editor of *P.S.* with seniority over . . . well, no-one in particular. There were only three permanent staffers to put out the supplement every week. Gabby, Francie and a young designer named Gus, who sat opposite her. He answered to no-one, and that wasn't just because he couldn't hear the questions through the iPod superglued to his ears. Francie suspected Gus spent most of his time at his work station playing *Warcraft* online. She was right. In fact he'd just won a gruelling orc battle in Gnoll Wood in the Frozen Throne Tournament and was through to the preliminary finals. He was celebrating with an icy cold can of turbo-charged caffeine.

So, spot the odd one out in this corner of the office! There was Gus in his shabby black Judas Priest T-shirt, Francie in her one good grey wool crepe suit with the jacket buttoned up because she had inadvertently worn a black bra under her white singlet, and Gabby Di Martino wearing a sleeveless emerald green satin wrap dress, silver pencil-heeled sandals and chandelier earrings. Give up? Francie already had.

Oddly enough, and for no particular reason that Francie could fathom, Gabby had decided to take on Francie's rehabilitation as a pet project. She inquired after Francie's wellbeing, brought her little presents. Francie sometimes imagined Gabby as a nurse, her marshmallow breasts stuffed into a tight white uniform. She was standing at the end of a pair of handrails while Francie shuffled along in her dressing gown: *Come on now, luvvie. Just one more step. You can do it. You're not tryyying.* Sometimes Francie wanted to say, 'Bugger off and let me crawl back to bed.'

Gabby thrust a pink velour leopard-print make-up case under Francie's nose and cooed sympathetically, 'I've got a sweet little bag here you can pack your g-string in, darls.'

'Big Night Out Beauty' was the name Gabby had given to a column she had created especially for herself. Even the piles of free stuff from cosmetics companies didn't make the extra duty bearable as far as Francie was concerned. She couldn't imagine the boredom of spending even three paragraphs waxing lyrical about 'triple alphahydroxy acnegenic fruit acid complex'. What was it anyway? Face cream? Or fireproofing treatment for Boeing 747 engine housings?

Francie opened the pink case and saw ten Bourjois lipsticks in shades from *C'est Moi* to *C'est Tout*. The sight of the ten little shiny torpedoes decorated with crystals penetrated Francie's black cloud.

'Oh, this is gorgeous! Are you sure you don't want to keep it?' Francie protested, sincerely hoping Gabby wouldn't change her mind.

'Hey, babe! Plenty more where that came from. It's my little lip-warming party for you. Pretty soon you'll have forgotten about Nick the Dick and you'll be on the smoocherama trail.'

Francie winced. 'Don't call him that . . .'

Gabby stood and jammed her fists into her skinny hips. 'Francie! Are you kidding me? The guy is a total loser! He screws your life. He takes up with Cruella De Vil. And you still think he's worth jack? Get a grip, girl. And that's an order.'

Bugger off and let me crawl back to bed. 'Thanks, Gabby. Keep telling me that. I know I've been a pain and really, truly, I am trying to get over it. In fact I went to therapy the other night and the counsellor said—'

Gabby's hands flew to her ears. 'NO! Stop! I don't want to know. My therapy is Appletinis, Brad Pitt in *Fight Club* and a honey bubble bath. The only counsellor I want is a new hard heat-seeking dick. Don't tell me. I know I'm shallow, but I've worked at it.'

Francie remembered she was supposed to smile. Gabby leaned down and placed one long acrylic fingernail under Francie's chin. Francie could smell perfume, breath mints and vodka.

'Look, doll, I think this move is really going to work for you. You know the house is stunning. Everyone knows Jessie! She's brilliant. And wait until you meet Dave! Too cute! Robbie's mad, of course. But they're all single and having a ball. You need this, Francie. You need to change your life. You're too sweet to let this whole bust-up wreck everything. Just be happy, that's all.'

Gabby kissed the top of Francie's head. *Thanks, nurse.*

'Now, I've had a look through this lippie selection and I reckon *Rendez-vous* is your shade. Try it. You could do with a bit of a lift. By the way, we're on deadline, so move it. Byeee.'

Gabby sashayed back to her office. You could see the guys in the sports department standing on the sidelines cheering her parade.

Francie's mind turned to the move tomorrow. The small removal van would be arriving at her house in Richmond at nine in the morning. There were still a few things to be packed tonight. Five years of her life with Nick was now in a pile of boxes by the front door. They were variously marked 'clothes', 'cutlery', 'computer'. Francie thought that perhaps 'shattered dreams', 'bittersweet memories' and 'abject failure' would have been more appropriate labels. She should ring a man to take the lot to the rubbish dump.

She looked at the next email on the list.

From: corinneMc@hotkey.com
To: ssingle@SunPress.com
Subject: Closure

Dear Francie,

My boyfriend left me for my best friend a year ago and now he wants me to come to counselling with him to help him get over the guilt. What do you think?

Once Francie would have thought it was a good idea. Two people sitting down like adults and resolving their conflict, moving on, being happy.

But not now. She typed: 'Take to his car with a hammer and tell him the only place you'll go with him is to a panel beater.'

Francie looked at this and couldn't decide whether to 'save' or 'delete'. She hit 'save' and decided she'd have another look at it when she felt more mentally balanced.

If indeed such a day was ever to dawn.

Three

Later that night Francie was sitting in the middle of her lounge-room floor where the rug used to be. She was draining the last of a bottle of Tia Lusso (low-fat chocolate liqueur) into a glass. As a final farewell she had decided to drink her way through what she and Nick laughingly referred to as their 'drinks cabinet'—a cane basket of sticky liqueurs they stowed under the kitchen table.

Francie had already consumed the dregs of the Frangelico (hazelnut), the Grand Marnier (triple orange) and Amarula (wild African fruit and cream). She should have been feeling numb by now, surely. But no amount of alcohol was going to anaesthetise her during this self-inflicted torture. She was looking through a box of photographs. She might as well have been sticking pins in her eyes.

In years gone by a woman who had split up with a man after five years would be sitting looking through a wedding album. Something bound in white leather with gold embossed letters on the cover—*Francie and Nick, 1999–Eternity*. She would have opened the cover and faded confetti would have fluttered out. Perhaps she and Nick would be quarrelling over who was going to get custody of that very special shot of them gazing at each other through a frosty champagne glass. Or the one with him taking off her beribboned thigh garter with his teeth. Maybe that would have been enough to convince them to give the whole thing another go.

But there was no such thing as a de-facto album. Francie supposed that's what she and Nick had been: 'de-factos'. Such an unpleasant term. She always thought of a de-facto as one of those tacky peroxide blondes who showed up to testify when 'colourful horseracing identities' had their day in court. And it was just as well they hadn't had kids. You can't show the kids a 'de-facto' album. 'Look, darling, here's a polaroid of the night Daddy moved his stereo into my flat.' But was it just as well they hadn't had a wedding?

Francie had a vision of what her wedding to Nick would have been like. It was one of her guilty secrets—flipping through *Modern Bride* magazine. It was chick porno. You could find these hefty volumes at the newspaper office library, and sometimes she sneaked them back to her desk under cover in much the same way as one of the sports writers might have done with a copy of *Penthouse*.

She had made a mental list of what she would have chosen to wear if she had been a bride, and at the top of that list came tulle sprinkled with diamantés. OK, she knew it was hopelessly girlie. That any modern woman should really have been thinking of herself in a simple, elegant slick of white satin, like Carolyn Bessette when she married JFK Junior. But Francie dreamed of the whole princess routine: the Big Dress, the Glittering Tiara, the Glass Slippers, the Lot!

Also on her list were the flowers: peony rose, tuber rose, iris and jasmine; the colours celadon, amaranth, titian and dove; the fabrics organza, duchesse satin, mousseline and silk. These elements, combined with pink champagne, redcurrant candles and a canopy of fairy lights, were interchangeable and could be endlessly configured into a million and one fantasy tableaux. And in the middle of each fantasy was Nick. In a classic black tuxedo. Waiting for his beautiful bride. Holding his hand out to take hers and fly her away to Always and Forever Land.

Actually, she had read that a Japanese businessman was building a wedding theme park on the Gold Coast in Queensland. He was investing $27 million to create 'Wedding World' on 116 hectares of reclaimed mangrove swamp. How romantic would that be? Staging your nuptials at Wedding World? With the knowledge that only 453 000 couples had shared the same identical special moment as yourself.

And imagine all the different 'lands' there—Profiterole Land, Whitney Houston Land, Candelabra Land. Great rides like The Cummerbund, where you're catapulted thirty metres into the air on a giant purple taffeta slingshot. Or The Bomboniera, where you whizz around incredibly fast in a little tulle bag tied with a ribbon. There would be a souvenir shop where you could buy bridesmaids' dresses bearing the legend: 'My friends got married at Wedding World and all I got was this lousy teal taffeta dress with puffy sleeves'. Mind you, thought Francie, with my luck I'd be fast-tracked straight through Wedding World and be queuing up for tickets to Divorce World and Custody Battle Park.

Francie was now, officially, drunk. She tried to focus on a photo of Nick taken on a camping holiday in Tasmania. He was putting up their tent on the edge of Wineglass Bay. He was on one knee, mugging for the camera, holding up a leftover tent peg. Remember that night? So perfectly quiet and still in their campsite hidden in the sand dunes that they could hear the flap of an owl's wing as it fanned the night air. More than this she remembered how she and Nick had squeezed into a double sleeping-bag in their blue nylon tent. How he had slid down her chilled body and his tongue had made a warm, wet trail from her knees to her . . . She chose another photo from the cardboard box.

This one was of Nick in a peacock blue-tiled hotel room in Morocco. He was lying back in bed, bare-chested, with the sheets swathed around his slim hips and his forearm shielding his eyes from the daylight. Remember that morning? She had risen early while Nick slept off the effects of a hash and brandy bender. It was not yet dawn when she took a chair onto their balcony overlooking the town of Fez and curled up nursing a cup of sweet mint tea, watching the *medina* come to life. As the sky faded from black to deepest purple, the first melodic yodel from the mosque called the reverent to prayer. She had seen the first puff of smoke from a whitewashed house, followed by another, then another. Until the bare hills beyond faded beneath a grey-violet haze. Through the lazy, drifting smoky trails she saw a small boy riding a bicycle and dragging three baby goats on a string behind him. She kept watching as the first truck piled with carpets roared up the dirt road in front of the hotel.

That was back in the days when she believed she and Nick loved each other enough to live anywhere. They could be airlifted from their lives and dropped into that whitewashed house over there and live happily ever after with the goats in their rocky pen. And as the new day was born she remembered bringing Nick to life too, with her fingers and mouth. Coaxing his inert body into consciousness. A call to prayer. And she remembered how his hands had reached for her breasts and . . . Every photograph in the box was like this.

Pictures of them from their trip around the world. In Rome watching the fireworks on New Year's Eve; standing in snow in Central Park; sitting on the step of a little shop which sold jewelled clay bangles in a Bombay alleyway. All of them were from a place she could never visit anymore. Nick and Francie Land. A land atomised by a neutron bomb which wiped out all living things and left the buildings still standing.

And then Francie was crying again. It didn't seem possible there could be any tears left! If humans were ninety-five percent water then Francie must have been at the low tide mark by now.

She looked around the bare room. The light shades were packed away and the naked bulbs threw a harsh light onto the ceiling. She could see deep cracks in the plaster up there. She'd never noticed them before. Maybe the fractures had always been there and it was only now she could see the deep fault lines.

There were pale squares on the wall where the pictures had been. The floor was a patchwork of dust indicating where the furniture had stood. She felt she was looking at the set of a movie which had wrapped. The whole team which had made it look real—the lighting guys, the make-up artists, the script-writers—had all moved on and her feature film with Nick was in the can. The photographs she held in her hands were stills from a movie no-one would ever see. *The Nick and Francie Story* had gone straight to video. Hah!

Eventually, Francie was in bed. Next morning she would remember crawling up the corridor on her hands and knees and wailing like an animal with its leg caught in a trap.

That night she had a vivid dream. It was not particularly allegorical, nor metaphorical. Her brain didn't seem able to conjure up anything that complex.

She was riding a bicycle on a yellow brick road through an emerald green valley. She was towing a wolf on a string. Ahead in this storybook landscape she could see a magical white castle, which looked exactly like Sleeping Beauty's in Disneyland. Francie walked across the castle's heavy wooden drawbridge under a portcullis tipped with iron spears. She threaded her way through a labyrinth of deserted cobblestone alleys. Past a market stall selling silver bangles. Past a pretty central courtyard powdered with snow. Wings flapped overhead and she looked up to see Harry Potter's white owl Hedwig leading the way.

And then she was looking through a tiny window down into a cavernous room arched with wooden beams. At the far end of this room up on a seven-tiered dais were two golden thrones. And there, draped in splendid royal purple robes and crowned with all the jewels of Arabia, were King Nick and Queen Poppy. They were a magnificent sight. So radiant with joy and privilege that it hurt your eyes to look at them.

It was then that Francie noticed her skin was brown and furry. Her reflection in a windowpane showed she was a mouse. She scurried down the hallway, her bald, pink tail twitching. Hedwig the owl swooped and her pink-clawed mouse feet scrabbled on the stone floor as she hesitated, then turned and crammed her furry body into a tiny hole in the wall. She brought her paws to her chest, curled into a ball of fear and fought for breath.

Francie woke with her hands balled into two fists in her cleavage. Her heart was racing, she was breathing hard. She saw it all, in an instant. Nick and Poppy were now the rulers of her kingdom. Francie was no more significant than a mouse. Somewhere a wise owl was waiting to make a meal of her.

But she wasn't ready to be caught. No, not yet.

Four

'So, this is the kitchen. And here is the broom cupboard, vacuum cleaner, all that stuff. Although I don't think Dave has discovered it yet,' laughed Jessie.

Francie dutifully inspected the broom cupboard. It was a very good broom cupboard and, amazingly, had a lofty ceiling, just like the kitchen. The kitchen itself, even more amazingly, had a working fireplace. There were alcoves in the wall on either side of it backed with leadlight panels. The ivy leaf design in the glass was echoed in the windows at the end of the adjoining dining room, which was furnished with a long old wooden table. It was a room of stately proportions and Francie had rarely seen a space quite as handsome.

The house was originally Victorian but had been made over in the 1940s with an Art Nouveau-ish, Deco facade. The name *Elysium* was picked out in gloriously extravagant script on the pediment. Francie remembered that, according to Greek mythology, Elysium was the place you went to after death. She couldn't think of a better name for the place she was moving to.

Jessie turned and crossed the hallway. With a flourish she opened a pair of panelled wooden doors to reveal a huge sunny room. It was comfortably furnished with a squashy cream linen-covered sofa and two old armchairs with loose covers of faded pink floral cotton. A television sat in one corner, facing no-one. The bookshelves went from floor to ceiling and were jammed full. Piles of magazines reached the windowsills. There were purple irises in tall vases standing on the floor either side of another fireplace edged with tiles embossed with fern leaves. It was altogether comforting, loved, welcoming.

The windows looked out onto blooming blue hydrangeas. In the rear wall another pair of French doors decorated with amber glass fanlights issued onto a wooden veranda. Jessie hit the stereo and the Rolling Stones blared from the speakers.

'ONE OF THE BEST THINGS ABOUT HAVING A SOUND ENGINEER LIVING WITH YOU—SHIT HOT STEREO SYSTEM!' she bellowed over the music.

'LOOK! OUR LOUNGE ROOM HAS A SPRUNG FLOOR. WE'VE TESTED IT OUT!'

Francie watched Jessie pogo across a red Persian rug.

'ALTHOUGH . . .' and Jessie hit the 'off' button, 'don't fuck with Robbie's stuff or he'll have a panic attack. Robbie's a bit precious, but he's brilliant to live with.'

'So . . .' Jessie folded her arms across her chest and regarded Francie with a pair of large, inquisitive hazel eyes. 'Sorry I wasn't here the other day when you came to check out the room. You should keep the key Gabby gave you. Now, what else can I tell you?'

Jessie walked back to the kitchen. Francie followed and wondered where to begin. Perhaps with the question: 'How come at the age of thirty-two I'm moving into a shared household in St Kilda with a trio of tragic singles when I should be in a two-bedroom brick veneer in Brighton with a baby on the way?'

Instead she opted for something she thought Jessie could answer: 'Um, who does most of the cooking?'

'Well,' said Jessie, peering into one of Francie's cardboard boxes, 'judging by the amount of kitchen utensils you've got in here, I would say it was *you*. In fact, you are the only person I've ever met, in my entire life, who has a melon baller, an ice cream scoop and . . .' Jessie reached into the box and pulled out a small rubber-handled device and held it aloft. 'What the hell is this?'

'It's a lemon zester. I do like to cook. Although I wouldn't say I'm very good.'

Jessie shook her head in amazement. 'At least with you it's a verb—"to cook". Usually with us it's a noun. Someone we can see through a glass wall while we're drinking at the bar! Speaking of which, I think we need a drink. A *welcome to the haunted mansion* convivial.' She took two glasses down from a shelf.

'Haunted? You have ghosts here?' It seemed possible in this rambling old place. It was the first time Francie had ever had a room in a house which had a cellar, a cloakroom, a vestibule and an attic. It was all much grander than she remembered.

'Yeah. Ghosts of relationships past. Spooky exes who ring the telephone, knock on the door, leave weird notes in the middle of the night. All very scary!' Jessie rolled her eyes in mock horror.

'Really?'

'Didn't you see the sign over the door: ABANDON HOPE ALL YE WHO ENTER? Vodka and tonic OK?'

She opened the freezer. Where Francie's freezer had always been stocked with raspberry sorbet and frozen dim sum, this one was stacked with chilled vodka bottles.

'Perfect, thanks. Exactly what does the sign mean?'

'I put that up back in June when I was halfway through the "Great Drought of 2004". Which, by the way, I hope will break before Christmas! It means that if you're looking for a relationship, you've come to the wrong place. The people in this house are cursed to endure an endless string of crappy one-night stands and dead-end affairs.' Jessie grimaced and offered a glass filled to the brim.

'Well . . .' Francie took her drink and sat at the dining room table. 'That suits me. About the last thing I need right now is another relationship. Crappy one-night stands sound like where I'm up to at the moment.'

Jessie opened a window, then sat opposite and lit a cigarette.

'House rules. The boys hate cigarettes inside, but I sit here and have one as long as the window's open. Want one?'

'No thanks. Don't smoke. How long have you all lived here?'

Jessie exhaled towards the window. 'It must be about three years now. I'm thirty-three, so yeah. I was like you, just out of the long relationship. I left. I guess we both wanted different things. I wanted a lover. He wanted a sister. End of story. As far as I'm concerned anyway. You'll get to meet Henry. He's one of the exes who haunts the place. So . . .' said Jessie, holding up her glass, 'here's to the single life. Enjoy. And may it last not a moment longer than you want it to.'

Francie gave her a friendly clink. On first impressions, she liked Jessie. Her face was, of course, familiar to Francie. She was the famous Jessie Pascoe, a stand-up comedian known for her sharp wit and acerbic views on life, love and men. She was one of the resident wits on the Friday night panel show *Talkfest* on Channel O. Everyone had heard of Jessie Pascoe! She was warmer, sweeter—and shorter—than she appeared on television. But both on screen and in person it seemed she'd tell you everything about herself in the first five minutes. Every detail of her life was offered up for a laugh.

She was not a classic beauty, but her big hazel eyes set in a plump round face and her utterly winning smile made her someone you felt you could share secrets with. She was shorter than Francie. Curvy, energetic. Her hair was a dozen different colours and spiked with gel. Overall she reminded Francie of a big-eyed, plump tabby kitten which had been pulled, protesting and wriggling, from a basket.

'But with you being on television, surely men chase you all the time?' asked Francie.

'Hah! I wish!' Jessie took another deep drag of her ciggie. 'When boys meet me they think three things. One: that whatever happens, their details are going to end up on national television—

which they are! Two: that I earn more money than them—which I do! And three: that I am smarter than them—which I am! So, there you go. Who wants to take me out for breakfast when I've just had them for dinner in front of a million people? Well, maybe a million people is stretching it, but you know what I mean.'

Francie did know what Jessie meant. If she was a male confronted with a woman who proudly confessed to being a rich, smart big-mouth right up front, she would have run for the hills too. But then again, Jessie was so bare-faced honest that Francie was mesmerised.

She jumped closer, a rabbit caught in the headlights. 'I never thought about it like that,' murmured Francie, 'I just assumed—'

Jessie talked over the top of her. 'All of which brings me to what we have to get straight, from the beginning.'

This sounded ominous. Francie put her glass down and met Jessie's eyes. She took another rabbit hop forward.

'Now. You write the *Seriously Single* column in the newspaper—which is brilliant by the way—' Francie squirmed with pleasure at the compliment—'and I am a panellist on *Talkfest* on television. Are we going to use stories from each other's lives and, for that matter, what happens in this house? Or, is it strictly *hands off*? Cos I'll warn you right now, I'm a comedian and I just sort of suck stuff out of the air. Everything around me—although it's heavily disguised to protect the innocent—*everything* ends up in a routine somewhere. It's all fodder . . . *material*. I can't help it. And, I suspect, you are exactly the same.'

It was a big question. Francie had never thought of herself as using her private life for profit. But she did, obviously.

'Before you say anything, I promise that I will never compromise your reputation. But the last thing I need is for *you* to tell anyone the details of the passing parade of losers through my life. And if you can promise me that, I'm basically happy. Because if I was a journalist and I met me, I know that the temptation to tell everyone that Jessie Pascoe, who comes over on telly as this worldly wise, smart-arsed chick, is in reality a fucking emotional basket case . . . well, the temptation would be hard to resist. Whaddya say?'

It may have been Jessie's expertise as a stage performer which sucked Francie in, but she felt as if she had found an ally and confidant. Francie also knew she was so unbalanced that she'd lost her ability to judge. In the end, she wanted to trust Jessie, so she did.

'Listen, Jessie, I feel the same. I'm trying to hold down a job as an agony aunt giving advice to the brokenhearted. If my readers knew that *I* was actually the one in agony, that I've just gone into therapy because I can't handle my life by myself . . . well, let's just say you've got a deal.'

Jessie sat back in her chair, stubbed out her cigarette and extended her hand. 'Good girl! Let's agree, it's open season on the "stuff", with no names, no pack drill.'

'That sounds fine to me.' Francie beamed and they shook on it.

'Welcome to the Last Chance Café,' Jessie added. 'You've trekked across an arid wasteland to get here, but it's friendly and we have frozen vodka.'

Francie laughed, but somewhere deep inside another warning bell was clanging. Again, she'd had just enough to drink to take no notice.

✳

Over the next two hours, as the sun moved off the windows and the corners of the old house retreated into shadow, Francie and Jessie unpacked Francie's boxes and found homes for every plate, glass and serving platter. Jessie expressed her delight and excitement as she unwrapped dozens of newspaper parcels. She was like a kid on Christmas morning.

'A lettuce dryer? They actually make such a thing? You're kidding!

'Wine bottle stoppers? You mean there are people who actually only drink half the bottle and save the rest? What for?

'A whole cookbook just on tomatoes? And another one just for garlic? If you've got a fucking pea cookbook in here, I give up.

'Jeez, Francie. Even my mother hasn't got this much crap and she's been married forty years!'

Francie was beginning to be embarrassed by it all. She thought of her own mother in the family house in Blackburn. A single woman living in a house packed to the gunnels with thousands of knick-knacks—doilies, ceramic ornaments, canisters, crystal vases, painted teacups, silver cake forks, gravy boats. Had Francie really collected all this stuff in the short time she lived with Nick? She was turning into her mother. She shuddered at the thought.

And then she recalled that both Nick and, twenty-two years earlier, her father had walked out the door with a few books, their shaving gear and the clothes they stood up in. In the end the domestic detritus had probably come to be a suffocating burden. She'd been collecting vintage embroidered table napkins while Nick was dreaming of escape.

'Francie? Sorry, I didn't mean it as an insult.' Jessie touched her arm. 'I just meant that I think you are incredible. The sewing basket, the tablecloths, the handpainted spice rack . . .'

Francie stood knee-deep in scrunched-up newspaper with her arms full of Tupperware containers and looked at it all. Jessie was right. It was a pile of crap.

'I know, I know. What you mean is that I'm some sort of 1950s Doris Day throwback. It's so dumb. As though, if you make a perfect home, a man will come and live in it. Like a polar bear enclosure at the zoo. It's utterly pathetic.'

She dropped the pile of pastel plastic on the floor and slumped into a chair. Jessie handed her another drink.

'Gabby told me all about it,' Jessie said in a soothing tone. 'I'm sorry. The way it happened really sucks. All this must be hard for you.'

There it was again. Everyone knew about her break-up.

'Gabby's a great chick to have on your side, believe me. She's a really good hater and that helps in a situation like yours.

'I first met her about five years ago, back when she came to interview me. We met up after one of my shows at the Comedy

Festival and about a million martinis later we were mates. She's amazing, isn't she?'

Francie wondered in what way she was 'amazing' . . . specifically.

'One of those chicks whose fingernails and toenails are always painted the same colour. Can you believe the amount of energy and concentration it must take to pull that off?'

Francie smiled and regarded her own fingernails. She hadn't polished them for months. What on earth must Gabby think of her?

Jessie went on: 'And her handbag always matches her shoes. Fuck! I'd need a month off and a forklift to transfer all the stuff that's in mine!'

Francie laughed. Jessie was going to be a fun housemate. Or should that be mansionmate? Which made her wonder: 'How did you find such an incredible place?'

'Just lucky. After I broke up with Henry I wanted to have my own place and I just stumbled across it. One of the last grand houses in St Kilda. The old gal who owns it is about ninety-two and the rent's cheap enough if we do the garden—by the way, your turn to dead-head the roses this week.

'Then I rang Dave, who brought Robbie. They've known each other since uni. My girlfriend Anna used to have your room. She's living in London. And now you're here. God, we've had some great bashes . . .'

Francie sat and listened to Jessie tell tales of ghosts of parties past. They put their feet up on the empty cardboard boxes and proceeded to drink half a bottle of vodka and a four-pack of tonic. Eventually the details of Francie's heartache with Nick and the 'passing parade of no-hopers' in Jessie's life were tabled for discussion. The two women reached the inevitable conclusion: Shit Happens, You're Worth More Than This, Men Are Fucked and Happiness Is Just Around The Corner.

Francie felt more content than she had in a long time. For a start she had been able to tell a brand new person all about her troubles. Finding a person who didn't know all the details of the Nick and Poppy thing had been a celebration in itself. Jessie's reaction had been comfortingly bitchy.

'Yeah. That's what men mean when they say: "I want to be by myself". Translation—"Well, we can't both sleep with my new girlfriend, can we?"'

Jessie also offered wise counsel on her own ex, Henry. 'He's always saying: "I'd still like to be friends". But what that means is: "I'd like to hang around long enough to ruin your next relationship". I mean, at least you know your boy is with someone else,' Jessie sighed. 'Every time it looks like I might have a chance at someone new, there's Henry.

'I remember the last time I got involved, with this boy, Mario—he was really, really cute, a definite *perhaps*—Henry started ringing me here every night at eleven o'clock, just as he figured we were getting into bed. After two weeks of these bloody phone calls, which were about absolutely nothing, Mario packed it in. Round eighteen to Henry. He just will *not* give up on me. I mean, you could see that as flattering. But mostly it's weird.'

In the end, and it might have been the vodka thinking for her, Francie was starting to see that Nick taking up with another woman, as painful as that might be, *was* some sort of blessing. Had Francie given up on Nick? Yes—no . . . perhaps . . . Whatever, the move into a new house where his absence wasn't a living, breathing presence was a good start. She felt she could begin to get some perspective on what her true feelings were.

Francie and Jessie were just at the point of concocting an elaborate revenge—'Someone told me you can put battery acid in a water pistol and write messages on the furniture or the carpet and then, weeks later, the message will slowly appear,' Jessie was saying—when there was a presence at the dining room door.

'Afternoon, ladies. Do I detect the whiff of saltpetre in the air? Powdered eye of newt, anthrax in an envelope?'

'Dave! Hi!' Jessie jumped to her feet and stubbed out her cigarette. 'This is Francie. She's in the Red Room. Say hello to our new inductee.'

Dave immediately dropped his briefcase and stepped forward with his hand outstretched. He was an impressive package. Medium height, dark hair cut close to his head. Dark green eyes and a wide, white smile. Francie immediately found him attractive. Was it his regular, finely made features? Or was it the cloud of intense feeling behind the eyes which reminded her of Nick?

For God's sake! Get over him.

Dave was wearing what looked to be an expensive black suit, white open-necked shirt, even more expensive shiny black loafers. Francie wished she was wearing something more elegant than old jeans, T-shirt and blue rubber sandals. And—damn! She also wished she hadn't knocked her drink over as she jumped to her feet.

'Whoops . . . Hi, Francie!' he said with a warm enthusiasm that immediately told her Dave was a charmer. 'So you work with Jessie's friend, the fabulous Gabby Di Martino, at the *Sunday Press*, is that right?'

Jessie was dabbing at the floor with a dishcloth. 'Dave's an architect,' she chimed in. 'Francie cooks,' she chimed again.

'You cook? Excellent!' said Dave.

Francie extended her hand. 'I'm not a great chef or anything. But, yeah, I love to cook.'

'Well, we love to eat, so this is going to work out fine,' he replied at once, taking her hand and pulling her toward him for a kiss on the cheek.

'Drink, Dave?' asked Jessie.

'Absolutely! I've spent the afternoon sucking up to clients and I'd love one. I'll just go and get changed.' And with that Dave ducked back down the hallway.

Francie turned to Jessie with wide eyes.

'Uh-huh! Cute as all get out. But watch him, he's a player!' Jessie turned her attention to fixing Dave's drink.

Francie considered the kick in her solar plexus, or somewhere lower, that she'd felt when she took Dave's hand. She hadn't experienced that in a long time. She'd thought the part of her brain which noted good looking men was dead and gone. So . . . Dave was in the bedroom next to hers. Jessie had the front room, which would have been the drawing room in the days when this old pile was in its glory, and Robbie, whom she was yet to meet, was across the hall.

She loved all of it. The soaring ceilings, intricate ceiling roses and moulded plaster swags of acorn leaves in every corner. It was too good to be true. Whenever Francie had imagined herself living in a shared household she had seen a dingy squat at the top of a rat-infested flight of stairs. The thought that there could be a room in an elegant mansion in St Kilda, directly opposite the rose garden in the park, had never occurred to her. And now she was here. Her bed was in the bedroom, her kitchen utensils in the drawer, her jars of chutney and herb vinegars in the pantry (a real, proper walk-in pantry) and her toothbrush was sitting in a glass tumbler on the windowsill in the bathroom. And this time there weren't just two toothbrushes in the glass, pledging their sacred troth (or whatever the saying was). There were four of them. All bristling with life and expectation.

Francie smiled. It seemed everywhere she looked there was a sign of hope—from the toothbrushes to the tangle of umbrellas and coats in the cloakroom. A new start. The doubled cell of Francie and Nick had now split into four single entities. She was excited at the possibilities of her new life.

Dave returned from the hallway, an even more arresting sight this time. He had pulled on a white T-shirt over a pair of black jeans, and Cuban-heeled boots. Francie caught herself trying to figure out whether his eyes were more hazel than green and quickly made a mental note: *Hands off.* Dave was to be her new housemate. As she had already told Jessie, meaningless one-night stands with strangers was all she was up to. The last thing she wanted to do was ruin her chance of a new start.

'So . . .' Dave picked up his drink. 'Saturday night, laid out before us "like a patient etherised upon a table".'

'TS Eliot?' Francie looked at Dave with a shy smile.

'Correct, Francie! Question is, is it Saturday night which will be etherised?' He drained his drink. 'Or will it be us? What's for dinner?'

'Dave!' Jessie protested. 'She's just walked in the door.'

'No, no, I'd love to cook,' burbled Francie. 'To tell you the truth, I haven't really cooked anything for ages and I'd love to get back into the kitchen. I'll just see if there's anything . . .'

Francie opened the fridge door. She knew there was nothing in the freezer but vodka. The cheese compartment was no better. It contained six bottles of nail polish and the butter compartment held a plastic bag of something suspiciously herb-ish. The shelves yielded two packets of chocolate biscuits, three take-away cartons of toxic sludge, four six-packs of beer, two four-packs of tonic water and, in the vegetable crisper, one lonely, dead carrot.

Francie smiled to herself. The last time she'd looked in her fridge there were only ice cubes and Diet Coke on offer. Not like when she lived with Nick and the shelves were crowded with fresh produce bought from the market and carried home in a basket. Two hands, taking a handle each. In the Nick and Francie Fridge of Love there had been dips and things to stick in dips, homemade jams, chutneys, sauces, sambals. And in the chiller tray, two lamb chops nestling together in a meaty heart.

When the door was opened the light had positively glowed on love's bounty.

So this fridge Francie was looking into tonight was a halfway house of hope. There was alcohol and evidence that food was actually being consumed, but it fell far short of anything you could make a meal from. Francie looked in the pantry. She found spaghetti, dried chillies and jars of pasta sauce.

'Um . . . I think if you can get me a packet of bacon, a lettuce, a bread stick and some butter, I should be able to whip up something worth eating.'

'No problem,' said Dave, flipping open the cover on his dinky mobile phone and dialling.

'Robbie? Bring home some bacon, would you? No,' he laughed, rolling his eyes. '*Actual* bacon. And butter and a bread stick and some salad stuff. Yep. The new chick's gonna cook!'

It was 10 pm by the time supper had been served and eaten. Dave and Jessie were pouring another glass of wine and Robbie was purring with contentment.

'Well . . . that was brilliant, Francie,' said Robbie, pushing away his plate. 'What did you call that again?'

'Spaghetti Matriciana. I mean, it's so simple anyone could—' Francie began.

'Forget it. There's this myth that all poofters can cook. Cliché. Like the cliché that all women have hormonal cleaning frenzies. We've been waiting three years for Jessie to have one of those. No such luck. She tends to shag complete strangers when she gets depressed.'

Jessie raised her eyebrows. 'Celibacy is getting to you, Robbie,' she drawled. 'Testosterone is eating away at your brain like mad cow disease.'

'You're celibate, Robbie?' asked Francie. 'I mean, I shouldn't be so personal . . . sorry . . .'

Because, looking at him, it seemed utterly improbable. Robbie was sitting back with his toned, muscled arms folded across an equally toned, muscled chest. He looked to be straight out of gay boot camp. Newly crew-cut, newly blonde hair topped a square-jawed, almost architectural face. His eyes were brilliant aquamarine studs, and Francie could see he was labelled from top to toe. Jean Paul Gaultier soccer shirt, Calvin Klein undies, Dolce & Gabbana jeans and Louis Vuitton slides. You could see his footwear because it happened to be propped up on the table. He was sporting ten perfectly square-cut toenails to match his head. If he was indeed celibate, Robbie had put in a lot of effort into making himself look attractive regardless.

'Don't be sorry! Yup, celibate. On *purpose*—unlike some!' Robbie grinned at Jessie, who poked her tongue out at him. He jumped up from the table for another vanilla vodka on the rocks from the fridge. Francie watched with fascination as his muscled forearm expertly wrestled a bottle from the freezer.

'I just can't handle the whole "gay" scene. I can't stand the intellectual posing, the drama queens, the whole Barbra Streisand Fan Club crap. It's just a licence to be intolerable, as far as I can see. About as relevant a stereotype as a bottle-blonde suburban hairdresser with plastic fingernails. Two years ago I got to the point where I just couldn't see the sense in pretending anymore. I knew what I wanted—a stable, long-term relationship. And I just thought that no amount of rough trade or casual sex with drama queens was going to make my life any better. So until I can find a "non-gay" gay man, I put my energy into my work. I have friends, I have pornography, and when it's right I'll know, and *then* I'll buy hostess soaps. Up until that time, I have better places to invest my emotional energy.'

Francie was surprised at this speech. She'd never considered the difficulties of a 'non-gay' gay man living in a gay, gay world. She was surprised because she hadn't exactly led a sheltered life. She was, after all, a journalist, she read newspapers, magazines, watched television. But then, she had moved out of her mother's home to set up house with Nick when she was twenty-six. Had five years of domestic bliss in Richmond put her completely out of the loop?

What were the chances, she wondered, of moving into a household with three single people 'having a ball' (according to Gabby Di Martino) and finding out two of them were celibate (whether by design or accident)? If Dave said he wasn't getting any action either, Francie thought she should probably ring the removal van tomorrow to take her away. She hoped the ABANDON HOPE ALL YE WHO ENTER sign above the front door was actually a joke, not the hideous curse Jessie had pronounced it to be.

Francie looked at Dave. He looked at the fat black watch on his arm.

'Well, what are we doing tonight? I suggest we frock up and get down to Honky Tonks in the city. Fluff Bat Central. I'm on a promise.'

Francie had been to Honky Tonks before, but Fluff Bat? What the hell was a Fluff Bat?

Seeing the look of incomprehension on Francie's face, Jessie explained: 'It's Dave's endearing term for the gorgeous little fluffy bits of nothing he's entertaining until Miss Right comes along. They tend to distinguish themselves by being young, blonde and . . . well . . . fluffy. I think he calls them "bats" cos you never seem them in daylight.'

'And,' added Robbie, 'because they have the intellect of slabs of pink ceiling insulation.'

'Whoa!' called Dave. 'Whoa, people! You're talking here about the women I love.'

'Women, plural?' teased Jessie.

'Look,' Dave said good-naturedly, 'the situation is this. We are all single, all in our early thirties, right? And we are all sitting here tonight, with each other, wondering where the fuck our twenties went. Obviously we're not millionaire wunderkinds, otherwise we wouldn't be sharing a house. And although we probably didn't think we'd be married with a couple of kids at our age, didn't we think that, at the very least, we'd have a relationship?

'Well the reality is that we *don't*, and there could be a good decade in it before we *do*. So, until The One gallops over the horizon—or, in fact, doesn't—we can tackle this in a number of ways.

'Celibacy is Robbie's option. Lurching between one crippling love affair and the next is Jessie's. Mine is to keep myself busy with mindless entertainment . . . and Francie?'

Three faces now turned to look at her.

'Um, oh . . .' Francie had been so engrossed in what Dave was saying she was caught out. 'Er . . . it all sounds good . . . celibacy, one-night stands, entertainment . . . all of it. But if I'm honest, I suppose I hope Nick and I will get back together.'

There was silence. Dave coughed and got up to fetch another bottle of wine. Jessie decided to clear the plates from the table. Robbie drained his glass.

'For your sake, sweetie,' Robbie drawled, 'I'd start thinking about Plan B.'

Five

It was about midnight, after Jessie, Dave and Robbie had left for destinations unknown, when Francie finally sat on the bed and surveyed her new room. It certainly looked like a Nick-free zone.

She had given her room a French bordello (think Moulin Rouge) theme, inspired by the long red velvet curtains already in place. They were why everyone in the house called it the Red Room. Francie had bought herself a red embroidered satin eiderdown and pillow covers to match from a Chinese emporium.

From the jumble of second-hand treasures she had assembled in the house in Richmond she had rescued an antique vanity set with a golden scrolled mirror, tiny glass-topped table and spindly chair. The vanity was so utterly feminine—it looked as if it belonged in a fairytale boudoir—that Nick had immediately banished it to the spare room. But here, it was perfect.

The old brown sofa from their living room had been disguised with a loose white cotton cover tied with extravagant bows. And on the floor in front of that Francie had placed the prized cream and pink rug. She had also taken possession of the bed, a chest of drawers, a pair of bedside tables, the stereo and the television. The rest of the furniture was Nick's to do with as he liked.

On the wall directly in front of the bed, where Francie could gaze at it, was her newest triumphant find from an antique shop just up the road. A huge old print in an elaborate gold plaster frame. A beautiful curly haired rococo beauty swathed in a flimsy nightdress was asleep in a carved wooden bed swagged with billows of silk. In through the window tumbled a dozen winged cupids with garlands of rosebuds on their heads. One cupid hovered in the air at the foot of the bed, about to fire a tiny arrow into the dreaming girl's plump bottom. It was titled *Reverie* and as soon as Francie had seen it she knew she had to have it. At five hundred dollars it was way more than she could afford, but she'd beaten the dealer down to four hundred and carted it away. And here it was on the wall. Hopelessly romantic. A symbol of girlish longing.

The trio of housemates had earlier traipsed into Francie's room for a viewing of the new boudoir. Their verdict was that a princess out of a fractured fairytale was now living amongst them.

'You know this room is terrifying for a man,' said Dave. 'It absolutely screams LOVE ME!'

'Or', said Robbie, 'leave fifty dollars on the bedside table before you take a towel and adjourn to the jacuzzi in the Elvis Room.'

The boys had both laughed. Francie ducked her head with embarrassment.

'Tell 'em to fuck off, Francie.' Jessie had come to her rescue. 'I think it's gorgeous! Very feminine. And now that you don't have to accommodate the tastes of a male, you can have it any way you want . . . Although this print is a bit of a worry. You know what's hilarious? I've got a print with cupids on it too. Come and have a look at mine.'

Francie and Jessie repaired to the front room for a look. It was a small print propped on the table next to Jessie's bed. The bed was covered in brown fake fur, as though a grizzly bear had expired there. The etching was in a silver frame. A host of cupids was massed in an avenging horde like orcs in *The Lord of the Rings*. They were firing arrows into a blood-red battlefield strewn with skeletons. In one corner a glossy black crow sat on a human skull.

'This is a bit bleak, isn't it?' Francie commented.

'Bleak—or realistic?' Jessie mused. 'I mean, how much human wreckage has been created in the name of love? It's a battlefield out there, baby.'

If it was a battlefield out there, Francie was now sitting here in the dark in Allied HQ a long way behind the front line. The Nick and Poppy Axis of Evil was stalled at the natural barrier of the Yarra River.

Francie hoped the defences at the Punt Road Bridge would hold. At the moment she felt she could walk freely anywhere south of the bridge while Nick and Poppy had colonised the north. She couldn't venture anywhere over the other side of the river without the horrifying possibility of running into them: at the Victoria Market buying strawberry jam; at a streetside café in Fitzroy sharing sweet pastries; at a bar in the city, gazing at each other over chilled martini glasses.

But now that she had moved into this house, Francie felt she had the support of coalition forces. She had an idea—she knew it was bizarre—that Nick had been taken hostage by some crack terrorist unit. That somehow he'd been spirited away from right under her nose and brainwashed into thinking he didn't love her anymore. How had that happened?

She sat and thought about this until her head hurt. But she couldn't stop herself from going through it again. It was as if she was sitting in a darkened theatre watching the same film over and over. The real world only appeared as a blinding, brief image through a crack in a doorway as someone occasionally got up and walked outside—or came inside and sat next to her.

When she looked at the screen she could see now that Nick had begun acting strangely pretty much from the first day he had come home from rehearsals and, presumably, met *her*. She could see how it had been between them. There must have been nights when Poppy had volunteered to drive Nick home and he had accepted, believing that the evening would end with a cheery 'goodnight' and a kiss on the cheek. Maybe it had once or twice. The car had pulled up outside their house and Nick had jumped purposefully out the door as if he was sitting on hot bricks.

But then, there would have been a night when he lingered. Poppy would have turned in the half-shadows and fixed her big dark blue eyes on him. His fingers would have reached out and searched for her pale neck through curling ribbons of hair. And as she leaned closer he would have looked into the black valley between her breasts.

A heartbeat away, in the bed under the front window, Francie would have been dreaming. Instead of half waking to check the clock—1.30 am—what if she had pulled on her dressing gown and walked into the street to look for him? What if she had noted the little silver car just beyond the streetlight?

Walking closer she would have realised it was a tangle of limbs she could see through the windows. A fog of lust making the glass run with rivulets of moisture. She would have crept nearer and spied them clawing at each other's clothes, breathing hard, groaning with frustration as they stopped themselves at a button or a zip.

If she had crouched down low and pressed her ear to the door, would she have heard as they willed each other's hearts to calm? Heard them whisper urgently about how they might get rid of her? Terrorists hatching a plan to plant a bomb that would rip Francie apart?

And then maybe she would have seen Poppy steal one last kiss from Nick. A kiss which belonged to Francie and had been cunningly thieved. Looking back at him standing under the streetlight, did Poppy smile with secret triumph as she drove away?

But Francie never did wake and walk into the street. Instead she slumbered on their bed under the window in a deep and trustful sleep. It was only when Nick crawled in beside her that she woke and noted the time: 2 am. He was guilty then, but still hard with desire for Poppy. Was Francie's body just an abstract of the female form to him that night? Skin, nipples, hair, holes? Like a blow-up sex doll?

Had he fucked Francie in the dark while his mind was full with the taste and smell of Poppy? Had he pushed himself into Francie's mouth—an innocent, compliant plastic 'O'—and thought of Poppy again as he groaned with the release of it all and the anticipation of even greater pleasure to come? It made Francie sick to her stomach to think of it. How pathetic it was that she hadn't seen it coming.

He had started to find excuses not to have sex: 'I have to learn these lines. You go to bed now, I'll come in later.'

Said he didn't want to go away to the mountains in July: 'I don't want to leave town then. Maybe something will come out of this play and I'll be offered another part. Do you still want to go with a girlfriend or something?'

Begun criticising everything she did in the house: 'What are these bizarre new cushions with the roses? Everything you bring home is so . . . girlie! I feel like I'm living in Hansel and Gretel's fucking gingerbread house.'

Started staying out late: 'The director took us all out for dinner and we kicked on back at his place. It's a whole cast "bonding" thing. I couldn't leave.'

Missed her birthday for the first time: 'Shit, Francie, sorry! This play is just taking up every bit of emotional energy I have at the moment. You have to give me a bit of space.'

And stopped complimenting her: 'You always look good. I don't know why you keep asking me. Does it make any difference what I think? You dress for your girlfriends anyway.'

And to the question she found herself asking, despite promising herself she never would—'Do you still love me, Nick?'—he had answered: 'Of course I do! I'm here, aren't I?' Which had immediately made Francie think he had other options—that maybe one day he wouldn't be.

So . . . all this had led Francie, inexorably, to the half-formed, terrifying thought that maybe she and Nick *were* on the way out. After all, they were the only couple who had been together five years in, as far as Francie could tell, the whole of Melbourne.

But she'd clung on, refusing to believe it was a possibility that they would break up. She had launched herself into a frenzy of domestic activity. Planted climbing red roses on the side fence, repainted the bathroom a blushing pink, made more jam— cherry, raspberry, blackberry—and trawled her cookbooks for ever more exotic recipes—Mexican chicken with chocolate sauce, black rice, stuffed peppers, devil's food cake. As if she could seduce him with talismans of love and dark flavours. And all the time she was doing this she was aware that Nick was slipping away. She didn't know why, but he was slowly drifting beyond her reach. If she could have boiled up a love potion on the old stove in that little wooden kitchen, with a toadstool and a hank of hair, she would have done it.

Then, one Monday night after Nick had again been distant and preoccupied all weekend, Francie broached the terrifying subject which had been haunting her for weeks. She was standing in the kitchen, about to deposit a joint of beef in a black iron pot of sizzling olive oil, when her question bubbled to the surface and burst.

'Nick, is there something you want to tell me? Has something changed between us? Do you still want to be here with me?'

She felt as if it was her heart she was carrying before her: a lump of bloody, throbbing meat on a tray. He had looked at the red-raw offering and then plunged a knife right through until it clanged on the metal beneath.

'I don't know, Francie. I just don't know anymore.'

And by that Friday, he was gone.

Now, six months later, Francie had gone too. She looked around her new room once more and then looked at the empty space in the bed beside her. She smothered her face in her embroidered pillows and cried. She hoped the cheap red dye wouldn't come off on her face.

✻

The digital clock read 3.49 am when Francie suddenly woke to a thumping noise coming from the room next door. For a moment or two she couldn't remember where she was, but focusing through the gloom she saw her heavy wooden chest of drawers and her gold scrolled mirror in this strange room. She held out her two arms and checked. Yep, they were hers too.

There was a thump, a squeal, a giggle, another thump, and Francie remembered that she was in her new room in her new house. And then she realised that the sounds she could hear from the room next door were being made by two people. Two people having sex. Dave and . . . ?

Oh, brilliant! Francie immediately thought of Nick and Poppy flinging themselves around in bed. To be more precise, a bed in a bedroom at 35 Everton Street, Parkville. A smart, renovated little house with a neat front path hedged with lavender bushes.

Francie knew exactly where it was. She remembered the first night she had driven there.

She hadn't gone *inside*. Alright, she'd admit that she parked up the corner of the street then sneaked down the side of the house and peered in through the window. But she didn't go *right* inside. She couldn't get in because she tried the back door and it was locked.

So, while she'd done a little trespassing that night, no-one could have charged her with *actual* break and enter. She had stood on a bucket and looked through the window. It was a bedroom, dark except for a small lamp shining a pool of light onto a bedside table and two pillows. This was Poppy's bedroom then. The bedside light was still on, waiting for them to come back here.

The bed cover was slate grey and the pillowcases were white with grey piping. It was all very grown-up and sophisticated. Nothing like Francie's adolescent jumble of pink, white and rose-print linen pillows. She imagined the rest of the house would be the same. Muted neutral colours with, say, a feature wall in aubergine in the designer kitchen. A kitchen perhaps installed with an impressive array of gleaming stainless-steel appliances.

In the living room she supposed there would be a large portrait in oils of the good lady herself—done by a *marvellously gifted, intelligent, intuitive* artist friend—hanging on the wall above taupe linen sofas. They would be decorated with cream scatter cushions and a chocolate-brown mohair throw rug. She imagined. She'd seen enough picture spreads of terribly chic living spaces to have a fair idea. In short, a home which looked the way Francie herself would have decorated it if she was a successful 43-year-old woman with impeccable taste. But at that moment that description didn't fit Francie at all. She was a deranged thirty-something stalker standing on an upturned plastic bucket at eleven o'clock on a freezing July night spying into someone's bedroom. Call the cops!

Francie had tried to pierce the shadows for more detail she could flay herself with. And there on the bedside table was a battered copy of Marcel Proust's *Remembrance of Things Past*. Again, predictable. The one piece of literature Francie had always been promising herself to get around to reading and had never found the time. If Poppy's copy had been in the original French, Francie would have opened a vein.

The next day she went out and bought the book. She sat up in her bed and tried to read it, but the words floated and swam off the page in a viscous pond of tears and snot.

Tonight the book was packed away in a cardboard box Francie could just make out across the unfamiliar space. Maybe she would read it one day, when the remembrance of things past wouldn't be just a reminder of what had once been possible and now would never be.

Thump! Squeal! Crash! More laughter! Well at least someone in this house was enjoying themselves! She thought of Dave naked and pounding away at some blonde Fluff Bat with her legs in the air.

Now there was an interesting development! It was the first time she could remember thinking about two people having hot sex who weren't Nick and Poppy. That had to be some sort of move in the right direction. As second hand and sordid as it was. That's what she needed more of. Less *Remembrance of Things Past* and more *Imagining of Things Future*! She wondered if thinking about having sex with Dave was a genuine expression of interest or just a cheap substitution racket?

Francie had to turn off her mind and get back to sleep. She finally hit on the image which was guaranteed to shut down her synapses. She was reclining nude on an elaborate four-poster bed swagged with billows of aubergine silk. In through the window, completely naked, with a garland of rosebuds on his head, tumbled George W Bush.

Six

Sunday morning found Francie in her new kitchen trying to light the gas griller without backburning her eyebrows. She had cleared a space for her new coffee-maker and it was burbling away. She was humming 'Sunday Morning Coming Down'—'Cause there's something in a Sunday, that makes a body feel alone . . .' when Jessie appeared, playing June Carter to her Johnny Cash.

The gals sang together in a nasal drawl:

And there's nothing short a' dyin'
That's half as lonesome as the sound
Of the sleeping city sidewalk
And Sunday morning coming down.

Francie turned her attention back to the griller.

'Oh Jesus, don't look in there!' Jessie protested. 'There's probably a family of mice using that griller tray as a 7-Eleven! I can't remember the last time we cleaned it.'

Francie, duly warned, took the tray out to wash it in the sink. Jessie was right. It was rancid.

'So,' said Jessie, pulling a juicer from the cupboard and a bag of oranges from the fruit basket, 'how'd you sleep last night? Any sign of ghosts?'

'Well, if it was a ghost it was a very friendly one. Dave sounded like he was having fun.'

Jessie laughed. 'Oh yeah, that would be the vision in pink sequins he stumbled over at the end of the night. She had perfect Fluff Bat qualifications. Cute as a button, dumb as a box of hammers. It was a case of "lie down, I think I love you" at first sight.'

Francie was surprised to feel a twinge of something she supposed was . . . jealousy? Envy? It was odd to have that feeling about someone who wasn't Nick.

'So, did the drought break for you?' Francie inquired politely.

'Nup! But there was a definite sprinkling of rain until he told me he played guitar. I have a "no musicians" policy in place at the moment. Henry plays trombone in this band called Diving Bell. And I have promised myself that, now I'm almost thirty-five and on television, I owe myself a man with a real job, a car *and* a suit and tie. You wouldn't think that would be too much to ask for, would you?' She held out a glass of fresh orange juice to Francie. 'But honestly, I might as well try to make a play for the Sultan of fucking Brunei! I dunno. I just don't get it anymore.

'Look at me, Francie.'

Francie looked. Jessie was a terrifying sight. She'd slept in her make-up and had two coal pits for eyes. She was still sporting her bright red Revlon Colorstay lipstick, which just looked weird at this hour of the morning, and her perky gelled hair had lain down and died. Francie wouldn't have been surprised to discover that Jessie had spent the night sleeping in the cellar in an open coffin.

Her housemate continued: 'Now you've just met me, so you should be able to give me an unbiased opinion. Wait, I'll turn around.' Jessie twirled. 'Have I got "loser" tattooed on the back of my head? Both heads?

'I mean . . .' and here Jessie turned back to her with an imploring look, 'what's wrong with me? This isn't a joke anymore. I'm in danger of turning into a caricature of a love-starved female comedian. I know that, traditionally, women comedians can't get a bloke, but that old routine is getting tired. Christ! *I'm* getting tired of hearing myself! So . . . you write a column in the newspaper about being single. Tell me where I'm going wrong!'

Phew! This had been happening to Francie a lot lately. So many women wanted her professional opinion on their love-lives. Which was ridiculous! Francie was just making it up as she went along. Couldn't everybody tell? Wasn't it obvious?

Her initial response to Jessie's inquiry was: The reason you're still single is because you're too loud, you're too cynical, you're wearing too much make-up. But she then realised this was exactly what her mother would say. Looking past all that, Francie saw a fabulous woman who had everything to offer. Jessie had a razor wit—everyone in the country knew that! She was alive, opinionated, passionate. In fact, Francie reflected, Jessie was everything she *wasn't* right now. She had beautiful big eyes and a very impressive cleavage spilling out of her singlet. She had a flat tummy and a curvy bottom fitting snugly into a pair of white footy shorts. Very nice legs. Francie guessed that being bad in bed was *not* part of Jessie's problem.

In the end she said: 'Jessie . . . you know . . . there doesn't seem to be any rhyme or reason to it. I mean, look at me. Miss Mousey nondescript blonde. Good, quiet steady job. Unthreatening. Crummy journo going nowhere in particular.'

Jessie wanted to interject in this litany of self-abuse, but couldn't quite find the space.

'I cook, I can put in a zip, I can even knit. Jesus, I'm a human doormat. And I'm single too!

'Don't you think that if I knew the answer—why none of us can find a decent relationship—I would have put it in my column or on a website and given it to the women of the world? In the end it's just got to be geographical or statistical or about demographics or marketing. Something!'

Jessie opened her mouth to speak again and then realised Francie was a long way from being finished.

'It can't be because we're unlovable. I mean, it *feels* like that, but it just can't be! First impression? I think you are adorable.

'I just think we're some weird blip on a radar. A bump on a graph. *Single, available women in their thirties in the year 2004 in Australia.* One day someone will look back at this anomaly, research us in retrospect and find that we were caught . . . I dunno, between song lines or tram lines or in some weird socioeconomic, demographic, romantic Bermuda Triangle and come up with an explanation. But, until then . . . we are a living, breathing mystery. All I can say is—I'd have a relationship with you!'

Jessie was now looking at her with surprise and even Francie herself couldn't believe where all this had come from, but there it was. She turned her back and began scrubbing furiously at the griller tray.

'Hey . . .' Jessie came up behind her at the sink and put her arms around Francie's shoulders. 'Thanks for that. That was amazing. If it wasn't against my religion, I'd have sex with you too.'

There was a delicate cough in the vicinity of the kitchen door. Jessie and Francie turned and there stood Fluff Bat. Tall, blonde, in a wildly inappropriate pink sequinned dress and jewelled high-heeled sandals.

'Hi,' she chirruped. 'Can I thmell coffee?'

Fluff Bat had the most adorable lisp which made you want to smooch her immediately.

Francie and Jessie quickly untangled themselves and switched to hostess mode. When Fluff Bat was comfortably seated at the kitchen table with a coffee and orange juice, Jessie sat opposite and began her interrogation. Francie had the distinct feeling that Jessie was not so much making conversation as gathering material, which was not to say she disapproved. They were both fascinated by this elegant, fresh-faced sylph who was now blithely piling strawberry jam on her toast.

By Francie's reckoning, Fluff Bat, whose name was in fact Antonia, had had five hours' sleep. But she looked—what was the word? Dewy? That look that cosmetics companies were desperate to bottle and get rough old bags to pay top dollar for. Antonia ('call me Ant') looked as if she had somehow managed to fit in a visit to a beauty spa between crawling out from under Dave and making her way to the kitchen. Her face was scrubbed and pink and her long blonde hair was brushed straight. Immaculate.

'So ... er ... Ant ... you're up early,' said Jessie.

'Yeth, I have to get to work.' She turned down her pretty mouth.

'And where's that? I don't think you told me last night.'

'A little cothmetic boutique on Toorak Road. Drop in, I'll give you a dithcount.' She handed out business cards from a tiny pink beaded purse.

'So, this is the first time you've ever met Dave. Isn't he gorgeous?' asked Jessie.

Francie squirmed. Next Jessie would be asking, 'Do you come here often?' or 'What's a nice girl like you doing in a dump like this?'

'Uh-huh.' Ant couldn't have cared less about Jessie's inquisition. Clearly she was used to post-coital interviews. 'He'th cute ... and funny. I've never met an architect before. I'm *tho* over lawyerth and thtockbrokerth. You know, guyth in thuits? They think coth they've got *tonth* of money it makth up for having no perthonality. You know what I mean?' She looked at the girls, her raised eyebrows lost behind her glossy blonde fringe.

Francie watched Jessie get up from the table and stagger to the sink. For one horrible moment she thought she was going to be sick in it.

'Yeah,' said Francie, covering the awkward silence. 'I know what you mean. You can get stuck in a groove with guys. For instance Jessie can't get away from musicians at the moment.'

'Eeeyew! Musoth . . .' Miss Fluff Bat waved a perfectly manicured hand under her wrinkled button nose. 'They thmell! They never have any money. They never take you anywhere nithe. They alwayth want you to come and watch them play . . . like ith foreplay or thomething. Ith never turned me on, watching a guy jerk off in public. No thankth! I try not to travel cattle clath if I can help it.

'Anyway, I've gotta run,' she sang as she fanned the air with a piece of jam toast. 'Theeya.' And with that she tottered out the door.

Jessie watched her go with open-mouthed amazement. 'That girl is a deadset genius—I mean, geniuth.'

'Yep,' agreed Francie, laughing. 'Those high-maintenance gals have got it made.'

'High maintenance, yeah . . .' repeated Jessie with a faraway look in her eyes, like Toad of Toad Hall. 'I'm going to do some work.' She took her cup of coffee and headed down the corridor.

Francie was sitting at the kitchen table with the weekend papers arrayed before her when Robbie made an appearance, radiating megawatts of white-blonde vitality.

'So,' he inquired between mouthfuls of fresh orange juice and bircher muesli, 'how's your Sunday looking?'

Francie replied that she was staring down the barrel of a day spent washing clothes and unpacking boxes.

'Hmm, and how did you used to spend your Sundays when you were a couple?'

Francie's first instinct was to be hurt by the question, but then she thought Robbie's bluntness was actually a refreshing change.

'You know, just the usual stuff. Maybe go to the plant nursery, a street market, wander around the antique stores . . .'

Robbie snorted. 'You mean shopping.'

'Well, a lot of the time we didn't actually buy—'

Robbie had no time for it. 'You know that's one thing I find incredibly sad about our society—we substitute genuine cultural interaction with consumerism.'

And that's how Francis Sheila McKenzie found herself spending Sunday afternoon in a church, in an outer western suburb of Melbourne she had never heard of, swaying to a Sudanese Catholic choir and singing *Hallelujah*!

Seven

The next Monday night Francie was to be found at Amanda and Lachlan's flat in East St Kilda. Johnno and Olga were there too, which meant there was just one person missing . . . Nick.

Amanda was bustling around the little kitchen preparing a casual supper of pasta and salad, demolishing a few vodka and cranberries in the process.

Olga was sitting on the bench trying to keep the voluminous skirt of her red 1950s sundress out of the way of the chopping board. She was fiddling and twiddling an armful of brightly coloured plastic bangles and her aqua cat's-eye glasses. Chattering away like a parrot on a perch.

'You two are going to *adore* this new range. I'm using all those old paste brooches I've been collecting and sewing them onto backings of antique lace. The ones I've already done look *divine*—especially on black satin. I see them pinned on the bodice of an evening gown of a movie star, because the biggest news is . . . guess what?'

Amanda was nodding, listening as she peeled avocados. She was stylish as ever in a plain black jersey dress which rippled around her bare feet. Her dark brown hair was brushed back sleekly and caught with a beaded clip. She heard the excitement in Olga's voice and turned from her preparations, her dark eyes twinkling with anticipation.

'What?'

'*Vogue* has already picked up a few of my pieces for this five-page fashion spread they're doing with—Naomi Watts!' Olga squealed.

'Really? Naomi Watts? That is *brilliant*, Olga! Imagine if they publish the pictures in American *Vogue*! You might even end up with your stuff in—'

'Neiman Marcus or Barney's! I know, I know! If they do, I am definitely going to somehow find the money to travel over there. Imagine walking around and seeing my jewellery in a display case in New York! Eeek!'

Francie applauded from the doorway, where she had been banished for treading on Amanda's toes with her high-heeled sandals. From her vantage point she could also see Johnno and Lachlan sitting on the balcony nursing beers and talking football . . . or cricket.

She thought of the times Nick had been part of this cosy domestic scene. He would have been leaning against the railing with his long legs stretched in front of him, arms folded over his chest. There would be an expression of intense concentration on his face while the boys discussed the monumental implications of a full-forward's dodgy hamstring or some earth-shattering umpiring decision. She shook her head to dislodge the painful memory.

This had been Francie's real family for the past five years. Not a biological family where you just made do with the genetic lottery handed to you at birth, but a family you had hand-picked and loved all the more for that. People you trusted and shared your life with more intimately than any mismatched brother, sister or parent.

Francie had known Olga since childhood and had met Amanda when they worked together as cadets at the *Daily Press*. The women were firm friends who had long ago claimed each other as part of the same tribe. They were, despite their inner city makeover, just ordinary suburban girls. A trio who had managed to find an independent, creative life their mothers could only have dreamed of—Francie as a journalist, Amanda now as a television producer and Olga as a jewellery-maker. It was only when they reached their thirties that they started to wonder when the rest of their birthright—the house furnished with husband and kids—was going to be delivered.

Over the years the friends had brought a number of men to restaurants and cocktails for approval, all of them possibilities, but all who *weren't quite what one had hoped for*. They were loved and lusted after all the same. But there had been a time— a golden era of contentment when you looked back on it now—when the three amigos believed they had found the men they were looking for.

Amanda had unexpectedly turned up Lachlan at work. She had started as a production assistant at Pretty Pictures, a local film and television production house, and one fine day Lachlan walked in the door in his disguise as a copyright lawyer. He was tall, loud, athletic. She was short, artistic, considered. He played golf, followed the footy. She practised yoga, loved the theatre.

It was like one of those bad chick flicks where she *hated* him, *hated* him, *hated* him and then, ohmigod, she *loved* him. It happened so fast it was almost between ad breaks. So here they were, three years later, living in a flat together, saving for a house, and every time Francie visited she expected a marriage date would be announced.

Then there was Olga and Johnno. There was nothing special about the way they had met. A dinner party. Francie knew Olga, Nick knew Johnno. Theirs had been one of those relationships where everyone *hoped* and *hoped*, but in their heart of hearts couldn't imagine it lasting. After all, if they had stayed together it would all have been so *neat*. It should have worked. He fashioned words into lyrical sentences and she took gemstones and beads and strung them into lovely necklaces. It had looked like they had a lot in common, but Francie could see that they were both so creative and intense, there was no-one to lighten the mood when things got dark—which they often did.

They'd broken up a couple of years ago. The group had survived that rocky passage and everyone had stayed friends. They ate out together at least twice a week, spent weekends away in the country and cosy nights in with a video. Then Nick left and kicked their comfy sitcom to the shithouse.

Whenever they sat at the dining table Francie noticed the space at the end where Nick would have been. She was reminded of the Chinese superstition in which the thirteenth place at the feasting table was always set, but left empty, for the ghost. The ghost of Nick was sitting there laughing, sharing stories, looking lovingly at Francie.

Nick's absence was even more glaringly obvious because Francie had not mentioned him once this evening. He had moved into Johnno's house in North Fitzroy and Francie dared not ask after him. Johnno's friendship had been a part of the furniture of Nick and Francie's relationship.

Francie adored him. She was a journalist, but Johnno was a *writer*! And with his declaration came poverty, rejection, humiliation, self-doubt and more poverty. On Johnno's desk were manuscripts for two novels, dozens of short stories, piles of poems—all unpublished. There were screenplays and television dramas, all on the road to nowhere. In the meantime he was keeping body and soul together by writing scripts for children's television.

Francie admired the way Johnno had cast himself as a struggling artist from another era. Something straight out of *La Bohème*. From the unkempt flop of dull black hair over his forehead and the threadbare T-shirt hanging off his chest, down to his battered black lace-ups, Johnno was a romantic who liked to *believe* in things. The innate goodness of people. The faithfulness of dogs. That right would always triumph if one just surrendered to the sweeping tide of the universe. It was a quality which was, by turns, endearing and irritating. His moral compass was always set, unerringly, to the same magnetic point of *natural justice*. Francie wished she could be so sure of herself.

For Johnno, Francie and Nick's break-up was deeply unfortunate. Francie could see he was truly torn between them, and she appreciated him trying to remain neutral, but she couldn't help making him suffer all the same. She had a list of questions for Johnno as long as your arm. She *wanted* to ask—starting with the innocent and moving to the insanely personal:

'So, Johnno, is Nick eating well?

'How's his mum?

'Has he found another job?

'Does he go out much?

'How many nights does he stay at *her* place?

'Has *she* been to your place?

'What's *she* like?

'Is *she* funny, smart, beautiful, clever, kind?

'What are *they* like together?

'Does he love her?

'Does *she* love him?

'Has he told you what *she's* like in bed?

'Do they fuck a lot?

'Does *she* give him blow jobs?

'Are they better than mine?

'WHEN IS THAT FUCKING BITCH GOING TO GIVE HIM UP AND LET HIM COME BACK TO ME?!'

But Francie didn't say any of this. She was trying, *really trying*, to push all this out of her mind and to be a cheery, sane human being. To step out of her dark place and engage with the real world. So all her questions were dangling over the dining table tonight like a chandelier of cut glass.

There was something else in the air tonight too. All through dinner Amanda and Lachlan exchanged long, loving looks with each other like a couple of doe-eyed . . . er . . . deer. It was making Francie, Johnno and Olga feel distinctly uncomfortable. Amanda and Lachlan's billing and cooing were almost intolerable. Francie could now see what Johnno and Olga had been complaining about since she and Nick had broken up. She'd never noticed it before, but they were right. It was an almost nauseating spectacle. Of course, Amanda and Lachlan's good fortune was a beacon of hope for the lovelorn in an otherwise blackened landscape. But did they have to flaunt it like this?

It couldn't have been more tasteless if they had been a bunch of homeless people paraded past the mansion of a millionaire. *See the double car garage, admire the huge entertaining area, gasp at the pool cabana! Bet you wish you had one of these!'*

The three singles were sitting at the table rolling their eyes at the flirtatious giggling coming from the kitchen when Amanda and Lachlan appeared at the doorway with a huge strawberry-topped cake and two bottles of French champagne. Amanda set the cake on the table and stood back with her hands clasped under her . . . uh-oh! Her stomach.

'We have an announcement to make,' said Lachlan, commanding a silent space in which to land his important proclamation. 'We're having a baby!'

There was a bomb blast of excitement. This was a testament to the devotion of the five friends because underneath the fireworks display of kisses, hugs and exclamations of joy was a deep, dark well of disappointment.

Francie immediately thought of the baby she longed for with Nick. Johnno thought of his fledgling scriptwriting career and wondered if he would ever be in a place where a family was possible. Olga remembered her two abortions and wondered if she would always feel haunted by their lost souls which hovered around her face now like butterfly wraiths. But these fears stayed under the surface as the effervescence of the moment was enjoyed.

A baby! Francie didn't have any other friends who had children. Which was bizarre when she considered how, just a few decades earlier, she and all her friends would have had two, three, four kids each by the time they were thirty. And a few decades before that they would probably each have produced a cricket team by now. Thirty was the new twenty. Forty was the new thirty. Fifty was the new forty! And when was the right time to have kids? No-one had figured that out yet. While women's magazines carried endless pages on which moisturiser and what hem length was appropriate for each decade, they were piteously short on details about what else should be happening in your life. They knew that after forty you shouldn't be showing off your cleavage or wearing frosty pink lipstick, but that's where their wisdom about the female condition started and ended.

Of course they carried the odd feature about supermodels and actresses who carted around babies like designer handbags. But have one themselves? Without a nanny, cook and cleaner? Francie knew enough female magazine journos to know that the prospect of nine months off the fags, cocktails and tuna sashimi were enough to make them schedule a four-page spread on the latest scientific advances in birth control. They saw the prospect of even *one* baby as a life sentence of drudgery. A blunt instrument which would bludgeon you into submission.

But Francie didn't see it like that. She had really, truly wanted a baby with Nick. She had spent hours imagining what their combined genes would have created. A dream baby which would have had his hair, her mouth, his eyes, her legs, his neck, her ears. His passion and intuition and her practical, calm logic. Looking back she could see this baby was more a vanity project than anything real. She even had names for this perfect phantom. If it was a boy it would have been James. Jimmy McKenzie Jamieson. That had a ring and rhythm to it. If it was a girl it would have been Jinx. Jinx as in 'charming spell'. 'One who can enchant with her beauty and grace.' She'd looked up the meaning in a book of *1000 Classic Baby Names*.

But now her baby fantasy, along with the walk up the aisle under a canopy of stars, had been vaporised. Francie reflected on all those years playing perfect plastic families with her Barbie dolls. It was ironic that Barbie was now in her mid forties, single and childless.

So one of her friends was having a baby! A baby that Francie could reasonably expect to be godmother to, or to babysit. One that she actually had the right to pick up. No, it was more than a *right*. It was an *expectation* that she would pick up the baby, and do . . . whatever you did with babies after you picked them up.

Putting aside her own preoccupations, Francie realised she was excited at the prospect. And, of course, she was delighted for Amanda and Lachlan. How any couple these days got to the point where they both agreed to have a baby and then actually made one! It was a triumph of . . . well . . . timing mostly. Francie sometimes thought it would be good to go back to the days when women could get pregnant accidentally.

Francie had always thought of Lachlan as being too stolid and predictable for her tastes. She rolled her eyes whenever she saw him heading out the door to play golf in his poly-knit shirt and tartan trousers. Now she saw him waving a handful of photographs of Amanda's ultrasound and grinning proudly, and couldn't imagine Nick ever doing the same. She felt envious. In a good way, she reminded herself.

'Have a look at this one! Look at the hands! Perfect golf grip!' Lachlan boasted.

Amanda swatted at him. 'We're having a baby, not a caddy!'

'And he's taking after me already . . . look . . . he's bald!'

'She's not bald!' Amanda squealed. 'She's blonde.'

They all bent over the grainy images which looked like aerial photographs of a swamp. Apparently the teensy blob of algae in the right-hand corner was human.

'Hey, I can see a foot,' said Johnno. He was lying.

'We'll have to have a baby . . . party,' said Olga. The word 'shower' had escaped her but, to give her credit, she was trying to grapple with a cultural ritual which was utterly foreign to her. Not so much because she was Jewish, but because she didn't know anyone with a baby either.

'Let's break open the champagne!' Francie clapped her hands.

'Well, you guys get into it. I suppose I'd better not.' Amanda rubbed her tummy.

And with this statement Francie realised that one of her dearest friends had already moved into a shadowy parallel universe. It was as if Amanda had stepped through the back of a wardrobe into the snowy land of Narnia and was now off on a fantastical adventure with a witch and a talking lion. Francie was still back in the bedroom looking at a rack full of clothes.

☼

It wasn't until the singles were on the way home in the darkened interior of the car, where they couldn't see each other, that any of them felt they could reveal their true feelings.

'Well, there goes the neighbourhood. Gone to hell in a baby capsule,' said Johnno. It was a half-hearted attempt at a joke. He didn't expect to get a laugh.

Olga was quiet in the front seat beside him. She was thirty-five. For her, this was just another whack over the nose with a rolled-up newspaper: 'Stupid, stupid Olga! Why aren't you married? What are you thinking? Where are our grandchildren?'

Francie, predictably, was in tears. 'Oh shit! I know I'm supposed to be happy. Well I am, but I'm not. I'm not jealous. I just . . .' She leaned her head against the car window and watched the darkened streets slide by. A low-lying black cloud settled in over the group. Johnno pulled the car up outside *Elysium*, Francie's new house, and they all sat there in the dark. It was quiet as Johnno and Olga waited for the inevitable question from the back seat.

'So . . . how's Nick?' Francie whispered. She knew she shouldn't ask. She wasn't even sure she wanted to know, but she couldn't see how she could feel any more wretched than she already did. As it turned out, she was seriously underestimating herself.

'Oh, you know, good, good,' muttered Johnno. He coughed and clutched the steering wheel with both hands. His position was truly unenviable. Now that he and Nick were housemates, he knew everything about Nick's life. Whether he whistled in the shower, what he ate for breakfast, how often he was home. Francie understood Johnno was sparing her the most gruesome details, but that he also didn't want to give her false hope.

'We . . . um . . . we had a party at our place last night for Poppy's birthday,' he mumbled.

Francie felt the champagne she had drunk bubble back up into her throat as bitter bile. She swallowed hard and finally found her voice.

'Who was there?'

'Oh, you know, the usual crowd. Some of Poppy's friends. Actually, they were a lot of fun, weren't they, Olga?' Johnno turned to Olga in a desperate attempt to drag her into the ring. She would rather have remained sitting outside the ropes as a spectator.

'You were there too?' asked Francie quietly.

Olga twisted her long black hair in her hands as she answered. 'Yeah. It was like Johnno said, all very . . . you know . . . fun.'

'So how old was she?'

Olga turned and looked at Francie over the top of the car seat.

'Don't do this, Francie,' she pleaded. 'You're just torturing yourself. You knew this was going to—'

'How old was she?' Francie's voice was louder now.

'You know how old she was! She was forty-four,' said Johnno as he stared at the windscreen. 'She looked great. She gave a speech saying that she'd never been so happy as when Nick came into her life. He looked happy too. They held hands all night and everyone there was pleased for them.

'Poppy's a good woman, France. Really, they suit each other and they're in fucking love. So there it is. You know all of it now, and if you were honest with yourself you already knew it.'

'Johnno, that is *so* cruel!' protested Olga.

'Cruel or real? You think I *enjoy* saying this stuff? But someone has to. We can't go on like this! None of us can. The Nick and Francie thing is dead. It's like this corpse that's starting to stink up the place. It's like dragging around a dead body everywhere we go!'

Francie jammed her fist into her mouth as her other hand felt frantically in the dark for the door handle. Johnno leaned back and grabbed her forearm a little bit more tightly than he needed to. Hard enough so it would get her full attention.

'Francie, I wanted you and Nick to stay together. We all did. But it's done! We can't change it! We all want you to get better and just get on with your life.'

'LET ME GO!' Francie tried to wrestle her arm from Johnno's grasp.

'NO! You can't just run off. You have to face up to—'

Francie pushed open the car door and fell out through the soft night into the hard bluestone gutter. She scrambled to her feet and ran down the driveway. Olga and Johnno watched from the car as Francie frantically fumbled with the key to the door and then finally gave up and slumped on the front step.

'Are you going to tell her about Nick and Poppy's new baby?' asked Johnno.

'I'll have to,' Olga sighed. 'The posters will be all over town in a few days. She'll see them everywhere she goes. I can't believe she doesn't already know.'

Johnno banged his head repeatedly on the steering wheel. 'Shit, shit, shit! This is a nightmare! When's it going to end?'

Olga walked up the darkened path and sat next to Francie on the front step. Johnno kept watching as the blow landed. He saw Francie curl into a small ball and bury her face in Olga's lap and was reminded of a mouse cringing in the corner of a cage.

Eight

'So, the shortness of breath, the nausea, the heart palpitations. It sounds like you had a panic attack,' said Faith Treloar of Faith and John-Pierre Treloar, Relationship Counsellors. It was Wednesday night—therapy night—and Francie and Faith were squaring off at each other in their respective blue and red velvet armchairs.

'I suppose that's what it was.' Francie now had a name for the unfamiliar and overwhelming emotion she had felt on Monday night. 'I've never had one before. I didn't know that I could feel so physically affected by something that's just emotional. It's all in my head, but . . .'

'Well, did you know—' Faith sat up straight and smoothed her embroidered cheesecloth top over her prodigious bosom; her voice took on an authoritative tone—'that centuries ago *griefe* was a notifiable disease? You can see it in the official records on the causes of death in London in the 1600s. It's next in the list after the plague and smallpox.'

Damn right! A plague and a pox on both their houses.

'People actually died of broken hearts in those days. Ladies took to their beds with draughts of laudanum. They sickened and just withered away.'

To Francie this sounded like a good plan. Laudanum had to be less fattening than Baileys Irish Cream. You'd be in bed a good year or two before you withered away drinking that stuff.

'So when are we to see Nick and Poppy's newest creation?' asked Faith. 'It often happens when people first get together. They come up with a joint project to express their commitment to each other. It's just unlucky for you that they're both actors.'

Francie thought she could detect a sardonic edge to Faith's voice which she found most comforting. There had to be some place in the world where she could find a sympathetic ear. Someone who didn't just tell Francie to 'face it, get over it, get better'. She wasn't paying eighty dollars an hour to hear that.

'Their show opens the week before Christmas. It's called *Stupid Cupid*.'

Faith pushed the box of tissues across the coffee table. 'And it will be about . . . ?'

Francie had a fair idea from what she'd read in the arts pages of the newspapers and gotten out of Olga and Johnno after intense interrogation. It was to be a late night cabaret outing which would portray Nick and Poppy as star-crossed lovers battling to find true love against the odds (one of which would be Francie, obviously). They'd written all of it—the songs, the vignettes, the dialogues, the monologues—themselves.

As Faith pointed out, it was all too predictable. If they were just a normal couple it would have been a real baby, or an overseas holiday. If they were musicians they would have started a band together. If they were architects they would have built a house. But as it was, they were actors. It was a stage performance. They were vain enough to think that anyone else in the world could give a flying fuck about their lives.

Francie could see her own life reduced to an even smaller pile of rubble. She would be merely collateral damage in a war of propaganda designed to keep Nick and Poppy on the front page with their story of grand passion. Francie would be a footnote.

'I saw the poster in the street today. Their faces were on it in two hearts,' said Francie.

'And how did that make you feel?'

'It was the same as the other night. I thought I was going to collapse. I couldn't breathe. I've never felt like this before.'

'I think you have.'

'What?'

'I think you have had this feeling before. When you were a child. It's something you've never talked about. When was it?'

This was odd. Was Faith a counsellor or some weirdo psychic?

'I don't know what you mean,' Francie stonewalled. She pushed the box of tissues back across the table and folded her arms over her denim jacket.

Faith leaned closer and brought her hand under Francie's chin. She tilted her face until they were eye to eye.

'You *do* know, Francie. I want you to tell me. When was the last time you felt like that? The shortness of breath, the nausea, your heart thumping so hard you thought it would explode?'

Francie knew alright. But it was such a long time ago in a land so far, far away that it seemed ridiculous to bring it up. It was more than twenty years ago. There had to be a statute of limitations on this stuff. But then the memory hit Francie with such force that she knew she was kidding herself.

'There's no point talking about it. It's history.'

Faith leaned back in her chair. She took a deep breath which made her mighty chest expand like a dugong about to dive into the murky depths.

'And that's why I want you to talk about it. It's not *history* . . . some ancient event that happened to someone else. It's your past, what made you. There was grief back then too, wasn't there? As I said, grief can kill you. Maybe not you, not literally, but what if grief was making you want to die? Have you thought about killing yourself?'

Francie looked into her lap and nodded.

'Why would a young woman like you, with everything in the world to offer, think she was worthless? That she wasn't fit to walk the earth?'

It was an extremely fair question and Francie had no answer.

'What if I told you that grief was something which crept up on you. That if you didn't deal with it properly it hid in the shadows, quietly feeding on your pain and doubling in size until it was immense and unstoppable. What if one day it caught up with you and knocked you out? Don't you think you should be brave? Turn and face it now, before that happens?'

It was true. The way Faith described it, it was like The Blob out of that fifties sci-fi movie starring Steve McQueen. *Indescribable . . . indestructible! Nothing can stop it!* Francie looked ahead to oblivion and knew she had to stand her ground.

'It was . . .' she began. She threw her head back and looked at the ceiling so her tears wouldn't cascade down the spillway. But it was useless. They couldn't be held back.

'It was . . . on the day of my father's wedding,' Francie sniffed. 'I can't believe I'm crying again . . . fuck, fuck, fuck!' She groped blindly for the tissue box. The words and the tears came in a torrent.

'Oh . . . God . . . I was the flower girl. I was ten. Dad picked me up and Mum was standing in the doorway watching me walk down the path to the car. I knew it was killing her. I didn't want to go. No-one, not one person in the whole wide world would listen to me! "It will be lovely, Francie. You look beautiful, Francie."

'It wasn't lovely! It was a nightmare! My dad married someone else. And I had to stand there and watch. I had to hold her horrible flowers. They were Christmas lilies. I've always hated those flowers.'

Francie drew her legs up and curled into the corner of her chair. The tears came down steadily.

'When I had to walk back up the aisle behind them—the new Mr and Mrs McKenzie—I thought I was going to be sick. I couldn't breathe. And I couldn't tell ANYONE!'

Faith listened to Francie cry. So much moisture in this little room night after night, it was a wonder Faith didn't have a problem with rising damp. She murmured in sympathy now and then, and placed a warm hand on Francie's heaving back. When there seemed to be a break in the weather Faith finally spoke.

'I'd like you to do a little visualisation exercise with me. Do you know what that is?'

Francie did know because Olga had employed it once in her search for the perfect man. Olga had regaled Francie with the story of how she had visualised this tall, dark and handsome husband and carried the image of him in her mind for months. One day Olga had seen him at the Victoria Market buying onions. She had approached him, breathless with anticipation. This was the man of her dreams and he actually walked the earth! She asked him something about the time or the weather and he answered—in Spanish.

'Next time I visualise, I've got to remember to put "speaks English" in there,' Olga said, shaking her head ruefully.

Francie remembered laughing. So she did know about 'visualisation', but doubted this New Age rubbish would be of any help. She leaned back in the chair and closed her eyes anyway.

Faith's voice was soothing, calming. 'I'd like you to go back to the day of your father's wedding. Imagine yourself as ten years old. Tell me what happened that day. Can you see yourself there?'

At first Francie could not see past herself sitting on the edge of her chair playing a childish game of 'pretend'. But as Faith went on murmuring 'relax' and 'go back' in a hypnotic tone, she was persuaded to go with the flow. She was back in the family house in Blackburn, standing on the swirly purple carpet in the dining room and looking at herself in the mirror-tiled wall. Her dress was cream taffeta with big puffy sleeves like Princess Diana's. Her mother was kneeling behind her fumbling with the matching satin sash at the waist. She looked like the old-fashioned bride doll which stood in the musty corner near the curtains in Grandma's bedroom. Staring eyes and rosebud lips painted onto a pale china face. Arms stiff and outstretched, fingers splayed.

When Mum finally stood, Francie could see her eyes were red. She knew her mother had been crying half the night. She had heard her through the bedroom wall. Her mother had been playing the same mournful Irish folk music over and over on the stereo. Sometimes Francie couldn't tell if it was her mother's voice or a tin whistle or a fiddle that was wailing and moaning. Francie had tried to block out the sound. She pulled the blanket over her head, stretched the sheet tight across her mouth and wondered how many times she could breathe in her same stale breath before she smothered herself and slipped into unconsciousness.

Where was Dad? What colour were his eyes? Blue? Brown? He'd been gone six months and she couldn't remember. Was that how it went? If people weren't right in front of your eyes they just faded away? Her father's boots were still in the bottom of the wardrobe. She had held them and tried to imagine there had been an actual pair of living fleshy feet which had pushed the leather into the worn contours, ground down the heels on one side. All she saw was a pair of abandoned old shoes.

That morning when Dad was getting married to someone else, Francie had found the empty wine bottles and the wedding album on the lounge-room floor. Francie made her brother Joel a bowl of cornflakes and he watched cartoons on TV. He was too young to understand.

Francie had sat on her bed for a long time looking at the wretched puffy dress on its hanger. Her dad's girlfriend had chosen it. She'd dragged Francie off to a bridal boutique with Stella, her new about-to-be stepsister—a sullen seven year old with big front teeth who didn't want to be there either.

Denise, that was Dad's girlfriend's name. What made him want to be with her instead of Mum? When she laughed she threw her head back and you could see right up her nose. She did this thing where she grabbed you and her orange fingernails dug into your arm and it really hurt.

Francie would tell her mum she wouldn't go. You were only supposed to have one wedding and that had been when her dad married her mum. If she went to the church it meant that Dad really wouldn't be coming home. If she didn't go, maybe he would see how Francie really felt and realise it was all a mistake. Maybe he would come back home to Mum.

She was still sitting on her bed when her mother shuffled in and sat next to her.

'You have to go, Francie. Your dad wants you to be there.'

'Do you want me to go, Mum?'

Mum looked over the top of Francie's head, and Francie had turned to see what she was looking at, but it was only the back of the door.

'Well, darling, it's not about what I want, apparently. You know I wish it wasn't happening. But sometimes things just don't work out the way we plan. We just have to try to go on with life as best we can.'

Francie had looked at her mother's tired face and puffy eyes and declared: 'When I grow up I'm only going to have one wedding. And *my* husband will never leave *me*!'

Her mother snorted as she took up a hairbrush and started pulling it through Francie's long fair tangles.

'Well, honey, I wish you luck! I really do. If you're pretty enough, and young enough, and clever enough, and perfect in every way, then maybe he won't leave you. But then again, maybe he will leave you anyway. Maybe you just have to be a better wife than I was. Because I tried, Francie, I really tried. But in the end I just wasn't good enough. And so he went and found someone who is.'

As the brush tore through her hair bringing tears to Francie's eyes, she made up her mind then that she *would* be good enough. She would be *perfect*!

Mum had sent her and Joel to wait on the front veranda until Dad arrived to pick them up in the station wagon. Joel was already pulling at the stiff white collar of his shirt, trying to loosen his tie, and tugging at his black suit jacket. He was a reluctant miniature groomsman to her miserable bridesmaid. She was clutching a stupid basket sprayed gold and filled with the ugly lilies. She would have liked to hurl it into the street so it would be run over by a truck. Then Dad drove up and got out of the car. He was wearing a tuxedo and bow tie. He told Francie she looked beautiful, and Joel that he looked handsome, opened the car door and they had dutifully slid into the back seat.

Francie hadn't wanted to turn to see her mother standing in the shadows. She knew she was crying. But now she watched out of the car window as Dad walked up the front steps and across the veranda to the flyscreen door. He looked like he was on his way to a ball. Mum, with her straggly brown hair tied back in a scarf and her old green dressing gown, was not invited.

Maybe Mum was right. Maybe she should have tried harder. Mum should have worn her best red dress with the pearly buttons, her pearl earrings, her white high-heeled shoes. Dad might have walked right on inside and never left.

But he didn't walk inside. Instead, Mum opened the door and said something to him and pushed him away. Her father shouted. Her mother shouted back. Don't shout, Mum! Ask Dad inside for a cup of tea! Show him the album with the photographs of me and Joel standing in front of the Christmas tree, then he will see we are a perfect family.

Then she saw Mum slap Dad's face. So hard she saw him take a step back. Francie remembered focusing on the steering wheel, wishing the car would drive itself away.

When Dad came back to the car Francie could see a red mark on his cheek. He started the car and it lurched so the basket of flowers flew off the seat. Francie looked out the back window and saw her mother fall to her knees on the wooden veranda. She looked as if she might never stand up again.

Francie had tried to wrestle the door open. Her father shouted at her to leave the door alone and drove faster until her mother disappeared from sight.

'So, can you see yourself there as a little girl?' Faith asked.

Francie still had her eyes closed. A picture of herself standing stiffly, clutching the ridiculous gold basket, was burned into the inside of her eyelids.

'Uh . . . huh,' Francie managed a choking sound through the tears which were now sliding quietly, smoothly down her face. As if they'd been doing that forever and had worn their own path.

'Well, what I want you to do is to go back now as an adult, as you are now, and take that young girl by the hand and comfort her. She needs you, Francie. I think she's a very sad little girl.'

In her mind Francie walked up the steps to where she stood looking so beautiful in her princess dress. She took herself in her arms and kissed her own blonde hair. She took little Francie's hand and they walked down from the veranda together. They walked away from Mum in her dressing gown. Past Dad in his black suit holding open the car door, and Joel already in the back seat. Away from the golden basket of dead white flowers.

They walked down the street, turned the corner and kept walking. They held hands and just kept walking until Big Francie and Little Francie eventually grew into each other.

Nine

'So, *Stupid Cupid*—are you going to go?' Olga was leaning over the table at Café e Cucina with the ribbon from her sleeve trailing in her gnocchi with mushroom sauce. Under normal circumstances Francie would have pointed this fashion faux pas out to her friend, but tonight she just watched as the olive oil seeped up the grey silk in a greasy tide.

'Oh . . . do you think I'll be invited?' Francie looked at Olga with a sick smile and then drained her wineglass. She was already halfway through a bottle of red while her seafood risotto sat in an undisturbed blob in its chunky white bowl.

'Well, you could come with me on my ticket,' Olga offered.

Francie threw up her hands in a theatrical gesture. 'Thanks, *dahling*! That would be *fabulous*! To come as an uninvited guest to a show about my own fucking life! What would ever make you think I'd sit and watch that pathetic luvvie prancing and dancing across a stage singing about *true love*? She wouldn't know about true love if it bit her on the arse! She's an actress,

Olga. She fakes emotion for a living. But she must be doing a good job because she's got you sucked in.'

Olga stuffed another forkful of gnocchi in her mouth so she didn't have to respond.

'You know what, Olga? The reason we are having dinner tonight is because I decided I at least owe it to you to tell you to your face that you are *really* pissing me off! First you go to *her* birthday party and now you are sitting here telling me that you are going to go to *their* show. Do you care about me at all?'

'Of course I do!' Olga protested. She tried to swallow and almost choked.

'I went to the party, I'm going to go to the show, *because* I'm your friend. An *embedded* friend. You know, like the journalists in Iraq? I'm operating behind enemy lines. I've told you everything, haven't—oh shit! Look at my sleeve!"

At that moment the waiter, in a long snowy starched apron down to his trouser cuffs, squeezed between the tables with a napkin. He dabbed at Olga's sleeve as she looked up at him with adoring eyes.

'There you go . . . *belissima*,' he crooned.

Francie watched with mounting annoyance. That was the trouble with Olga. She was so desperate for affection that it was like sending a cocker spaniel on a reconnaissance mission when you needed a Doberman.

'Ohmigod! How cute is he?' Olga exclaimed as she watched the waiter go.

Francie sighed. 'Can you just concentrate for *one* minute?'

Francie was becoming even more isolated with this Nick and Poppy thing. Her best friend Amanda was pregnant and could now be counted on to have a care factor of nil about Francie's troubles. Johnno was utterly compromised as Nick's friend and now housemate. Even Olga was showing that she couldn't be trusted to maintain the rage.

Francie took another hit of her drink, regarded Olga and decided to give her one last chance. Olga's brown eyes were wide with alarm and she raked her fingers nervously through her hair.

'Can you begin to understand why this whole thing is freaking me out? I mean, what part of this don't you understand? They are going to do a show in front of everyone in this whole city about the most painful thing that's ever happened to me. I feel ill just thinking about it. OF COURSE I CAN'T GO!'

Olga's slender hands flew to the front of her silky blouse. She was twiddling the self-covered buttons and looking at the tables to either side of her in case someone had overheard.

'Yeah, I knew you would think that,' she leaned over to Francie and whispered, 'but imagine if you turned up on opening night? Sitting down the front, looking utterly fabulous. You know, really amazing? And imagine if you weren't with me. I mean, imagine if you were sitting next to some incredible man. Think about the message that would send to everyone. It would say: *I'm so over all this. I've grown up, moved on, it's a pity you two can't.* Don't you think?'

Francie paused before answering. Olga could see that her dinner companion was trying to overcome her first impulse, which was to stab her in the eye with a fork. She could see that Francie was trying to marshal her thoughts to make them as clear and unequivocal as possible. All this made Olga stop twiddling her buttons and instead begin nervously tracing the outline of her antique peacock brooch.

Francie finally spoke: 'No, I don't think it would say that. I think it would say to everyone: *Look at poor screwed-up Francie. She can't stay away. How pathetic!* And you know what, Olga? They would be absolutely right.'

Francie was reaching behind her and wriggling her arms into the sleeves of her coat as she delivered her 'goodbye' speech.

'I know everyone wants me to be *better* by now, but I'm not. And I don't know when I will be. I'm sorry if I'm not everyone's perfect cardboard cut-out *balanced human being* anymore. I'm sorry if I've thrown everybody's schedules out.

'I wish I could give you a completion date: *Francis McKenzie's personality repaired, renovated and open for business January 2005.* But I can't. Sorry about that. Sorry to inconvenience everyone.

'So . . .' Francie was standing, pulling her bag off the back of the seat, 'here's the money for dinner . . . and keep the change for a bag of popcorn to enjoy during the show. Meanwhile, I HAVE TO GO OUTSIDE AND BE SICK!'

Olga covered her face with her starched napkin and sank into her chair as every head in the restaurant turned to look at their table. There was a stagy silence as forks and glasses paused in midair. They didn't pause long. This was Chapel Street, Melbourne—the hip, urbane clientele prided itself on being unshockable. And, after all, they were in an Italian restaurant which thrived on such marvellous melodramas.

In a Melbourne minute Francie was marching up Chapel Street in the dark, wrapping her cherry-red trench coat around her. It was November, but an unusually chill wind was blowing down the street from the bay to the river. She didn't turn to see if Olga was following her and guessed she wouldn't be. She imagined Olga was accepting a complimentary glass of port and a consoling flirtatious chat with the hunky maître d'.

To hell with her, thought Francie. She knew she was on her own. There was no-one to whom she could admit her deepest fear: that Francis Sheila McKenzie, thirty-two, resident of St Kilda, was about to be revealed to the world as a deranged psycho. For a moment she allowed herself to recall her night of shame and the episode she feared would one day be exposed. But she quickly pushed it back into the dark recesses of her subconscious mind. It didn't bear scrutiny during waking hours.

She hadn't been normal then, she reasoned. In fact, she was barely functioning now, but six months ago she had truly lost control. Looking back, she could forgive herself. It was not like there had been a list of options in boxes where you could tick either 'tremendously brave', 'mildly upset' or 'totally irrational'. There seemed to be only one logical course which took her down a dark road. She didn't hold out much hope that anyone would understand.

The wind was blowing up dust and rubbish around Francie's knees as she struggled with her flapping coat and finding her car keys in the bottom of her bag. She could hear pieces of tin banging on shop awnings and the sharp flailing of paper. And there it was on a brick wall near the railway bridge, illuminated by a streetlight—another poster with Nick and Poppy looking out at her! Their faces were framed in two pink hearts like the King and Queen of True Love.

She ran over and ripped the poster off the wall. She was crying, scrabbling at the bricks, tearing her fingernails. As she scraped away the last fragments of paper she wished she could do the same to her own body. Scrape away her eyes and face and flesh until she was just bare white bones that didn't feel anything at all.

Ten

From: Kyles@bigpuddle.com.au

To: ssingle@SunPress.com

Subject: Revenge

Francie, I know someone who superglued cigarette butts and rubbish all over her ex boyfriend's car. What's the best revenge story you've ever heard?

Kylie

Hah! How about the one where the ex and his new girlfriend put on a show and invite everyone in town?

Francie was sitting in the newspaper office with her head in her hands when Gabby Di Martino came to take up her favourite perch on the corner of her desk. Today she was a vision in fawn suede. Fawn suede, fawn hair, fawn tummy. She reminded Francie of a baby antelope as she folded her long limbs and licked at her lip gloss.

'So, how's the column coming along? Can you have it in by five so we can split this joint on time? I've got a hair and nail appointment.'

'Sure, almost finished,' Francie replied wearily.

Gabby leaned over and read the email on the screen.

'Oooh, revenge! Sex it up, will ya? The punters love all that revenge crap. Personally I think the best revenge is just looking fabulous and totally ignoring the bastard! But I'll admit I've had years of practice and it's not something everyone can manage.

'Speaking of looking fabulous, watcha wearing tonight? Something glam? It's always *so* much fun after the show. We all sit in the Green Room and watch Jessie as the program goes live to air, then she comes in and we all tell her she's *brilliant* and then we hit the town and get wasted.

'And the most compelling feature of the *Talkfest* Green Room is the talent. All those hot international musos, movie stars and their entourages in town for the weekend! So lonely and all looking for a tour guide to the local sights!

'Can I help it if the best attraction in this dump is my bare arse?' And here Gabby laughed so hard she slid off the desk. Francie managed a smile.

'Awww . . . c'mon, Francie! You've been in the fun house a week now. Please tell me Dave has at least crossed your radar.'

'He seems really nice,' Francie replied. *Fuck off and leave me alone. If I want a nurse I'll push a call button.*

'Oh Jesus.' Gabby's head pitched forward towards her lap. 'You know what, Francie? Being single is not a life-threatening condition, but being celibate is. If you don't have sex with someone soon, YOU WILL ACTUALLY DIE!'

Francie refused to be entertained. 'I don't think I should get involved with anyone in the house. I'm not really ready for a relationship.'

'Whoa, girl! Involved? Relationship? How much time have you spent with Dave? Those words aren't in his vocabulary. I'm talking about a late night *oops . . . I seem to have stumbled into the wrong room and fallen face down on your dick, Dave . . .* He is *seriously* cute.'

Francie was surprised to register a twinge of possessiveness over Dave. That was a laugh! As if anyone would be seen dead with her after the opening night of *Stupid Cupid*. Which raised an interesting point. Gabby must have seen the posters and advertisements. Was it like when she and Nick broke up? Everyone knowing about it but too polite or embarrassed to mention it. Or too afraid to say anything in case Francie fell apart.

Would Gabby go to the show if she were Francie? Francie was just about to ask her advice when Gabby snapped to attention.

'Uh-oh, I've gotta go. I can tell by the look I'm getting from the boss that we've had a visit from the fuck-up fairy again. This isn't an office. It's hell with fluorescent lighting!' She leaned over and squeezed Francie's hand.

'I wanna see you trashed tonight, Francie. Sitting on some divine man's knee, with his hand up your little black dress and your tongue down his throat. Let yourself go, for God's sake. The way you are, you're shit for morale around here.'

109

And thanks for that caring speech.

Francie watched Gabby go. There was no-one in the office who could *not* watch her traversing the expanse of green carpeting as if she was loping across the grasslands of the Okavango Delta.

Francie turned her attention to next Sunday's column. Revenge—that was the topic at hand. You could talk about crustaceans in the curtain rails or watercress seeds in the shag pile, but the reality was that revenge was all in the eye of the perpetrator. One could sit and imagine the havoc wreaked by a violent, ingenious or expensive revenge, but truly, did it change anything . . . ever?

Did you ever hear of a bloke who came running back after his windscreen had been smashed by a harridan with a house brick: 'My God . . . I spent all morning waiting for the repair truck to arrive and I just realised that I do love you after all?' No. Did you ever hear of a man brought to his senses by a dead rat nailed to the front door? 'What was I thinking? She probably caught that rat with her bare hands. I've made a hideous mistake. I love her, not you!' No. What actually happened was that the lovers huddled closer together as the storm of vengeance wheeled around them.

Francie wished she had been able to play it cool like Gabby. She'd always admired those women who were able to loose the cold steel and execute a bloodless decapitation. Women who were able to say, 'Fine, I will never see you ever again and don't even think of calling.' But that wasn't Francie. She had called and called again, begged, cried and staggered around all over town making a sorry, soggy spectacle of herself. And she could sit and regret what she had done for as long as she lived, but it was over. Done and dusted. So, what to say to Kylie? She typed:

Dear Kylie,

I don't actually believe in revenge. All the best ones have been done—filling cars with cement, posting nudie pix on the internet, prawns in the hubcaps—done, done, done!

To be a witty and original bitch takes a lot of time and money. Why spend that on your ex? Spend it on yourself and leave it to a higher power to exact karmic retribution. Have faith, my child!

As ye sow, so shall ye reap . . . (and the only thing you'll attract with dead prawns is flies).

Love, Francie XXX

Francie shut down her computer terminal and collected her handbag. Of course she was wise about all this revenge stuff—in retrospect. She didn't want to think about that night anymore. She must—she was determined to—start looking back on the break-up with a bit more detachment. Be kinder to herself. It wasn't the first time she'd thought this, and it wouldn't be the last. It seemed you had to say this stuff to yourself over and over until you nursed every damaged brain cell back to health individually. Francie figured that meant she only had to tell herself this a few million times more.

Tonight was Friday night. Maybe Nurse Gabby was right and she should start kicking up her heels. She knew exactly which heels they would be—the sweetest little pair of strappy silver sandals with pearls on the toes that she'd seen in a window in Toorak Road. If she ran now, she'd still have time to get them on the way home.

Eleven

The Green Room at the television station was in party mode and it was only halfway through *Talkfest*. Francie was sitting with Dave, Robbie, Johnno and Gabby watching a massive plasma screen on a wall. Everyone talked through the advertisements and all shooshed each other whenever Jessie appeared on camera. They had already raided the refrigerator for three bottles of white wine and made short work of a cheese platter.

It was all very glamorous. The Green Room was *actually* green. The recessed lighting in the ceiling and the table lamps rendered the space theatrical, dramatic, and everyone there was superbly cast.

Gabby looked edible in a cinnamon coloured mini-dress dusted with transparent beads—like a sugar-coated cookie. She was balanced (she always seemed to be perched, as if she was about to take flight at any moment) on the arm of Robbie's black leather chair. Her long legs were crossed at Dave's eye level, so that if he turned even slightly he was presented with yards of tanned bare skin. Francie idly wondered, not for the first time, whether Gabby and Dave had been lovers. But tonight it was Robbie who was sitting on a chair next to her, his arm around her trim waist with that easy privilege gay men seem to have as a birthright. Perhaps they were all just good friends.

The spotlights shining on Robbie's hair turned it translucent white and threw sculpted shadows on his muscular chest and arms. Francie had already noticed a frisson of interest between him and the equally hot, dusky Cuban percussionist who was here with the band—tonight's guest musical act on the show.

Johnno had come along as Francie's date and he was reclining on a leather couch, beer in hand, in his usual scruffy uniform of ripped jeans and equally desiccated black suit jacket over a T-shirt with political protest. Tonight his cause was battery hens and a cross-eyed chicken peered out at the room from between his lapels. Francie glanced at him and smiled. With his big dark eyes and thick hair flopping over his forehead, he looked the arty poetic type that any number of women would be unable to resist taking home. And Johnno was so loyal, so loving. It would be like rescuing a puppy from the pound.

She took another peek at Dave from under her fringe. Oh yes, Dave was *seriously* cute alright. He was so easy and confident he didn't need a prefab slogan to announce his arrival. He was wearing beautifully cut plain black trousers, a white shirt and a black leather jacket which reminded Francie of fresh liquorice. Dark, sweet and substantial. She realised she wanted to lick him.

Francie had run into Dave a handful of times in the house this past week. Each time she'd felt awkward while he had regarded her with calm interest. Their conversations hadn't gone much past the *bathroom's free, light switch is here, bread knife is there* stage, but there was definitely a mutual flicker of fascination which went beyond banal domestic exchanges.

Francie, sitting on the floor, had bought the pearly toed sandals and she looked at them appreciatively as they peeked out the bottom of her jeans. She'd also piled fake pearls around her neck and in this light they were almost luminous over the tiniest little black top in her wardrobe. Her blonde hair was sleek and just so, her lips a delicious, glossy, pinky beige. She was watching the screen, but felt Dave's eyes on her whenever she moved.

She remembered reading once that the way to feel happy, when you weren't, was to imitate people who were. So that's what Francie was doing. Watching the people around her laugh and smile, and imitating them like a small child. It seemed that no-one could tell the difference.

'Shoosh, shoosh, Jessie's talking,' someone hissed and all eyes turned to the screen.

The five members of the *Talkfest* panel were sitting behind a glass desk in front of a modestly sized TV studio audience. The three regular male hosts were in the middle and a woman sat either side of them. One was an Olympic medal-winning water polo player who was clearly out of her depth in the witty conversation being bounced back and forth in front of her, and the other was Jessie.

Jessie's eyes were glittery purple and matched the streaks in her hair. She was wearing a neat little black jacket scattered with miniscule silver and blue sequins which sparkled as she waved her hands at the studio audience and the camera. Jessie the comedian was in full performance mode. Her big eyes flashed with enthusiasm and everyone was captivated, waiting for her next witticism.

'The thing is, my flatmate,' she was saying, 'he keeps bringing home these high-maintenance chicks . . .'

Francie shot another look at Dave, who was suddenly staring very intently at the screen.

'High maintenance? What does that mean?' one of Jessie's male offsiders on the panel interrupted.

'You know,' she exclaimed, waving her hands, 'they always want to go somewhere expensive. They like lots of little gifts—flowers, perfume, jewellery. They're always *perfectly maintained*. Their Chanel fingernail polish is the exact same shade as their toenails. Their handbag matches their shoes.'

The men were puzzled. Why would anyone devote a nanosecond of mental energy to matching her shoes and handbag? They were keen for Jessie to get to the point.

Francie then sneaked a sideways look at Gabby and caught her regarding her own coordinated fingers and toes. Gabby recrossed her legs, tossed her hair once more and purred with contentment.

'Well, I've now realised,' continued Jessie, 'these high-maintenance chicks have got it made. My problem is that when I meet a bloke, I *look* low maintenance and, it's true, I *am* low maintenance. I'm happy with an afternoon at the footy and a beer. I even cut my own hair!'

There was general guffawing from the audience and the panel members as they fought to get in the next line.

'Jeez, doesn't look it, Jessie!'

'Whaddya use? An angle grinder?'

Jessie squealed with mock indignation: 'Shut up! Shut up! You are all so RUDE! The thing I want to say is that, OK, I don't look like I cost much to run, BUT I am actually a *high performance* unit! So it's like buying a Nissan Pulsar and then finding out it goes like a Formula One—and you don't have to fill it with racing fuel cos plain old unleaded will work fine.'

There were more hearty laughs all round.

'Don't laugh—it's a pain! What's the point of a bloke having a crappy looking car that goes hard? No-one ever believes you— am I right, guys? How boring is that?'

The men had to admit Jessie had a point.

'But if you are a high-maintenance chick and you *under*perform, you totally get away with it! I mean, what bloke is ever going to admit that his gleaming Ferrari actually goes like a Holden Barina? No way! So, girls, I reckon the solution is over-promise and under-deliver every time. It's the way car yards work. Oh, and don't have too many owners!'

There was more laughter and applause. Jessie was sitting back smiling, pleased with her efforts.

The camera cut to the host. He was shaking his head with admiration. 'We'll take a break while we get Jessie up on the hoist, check out her donk and rear end, and we'll be back with *Cuba Cuba!* and some high-octane rhythms to finish the show.'

There was a last shot of Jessie feigning outrage and the screen cut to an ad break. Francie looked over at Dave, who was looking back at her with raised eyebrows.

'There you go, Francie. Just be careful what you tell Jessie—it will all end up on national television!'

'Do you mind?'

'Nah, not really. That's our Jess. She's got a big mouth and a heart to match, but I'm a tough guy. I can handle it. Anyway, I guess it pays to advertise. Can I get you another drink?'

Francie smiled at him. He was becoming more attractive by the minute and it didn't seem to be the wine talking. Dave was so relaxed and open. He was definitely more sure of himself than Nick ever was.

'Ooh . . . I'd love another drink too, Dave.' Gabby leaned over to him so he had a view of her impressive cleavage.

Everyone in the room, which also included the assorted guests of the other panel members, mingled and chatted while the ads were playing. Johnno sidled up to Francie.

'So . . . Jessie. Is she single?' he asked and drained his beer.

Now Francie thought about it, Johnno and Jessie would make a very handsome couple indeed. There was certainly something in the air tonight. Expectancy, sexual tension everywhere you looked.

'Yep, she sure is, Johnno. Go for it!' Francie whispered in his ear. He smiled broadly and headed for the fridge.

'OK, everyone, SHOOSH!' This time it was Robbie who was glued to the screen, taking a very keen interest in the band—or more particularly, the hunky coffee-skinned man with the black dreadlocks who was sitting behind a pair of bongo drums. The music started and everyone in the room was up on their feet, unable to resist the Latin grooves of *Cuba Cuba!*

Dave shimmied over towards Francie with her drink and they quickly fell into a synchronised step. Gabby was there in a flash with her arm around Dave's shoulders. Dave reached out for Francie's waist and she felt a warm tingle of excitement down to her pearly toes. The night was becoming more interesting by the minute!

The music stopped and everyone clapped. The noise subsided just in time to hear the host wrap up the program. 'And join us next week when our special guests will be stage legend Poppy Sommerville-Smith and her partner Nick Jamieson, who will be telling us all about their new show *Stupid Cupid . . .*'

Francie didn't hear any more. Her world stopped in that instant. Her heart sank to her sandals. She wriggled out of Dave's grasp and looked wildly around the room for Johnno, who, at the same moment, was crossing the room to her.

'Hey, hey, hey, France, it's OK, it's OK,' he was mouthing as he came closer. He was already in full damage-control mode.

'Just come outside for a moment and settle down, baby. It's OK.'

Francie let Johnno take her by the hand and she stumbled blindly after him into the shabby corridor. They found a dressing room door with Jessie's name on it and ducked inside.

Francie was breathing heavily as she paced the small room strewn with clothes. Johnno sat in front of the mirror on the bench piled with make-up and jewellery and watched her go.

'They're *everywhere*! I can't go *anywhere*! If I drive down the street they're *there*. If I open a newspaper, they're *there*. What am I going to do? Where am I going to go?' Francie's voice was high-pitched and strangled, but mercifully there were no tears.

'This was always going to happen, France. But you can't take it personally, it's not about you—'

Francie rounded on him: 'DON'T YOU GET IT EITHER? IT *IS* ABOUT ME! IT WILL ALL BE IN THERE . . . EVERYTHING!'

Johnno looked at her for a moment, uncomprehending, and asked, 'Why are you so terrified? What do you mean *everything*? What the fuck happened?'

Francie looked down and stared at her stupid Noddy shoes.

'Nick must have told you.'

'Told me what?'

'You'll know soon enough. I just hope that you can find some way to understand. I . . . just wasn't me then. I was . . . I can see now. It was about something that happened to me a long time ago. I . . .'

The door banged open before she could say any more and in whirled Jessie. 'Phew! Hi, hi, hi Francie!'

Johnno jumped off the bench and Francie stood to attention. They were trespassing, after all, but Jessie didn't seem to notice. She was on an adrenalin high. Francie was glad of the interruption and gave her an extravagant hug.

'Jessie, that was great! You were great! Oh, and this is Johnno Purcell. He's one of my best friends. Johnno, meet the gorgeous Jessie Pascoe.'

Johnno Purcell and Jessie Pascoe. Here was a match! Even Francie, who didn't have much time for spiritual mumbo jumbo, could feel the earth's spin slow for a millisecond as their fates collided.

Johnno extended his hand and pulled Jessie towards him for a kiss on the cheek. 'Hello, the gorgeous Jessie Pascoe! How nice to meet you at last,' he said smoothly. 'Long time admirer. Love the show. Love your work.'

Francie could see Jessie was impressed. She even blushed, which no-one in Australia would have thought her capable of.

'Thank you very much. Eeyew! I've put vile orange make-up and lippie all over you.'

Jessie wiped a thick smear of gunk from the side of Johnno's face with her fingers. It was a typically spontaneous and intimate Jessie gesture, but Johnno didn't seem to mind and offered himself up to her ministrations.

'There, gone. I'd better get myself out of this disguise.' She flapped her hands theatrically.

'I'll see you in the Green Room for drinks in a minute . . . and then the night is ours, kids. OK?'

Johnno and Francie were kindly dismissed. They took a little time to walk back down the corridor. If Johnno hadn't had such a tight hold of her hand, Francie might have made a run for it. When they saw the door to the Green Room up ahead and Johnno had regained the power of speech, he turned to her.

'Look, France, I think you're worrying too much. Why don't I talk to Nick. The fact is no-one wants to see you fucked over any more than you have been.'

'Except for Ms Poppy Sommerville-Smith. I mean, what does she care?'

'You know she's not as bad as you make out. I think she's pretty mature about it all.'

'Meaning that I'm not?'

'Well . . .'

'Don't answer that! It would be great if you talked to Nick. Can you? Can you ring me when you have?'

'Yeah. I promise. Now, I can see Dave's got his eye on you and I definitely have mine on Jessie! Let's just have a good night,' he said, nuzzling her neck.

Francie shoved him and sighed. He was right. Despite everything, she should try to do just that.

When they were back in the Green Room they could both see that the night was moving along satisfactorily. Robbie was conducting an animated discussion with Mr Dreadlocks Bongo. Sound engineer and musician? Or was there something more? Francie hoped for Robbie's sake there was. Francie could also see Gabby and Dave chatting in another corner. And why not? What a great looking couple they made. It was stupid to think of herself with Dave, Francie reprimanded herself. In her current state of mind she was a liability to any man. She was a liability to herself, for God's sake. She felt that she could dress herself up and put on make-up, but in the end it was just cheap wallpaper covering up the cracks.

Oddly enough, at that very moment Dave and Gabby both turned and looked at her. Erk! Francie grabbed Johnno's hand and dragged him to the buffet. They took fresh drinks and began devouring hot party pies like they were going out of fashion (which they were).

Francie had a mouth full of hot pie when she felt a large pair of hands insinuate themselves around her midriff. She almost choked when she turned around and found herself face to face with an expanse of black liquorice leather. She spluttered and watched, horrified, as bits of pastry and mince sprayed out of her mouth and all down the front of the soft, no doubt expensive, hide.

'Oh . . . goodness . . . sorry!'

'Don't worry, fine, fine,' said Dave, brushing his chest with a napkin, and Francie could see that it was.

'Where's Gabby?' She was genuinely surprised not to find her hanging off Dave's arm.

Dave whispered: 'I'll give you ten seconds of thinking music . . . is she heading for the waitress serving the party pies? The bloke on camera three? Or the lead singer of *Cuba Cuba!*, which is currently supporting Lenny Kravitz on tour?'

Dave then began humming a refrain from *American Woman* in her ear.

'Hmm . . .' Francie leaned back and almost put her hand into a large bowl of avocado dip. 'These party pies *are* very good . . . um . . . it's a tough question . . .'

Dave leaned over her and Francie could smell him. She couldn't tell exactly what the smell was, except that it registered somewhere in the back of her primitive woman brain as 'gorgeous, fuckable man'. Her hair felt hot.

'I'm HERE!' It was Jessie, who bounded up and grabbed Dave and Francie in a big hug. 'Hi, flatmates! Just working out who's turn it is to clean the loo?'

Not quite, thought Francie, but it was a timely reminder. She and Dave were sharing a house, after all, and she'd only been there a week. The last thing she needed was a disastrous one-night stand and the removal van backing up again.

Dave turned and gathered Jessie in his arms and kissed her while looking meaningfully at Francie over the top of a purple tuft of hair. Then Johnno was on the scene too, with a drink for Jessie, and the stage was set for a night of fabulous flirtation and foreplay.

✳

It was probably about 2 am when they all staggered through their front door in St Kilda.

Once in the kitchen Francie was automatically in hostess mode and went for the vodka to offer a round of drinks, but by the time she'd pulled the bottle from the icy clutches of the freezer, retrieved potato chips from the pantry and glasses down from the cupboard, she and Dave were alone.

Jessie and Johnno hadn't made it up the hall past Jessie's bedroom. Francie also noted that Robbie was alone and seemed content to share his bed with the weekend newspapers he'd picked up at the 7-Eleven on the way home.

There was a certain inevitability to proceedings. Dave and Francie could have sat around the table and made small talk for another hour and ended up at exactly the same moment they were at now. But they both knew the last thing they needed was more small talk or alcohol. Time to move things along.

'So,' said Dave in a most seductive voice, holding out his hand, 'your place or mine?'

'Well, I think mine's closer but I'm too drunk to . . .'

'Too drunk to fuck?' Dave hummed that well-known Dead Kennedys tune.

'Oh no . . . not at all.' Francie smiled. 'In fact I'd say I'm just the right amount of drunk not to give a fuck. I was going to say too drunk to drive . . . so let's walk.'

'Then fuck?'

'Why the fuck not?'

It wasn't what you'd call the most romantic seduction in the world but Dave and Francie had been working up to this all night. They had danced and touched and whispered until their bodies were tuned to the same frequency. Neither of them had mentioned 'love', 'romance' or 'relationship'. This was about sex and they both knew it.

As it turned out they didn't walk down the hall. They ran. They fell into her room and onto her bed in the dark.

Francie couldn't believe she was doing this. Was about to have sex with a man who wasn't Nick for the first time in five, no, more like six, years. She figured this would be a more efficient way of wiping out memories of her ex than any number of hours spent sitting in Faith Treloar's blue velvet confessional chair.

Everything about Dave was different. For a start there was his chest. It was broader than Nick's, and hairy. Where Nick's body was lanky and boyish, Dave's was muscly and powerful. Then there was his tongue, which seemed to be much more expert than Nick's, and paid attention to places Nick hadn't visited with great enthusiasm for a long time. And there was his voice. Dave was a talker where Nick usually conducted himself in silence.

Over the next hour Dave showered Francie with words of appreciation which fell on a parched landscape. She could feel herself blossoming, every petal unfurling.

'Ooh . . . you smell . . . I can't even think of a word to describe . . .

'Your hair is *so* . . .

'Now let me see, if we can just get rid of this . . .

'And these . . .

'Can I turn on the light?

'Oh God . . . perfect . . . just perfect . . .

'Gorgeous breasts . . . mmm. Sweet little nipples. I might just . . .

'Take your hands away and lemme look . . .

'So pretty. You're so pretty. Did you know that?

'Now, if I can just put this here . . .

'Oh, keep doing that. That feels *very* nice. Do that again.

'And while you're doing that, how about if I do this?

'Oh . . . so you like that?

'Well, how about if I keep doing that while you take this and . . .

'Now turn over and I'll . . .

'Not yet . . . in a minute . . . shoosh . . .

'I love this curve here . . . these cute dimples . . .

'I wish you could see yourself . . .

'So tight . . . so very . . . very . . . tight . . .

'God that feels good . . .

'You'd better stop or . . .

'I'm telling you . . . you move like that again . . .

'And I won't be able to . . .

'Uh . . . huh . . . uh . . . aaah . . .

'Mmm . . . mmm . . .

'Can we do that again?'

So they did that again and a few other things as well. Francie felt that she wasn't watching an old movie in a darkened room any longer. She was starring in the premiere of a new blockbuster production. She was a newly discovered ingenue playing opposite an experienced, extremely talented leading man.

Within a couple of hours she wasn't comparing Dave with Nick anymore. Dave was there in his own right. Full frame, front and centre.

Twelve

By the time breakfast came around next day, it was after lunch. And if Elysium was the place you went after you died . . . well, it wasn't a bad option.

Francie straggled into the sunny kitchen mid morning and found it more like a cosy corner café than her own home. The sound of the Rolling Stones' 'Satisfaction' was blaring from the living room. Robbie was serving scrambed eggs and bacon, and holding forth to Johnno, who was sitting at the table in front of a large jug of bloody marys with an entire celery tree sticking out of it. Jessie was blowing cigarette smoke through the open window in between looking at Johnno with big, limpid, hazel eyes.

Francie fished in the fridge for ice for her glass of water as she listened to Robbie's Saturday morning lecture.

'The trouble is that prosperity has come at the cost of originality,' he was saying as he waved a wooden spoon. 'With today's music you have to look hard to find that intellectual and physical risk. Now the Stones had it—you could still find that raw energy of African rhythm in their early days, like you could find the blues in Elvis Presley. But today, because of the politics of blame, everything has to be safe, safe, safe. Urban living has transformed that raw energy into banality. What do you like listening to?'

'I like the John Butler Trio. I think he's—' began Johnno.

'A hippie. Back to the womb stuff,' said Robbie dismissively.

'Yeah, well back to the womb isn't such a bad place to go, you know. Safe, warm . . . a place to be nurtured, to grow,' and here Johnno looked at Jessie with a wink and a sly smile.

'Yeah,' Jessie cut in, 'climb down off your soapbox, Mr Homo Man, and give us breeders a bit of respect.'

'Morning,' said Francie. She could feel herself blush. This was a new sensation after a night of wild sex—being greeted with a panel of inquisitive eyes.

'Morning.'

'Hi.'

'Hello, darls!'

Don't ask me, don't ask me, don't ask me.

'So how was last night?' Jessie and Johnno chorused together. They looked at each other and giggled.

Well that, Francie supposed, was inevitable. She reached for the jug of tomato juice and poured herself a drink. After a procession of cocktails and five hours' sleep Francie should have felt a lot worse, but she felt energised, alive.

'Hey . . . I could ask you the same question.'

There was a short pause for meaningful looks all round and Johnno and Jessie dived on the toast and eggs. Then Francie heard Dave cough as he walked up the hall. She ducked her head and retreated into the pantry looking for raspberry jam.

'Morning, all.' Dave sounded very hale and hearty. Francie walked out of the pantry straight into him, and was rewarded with two big hands reaching down the back of her baggy pink pyjama shorts to give her bottom a squeeze.

'Mmm . . . hello there, you . . .' he crooned into her neck.

He was still warm from the shower, his hair wet and glossy black. His dark green eyes were fringed with the longest black eyelashes and Francie could feel them brushing her skin. He was as handsome in broad daylight as she had last seen him in shadow.

He didn't seem embarrassed at all. But why would he be? He does this all the time, thought Francie. From what Jessie and Gabby had told her he was the one-night stand expert. Was Francie just another goodtime Fluff Bat? Before last night she thought that all she wanted was a meaningless one nighter. Now she wasn't so sure.

Over the next hour two more plates of toast and more bacon were eaten, Johnno had cleaned out the juice and everyone was now on vodka and tonics. They'd moved on from discussing music and gotten into art, politics and architecture.

Francie loved hearing Dave talk. The theme of 'dumbing down' seemed to come up a lot. Dave talked about contemporary design: 'You see it all the time. The ironic quotation of the past. In the end it goes nowhere. It's a stand-in for creativity and intelligence. An excuse for not taking up the challenge of originality. Irony is the subtle threat of post-modernism. Whenever post-modernism is questioned, the easy answer is: "It's a joke, it's not serious". But that answer robs people—artist and audience—of initiative. At its worst it's a confidence trick.'

Said by anyone else this would have screamed 'wanker', but Dave was actually extremely well read and frighteningly intelligent. But he wasn't condescending. His face was alive with enthusiasm whenever you caught an idea and wanted to hear more. But despite his friendly and patient inclusion of her in the discussion, Francie did feel dumb when he talked. This was nothing like the household of singles you saw on television's *Big Brother*: 'Shite! What dickhead drank all the beer?'

She was transfixed listening to Robbie and Dave vigorously exchange provocative views on modern life and culture, Jessie interjecting with her sharp wit and Johnno defending his leftie orthodoxy with passion. If last's night's physical encounter had restored Francie's thirsty body, then this conversation was feeding and watering her very soul.

Of course it wasn't fair to compare, but Francie was now wondering whether her long, settled relationship with Nick had deprived her of something far more stimulating. Maybe that's why he had buggered off. Maybe he'd just realised this months before Francie had. Maybe that's what he now had with *her*.

She found herself entertaining a quick sound bite of Nick and Poppy at their breakfast table in Parkville.

'*So, Nick, do you think Australian theatre must be more protective of our unique voice in the face of globalism? Or will such protectionism render us a cultural backwater?*'

'*I'm glad you asked, Poppy. I feel that without a more rigorous approach, a renewed effort to place our voice in a global context, we are in effect trying to preserve a dying culture. It's imperative that we embrace the new realities or become irrelevant.*'

And then, the oddest thing happened—the phone rang and Jessie announced that Nick was on the line and wanted to speak to Francie. It was odd because, although she had given him her new number, she had never expected him to actually use it. It was also strange because in the six months since she and Nick had busted up, he had hardly rung at all.

The sound of Nick's name in the kitchen was like a rifle shot in a duck pond. Everyone stopped talking and stared at Francie. She grabbed the handset from Jessie and quickly scurried out the French doors onto the veranda where it was quieter. She could hear her own heart drumming an erratic beat.

'Hello . . .'

'Hi . . . Francie?'

'Nick?'

'I just wondered, if you're not doing anything tonight, do you want to go out? Go to a movie maybe? I think it would be good . . . we could have dinner, talk.'

Francie, as if in a trance, heard herself agree to meet Nick in town tonight at 8 pm. She clicked off the phone and gazed at it with amazement. She was startled to find Jessie beside her.

'Bloody hell! What was that about? Are you OK?'

It was a lot to answer. Francie could only manage to mumble something about Nick wanting to know where to send the refunded bond on their old house.

Jessie was scarcely interested. She wanted to talk about what was really on her mind, hopping from foot to foot as she spoke: 'Don't you feel this whole house is just *alive*? God, imagine . . . you, me, Dave, Johnno . . . All of us on the one night? What are the odds of that happening?

'Oh, Johnno is *so* gorgeous! We had the most brilliant night! He's too funny, and smart and *thank you* for introducing me. Maybe my luck is changing. I told you the great drought of 2004 would break before Christmas!

'Isn't it a beautiful day? Isn't Dave the best? I can tell he really likes you. Do you like him? All we need now is for Robbie . . . Well it's a good start, don't you reckon?'

Jessie didn't wait for an answer to any of these questions. She hugged Francie and skipped back inside to take up a position on Johnno's knee.

Francie looked at the sky. It wasn't a beautiful day. It was sunny, but that chilly wind was blowing up again. She could feel bits of herself coming loose, flapping like the posters on the brick wall in Chapel Street. She crossed her arms over her chest and stumbled back inside. She sat down, ignoring the quizzical looks from the boys. She tried to tune in to the conversation once more, but the spell was well and truly broken. Francie talked, but meanwhile thoughts flashed through her mind as if they were bulletins being pulled through at the bottom of a television screen.

'Breaking News: Nick Jamieson seeks talks . . . Experts confused why talks scheduled at this time . . . What is nature of demands? asks McKenzie . . . Analysts say could be détente both sides hoping for . . . Stand by . . . more details in late news. Tomorrow Fine . . . 26 degrees.'

All thoughts of a languid Saturday afternoon in bed with Dave disappeared. He kept looking at her and she knew he sensed it. What did he know about Nick and her? She recalled telling him that she hoped she and Nick would get back together. She guessed Gabby Di Martino had filled him in on the details.

She thought back to the Green Room last night and the sight of them with their heads together. She wondered if Nurse Gabby had told Doctor Dave that a night of mind-blowing sex was just the tonic the patient needed.

'Well,' sighed Robbie, looking at the wall clock, 'gotta crank up for an afternoon recording gig at Manchester Lane. So I guess it's adios, one and all.' He looked at the two couples with a knowing smile. 'Enjoy your respective Saturday nights.'

After kisses all round he was gone, but just for a moment. He was soon back with someone Francie had never seen before— a shortish, tubby bloke wearing neat black trousers and a natty green embroidered waistcoat over his white shirt. He looked Greek, Italian or something more exotic. He registered Jessie sitting on Johnno's knee and Francie could see a flash of annoyance in his eyes until his forced smile ran interference.

'Heeere's Henry,' Robbie announced. Ah, so this was Henry! Jessie's ex. The one who apparently had an uncanny knack for ruining all Jessie's efforts at finding a new beau.

'Good afternoon, people,' said Henry. 'I have cakes.' He ripped the white paper bag which read 'Mozart's, Acland Street' off a cardboard tray and dumped chocolate éclairs and icing sugar-dusted almond crescents on the table.

Francie shot a look at Johnno, who had obviously heard about Henry too, because he quickly stood, almost throwing Jessie off his lap onto the floor.

'I've gotta go,' Johnno blurted. 'Things to do. See you, Robbie, Dave, France. Thanks for the drinks.'

'I'll walk you to the door,' announced Jessie, and as they headed out of the kitchen she turned back to Henry with a face which was pure poison.

Henry merely shrugged. 'Who wants a cup of tea?' he asked as he reached for the kettle.

'Thanks, Henry, but no, I've got to get going,' said Robbie, following Johnno and Jessie.

Then it was Dave's turn to make excuses. He stood and stretched his arms. 'Uh yeah, got some work to get through this afternoon. I'll take a cake though, Henry. Sensational éclairs . . . I need a sugar hit.' And then he was gone too.

So, that was that! Ten minutes ago there'd been two new couples in the room basking in a comfortable post-coital glow, and now there were just two morose exes looking at a kitchen table piled high with dirty dishes.

'Um . . . I'll have a cup if you're making one, Henry. I'm Francie, by the way.' She smiled weakly.

'Oh I know who *you* are,' said Henry as he busied himself in the kitchen with an easy familiarity. 'I play trombone in a band called Diving Bell. We've been doing some work with Nick Jamieson and Poppy Sommerville-Smith on their new show.'

Francie stood and looked at his back as he spoke. Nick and Poppy couldn't be here *too* . . . not in her own kitchen! She started to noisily stack glasses on plates. *Just shut up, shut up, shut up!*

But Henry either didn't understand or didn't care about Francie's feelings as he ploughed on: 'Yeah, it's going to be really good. There's a great song in there about revenge. Poppy wrote it herself. There's a few surprises in this show. I think people will be blown away by how good a singer she is. I think . . .'

Francie considered throwing a coffee mug at the back of his fat head. Instead she banged the mug on the table and was heading out the door when Jessie pushed past her into the kitchen and started shouting.

'What the fuck are you doing here, Henry?! HOW DARE YOU JUST WALK IN ANY TIME YOU FEEL LIKE IT . . .'

Francie could hear their argument echoing down the hall as she found the sanctuary of her room and closed the door firmly behind her.

In the Red Room thoughts of Nick crowded in on her. Why now? What did he want to talk about? Francie saw her hands were shaking. She was nervous already at the thought of seeing him. She ran through what he might possibly say. The first scenario was: 'I want us to get back together. It was a mistake. I still love you.'

Is that what she wanted to hear? Twenty-four hours ago it would have been 'yes, yes'. Now it was 'yes, no, yes, maybe . . .'

She honestly didn't know how she felt and wouldn't until she heard the words actually come out of his mouth. But then, because Francie wasn't a complete idiot, she also entertained the other possibilities.

'Poppy and I are getting married.

'It's a medical miracle, she's pregnant. It's twins!

'They want to make a movie of our stage show starring Meg Ryan and Tom Hanks!

'I've finally realised, I'm gay.

'My mum wants you to send back the champagne glasses she bought for your birthday.

'Can I borrow some money? You wouldn't believe how much our street posters cost.

'We're going away—can you feed Poppy's piranhas?

'I suppose a threesome . . . nah . . .'

How many false starts and blind alleys would there be on the path to getting over all this? She remembered Olga telling her that the rule of thumb was that you had to take the length of time you'd been together, divide it in half, and that's how long it would take to stop feeling the pain. So that meant two and a half years. Even in Victorian England you only got two years' mourning for the death of a husband. And that was when you had an actual body to bury. Francie wished, not for the first time, that Nick *had* died in some horrific mishap. Then there would have been some dignity in all this. She would have been a noble widow instead of just a useless cast-off.

In two years' time she would be . . . who? What? Francie couldn't imagine the person she would find after all the layers of hurt and confusion were peeled away. Maybe she was like an onion. You peeled and peeled and all that was left was a tiny small space of nothingness.

She was straightening the bed, picking up hurled underwear and ripped condom foil packets off the floor when there was a tap-tapping at the door.

'It's me—Dave. Can I come in?'

'Yes, sure, come in,' she stuttered as she dumped the detritus from their lovemaking behind the couch.

'Hope I'm not disturbing you . . .'

Was he kidding? Of course seeing Dave was disturbing. The sight of him sent every molecule in her body into violent collision. The memories of last night with him crashed into memories of nights with Nick and created a chain reaction of anxiety. Her thighs still ached from the hours Dave had spent between them. Her face was red and grazed from his stubble and her breasts felt tender. He had imprinted himself on her body. She felt as unmade and rumpled as the bed he was now sitting on.

She didn't want him sitting there! It was the bed she'd shared with Nick. Maybe Nick would be sleeping there again and would know she'd been unfaithful. And there she went once more, having completely irrational thoughts. She looked at the clock—3 pm—and suddenly felt very tired.

Dave reached for Francie's hand and tried to gently pull her in between his thighs. She ducked away and sat at a safe distance on the couch.

'Um . . . I haven't had the chance to tell you yet, thanks for an amazing night.' He glanced at Francie who was taking a keen interest in the floor.

'I had a great time too,' she murmured without meeting his eyes.

He hesitated before going on: 'I thought we should have a talk about how we are going to work this.'

'We don't have to have a talk. It's fine.' She picked bits of fluff off the couch as she spoke.

He was looking straight ahead at her embarrassing cupid picture when he asked: 'Would you like to come out to dinner with me tonight?'

Dinner *after* sex! What was the etiquette here? Were you obliged to have dinner with a man after he'd spent so much time on you in bed? Somehow sitting and talking to him all night over a dinner table for two seemed more intimate than what they'd already done. How could a dinner date imply 'relationship' more than having abandoned sex all night?

'I dunno, Dave,' Francie sighed. 'I mean, thank you, but maybe we should leave it there. It's just . . . too complicated right now.'

'Is it because of Nick?'

Francie didn't want Dave to say his name! It was none of his business. He had no right to ask.

'No,' she lied. 'It's . . . it's because of me. I'm just in a weird place at the moment. I don't think I've got anything to offer . . . anyone. So . . .'

'Hey, I understand! It's fine. Fine. It's all just, you know . . . fine with me.' Dave jumped to his feet. 'So I guess I'll see you round . . . probably in the kitchen . . .'

He backed out the door awkwardly and closed it softly after him.

Francie threw herself onto the bed and pulled the covers over her head. The emotion came in waves, flooding and then receding. A tidal pool of tears. Soon she slipped under the surface and was asleep.

☼

Francie dreamed she was a mermaid. She was sitting on a rock in the middle of the ocean. Her wet hair was wrapped around her face and when she scraped it away she could see she had a tail of glittering scales carved from solid emerald.

She was listening to the waves sighing the loneliest song in the world. This song was so lonely that one of every kind of creature in the ocean came to ask her to make it stop.

They crowded around Francie's rock looking up at her. One seal, one whale, one dolphin, one turtle, one of every kind of fish in the sea. And there were shells, again one of each kind, floating just near her. There was a starfish, a seahorse, a spiny shelled lobster, all staring at her with despairing black eyes.

Please make it stop, they all pleaded with her, but the song went on without end. Every peak of every wave sounded another desolate note.

Then out on the horizon a sailing ship with golden masts appeared. As it came closer Francie could see two figures in white robes standing on the deck holding hands. It was Nick and Poppy. The ship came so close to the rock she was sitting on she could see they were wearing braided wreaths of silver seaweed and pearls on their brows.

Francie tried to cry out to them, but the keening song of the ocean drowned her calls. Nick and Poppy were smiling at her and waving as the ship sailed right on past and into the setting sun. The last she saw of the ship was its black silhouette disappearing from view. The wash from the mighty vessel churned the water around Francie's rock, washing over it and sweeping her away.

As she fell back through the depths Francie tried to move her emerald tail but it weighed her down like an anchor. She reached her hands for the surface as she went down, down into blackness. Looking up through strands of her own hair, as thick and heavy as kelp, Francie opened her mouth to take a breath. All was liquid. As her lungs filled with water she saw the sun shining on the sea's surface for the very last time.

Francie sat up in bed with her damp hair plastered to her face and gulping for air.

This time she saw that Nick and Poppy not only ruled her waking life, but the unfathomable immensity of her subconscious as well. She knew she had to make a swim for it or at least drown trying.

Thirteen

Francie watched Nick dodge the Saturday night traffic on Bourke Street. His hands were captured in the pockets of a charcoal coloured three-quarter length overcoat. His head was battened down against the wind. She'd never seen the coat before and thought how odd that was. She had once known every item in Nick's wardrobe. He was like a snake, shedding his five-year-old skin and growing a new one.

She felt she could recognise him amongst a million people by the way he walked. He strode purposefully and always looked as if he was late. Francie remembered that she had always called 'slow down'. He had always called 'catch up'.

Even when they walked the streets of Paris and London, they were never quite together. He would walk to the corner and wait for her by a lamppost and she would stop halfway down the street to look in a shop window, waving at him to double back. The result was that it always took twice as long to get anywhere. Two steps forward, one back.

As Francie watched she was reminded why she had first been attracted to him. He stood taller than most of the people strolling in the street tonight. They walked with blank, open faces while Nick's brow was furrowed, as if he was pondering one of life's big questions. She used to ask him what he was thinking about and was always surprised to find it was nothing in particular: the pattern of shadows on a wall, the beat of the windscreen wipers, the colour of leaves piled in a gutter. After a while she had stopped asking.

And then there was his colouring. Most people were faded facsimiles of humans compared to Nick. His skin was an even, warm olive. His eyes a warmer, sweet caramel. A crow's wing of straight blue-black hair fell over one eye. There was a branch of the Black Irish somewhere in the Jamieson family tree. It wasn't until she saw him stalking the streets of Dublin that she finally placed him. He was a turbulent mix of the sailors of the Spanish Armada and the fishermen of the Gaels. In her mind's eye he was often standing on a rugged Irish cliff looking out to a darkened sea.

Of course, this was all fanciful romantic nonsense. The Jamiesons were actually from Bairnsdale, a fair sized pedestrian country town in Victoria. His father was a panel beater—a booze artist and bore. His mother was a teacher at the secondary school Nick had attended. On weekends she rescued Nick from late-night drunken inquisitions. On weekdays she marked his school essays with a thick red pencil. When Francie and Nick visited the family's old weatherboard house during holidays, she saw how far his journey had taken him.

In this blokey landscape of flannelette shirts, Blundstone boots and beer guts, how was a boy like Nick to survive? He once told her he was bashed by the local hoons when he landed the role of Sky Masterson in the high school production of *Guys and Dolls*. They'd broken his nose and two ribs. Almost fifteen years later Nick and Francie had driven through the outskirts of the town on their way to spend the weekend with his parents— past the ugly fast food outlets and tyre marts—and Francie had felt Nick's past begin to weigh him down. As if someone had put a brick on his head.

When they first met at the cocktail party for the opening of the Melbourne Film Festival, there was a moment (Francie could not now remember why) when they both talked about 'escaping and surviving'. At that moment their eyes locked and their romantic pact was sealed. Now, here they were, almost six years later, attempting to unglue themselves and ripping off sheets of skin as they tried to pull away.

Nick looked up to see her and smiled. Francie felt her heart rush out to meet him.

'Hi, hello, hi, good to see you,' he said. He pecked her on the cheek. She would always remember that dry little peck.

For her own part, Francie wanted to wrap her arms around his neck and smother him with luscious kisses. Instead she stood on tiptoe, her arms stiffly to her sides, and pecked him back.

'It's lovely to see you too. I . . .' She stopped herself from saying it. 'I like your coat. It suits you.'

'It's new.'

Francie saw up close that it was expensive. Cashmere? She guessed Poppy had chosen it for him.

As they walked down the street Francie realised they were actually in step. She sensed that Nick was concentrating on matching her, allowing her to set the pace. It made her feel once more as if she was a patient. This time she was being walked down a hospital corridor by a concerned relative. *Thanks for coming. Yes, I'm doing fine. Almost better. Not long now and I'll be my old self again.* She knew then that Nick wasn't coming back to her. She was blinking away tears as they walked, hoping he would think it was the wind blowing dust in her eyes.

'So how are you?' he asked.

'Oh, you know, fine. How have you been?'

'Pretty good.'

'It's cold, isn't it? For late November.'

'Yeah. It's usually warmer by now.'

They talked about the weather. How fucked was that? It seemed to be the only safe ground. Any other avenue of inquiry led straight over a precipice.

Global warming, the drought, the science of long-range forecasting and the arcane practice of water divining were all pretty much played out by the time they got to Rosati's Italian restaurant and bar. Patrons entered off a dark lane into an echoing space with an intricate terrazzo floor and walls featuring a Mediterranean trompe l'oeil of archways framing unnaturally blue water. It wasn't an intimate setting. It was bright and busy and Francie knew Nick had chosen it precisely for its lack of intimacy. They filled up the next ten minutes with ordering their meals and taking turns to dip warm bread in a little dish of olive oil with an ease which Francie found heartbreaking in its ordinariness.

While they sipped their martinis they reminisced about the meals they'd shared: a garlic and parmesan spaghetti at a Sicilian restaurant in Rome—utterly plain but unforgettable; a spicy goat and lemon tagine from a roadside stall in the Atlas Mountains in Morocco; and a hilarious Christmas dinner in India.

'Remember that?' Nick smiled. 'The toasted raisin bread masquerading as Christmas pudding?'

'And the skinniest Santa in the world?' Francie was smiling too.

'Do you remember what he gave us?'

Francie did. 'A little painted erotic cameo.'

The word 'erotic' hung in the air like a blown light blub. She didn't mention that she still had this memento strung on the end of her bed. Thankfully the meal arrived—mushroom risotto, spaghetti carbonara and green salad. Francie picked at her food.

As she watched him eat she knew that she would probably never be this close to him again and she knew she had to say it: 'I miss you, Nick.'

He pushed his food away and said softly, 'I miss you too.'

Francie was about to reach her hands out to him, but she stopped herself.

'I don't think I can do this. Sit here as though nothing's changed. And I'm not that hungry, so what did you want to tell me?'

Nick sat back and pushed his black hair out of his eyes. He looked past Francie to somewhere in the blue water off the Amalfi coast. What did he want? She would wait until he found the courage to say what was really on his mind.

'I just needed to see you. It's great being with you here tonight. I mean, we can't just throw away five years . . .'

'It wasn't me who threw it away, Nick. Remember?'

'Uh-huh.'

He began arranging his cutlery at perfect right angles to the patterned border on the damask tablecloth.

'It's just that it makes it so hard on all our friends when we can't be in the same room together and I thought, now that we're both single . . .'

Both *single*? Oh this was good! Really good! She'd seen him with Poppy, kissing, holding hands, and he still wanted Francie to believe he was single?

'But you're with . . .' Francie could not say her name in his presence. '*Her*. And you were with *her* even before you left *me*. What are you talking about?'

'We're, um . . . having a few . . . *problems*. It's hard to explain but . . .'

Francie felt a hand grenade of hope detonate in her chest. The impact took her breath away and made her hands tremble. She quickly slid them off the table and folded them into her lap, where Nick couldn't see.

'I want to tell you first that I'm sorry for what happened, Francie. How it happened. It's the worst thing I've ever done to anyone. And you deserved better. I really am more sorry than you'll ever know.'

Francie rehearsed his next words for him. *I made a mistake. I still love you. I want us to be together again.*

And then she saw his face crumple and realised there were tears in his eyes. For the second time in this whole sorry saga there were tears. The first time was when they'd fallen into bed together and the tears had come just before he delivered a body blow which had made her want to die. What was coming this time? She dug her nails into her palms.

Nick sniffed hard and cleared his throat. 'Jesus . . . I feel like shit! My whole fucking life is unravelling! Johnno told me that you're in therapy and I know it's because of me. I need to know that you're OK, Francie. I can't sleep for feeling so guilty.'

'I don't want this show Poppy and I are doing to push you over the edge. It's just a few songs and stuff and I know when you see it, you'll get it. It's not just about me and Poppy, it's about love, loss, forgiveness . . . you know, universal themes.'

Francie's hands stopped shaking and balled into fists. The warm spot in her chest hardened into a rock which was sinking fast. Her descent was so rapid she couldn't breathe. Nick saw her falling away from him and reached his hands across the table. They clutched at thin air. He'd been good in that medical soap opera on TV, Francie remembered.

'You have to understand! It's not about us, as such, but I want to do the right thing. I've told Poppy that I don't want to do it unless you're fine with it. So, do you think . . . ?' And here Nick faltered.

You totally insensitive . . . Francie looked around the restaurant to see if anyone else had heard him. She had to be imagining this!

Francie looked at the painted balcony on the wall and thought, that's what this conversation was. Two-dimensional. A scene painted on a concrete wall that was supposed to look real, but was obviously fake.

At last Francie heard herself speak in a thin squeak, as if she too were a cartoon.

'You want *my blessing*? How would you like it written on the program, Nick? *Inspired by*? *Dedicated to*? *By royal fucking appointment*? You can shove your *universal themes* up both your arses. I'll tell you something everyone understands— lying, cheating, cowardice. Just plain cruelty is something everyone knows about too. Why don't you call it *The We Don't Give a Fuck About Francie's Feelings Show*? That's got a nice ring to it!'

And then she was standing, wrestling her scarf from the back of the chair, dragging her bag over her shoulder, while Nick slumped down in his seat.

'Yes, I am in therapy,' she hissed. 'But not because of you. I'm just starting to realise this isn't about you. In fact, none of the past five years have been about you *at all*. The last time we saw each other, Nick, you said we were finished. Even as friends. I think you were right.'

From the footpath Francie looked back one last time to see Nick already talking on his mobile phone. She walked down the dark lane towards the lights of Flinders Street glowing brightly ahead of her.

Fourteen

'Well, what we have here is a classic case of a *clinger* and an *avoider*.'

Faith Treloar was pontificating from the red velvet thinking chair. Francie was opposite her in the blue chair and she noticed that, for the first time since she'd been coming here, Faith hadn't pushed the box of tissues across the small table. She was instead sitting back with her hands folded over her ample bosom. The row of amethyst rings twinkled in the lamplight.

'I want you to answer a few questions, Francie. Try to be clear. Try to be straight.'

Francie shifted in her seat and sat up as if she was in school.

'Did you ever feel that you loved Nick more than he loved you?'

Well, of course! Francie had always felt that. But not just about Nick. She had felt this way most of her life . . . about everyone. There was an intensity of feeling that was never requited. She loved so fiercely that no-one could be expected to return what she felt. But this, surely, was the way it would always be. If someone had returned her love with the same fierce passion? She couldn't imagine it was possible.

'In what ways was he emotionally unavailable to you?'

Photographs. There was always an argument about photographs. Nick always said he preferred to remember things as they happened—catch the emotional moment in his head. Looking back, Francie wondered if it was because photographs were evidence that they were a couple.

The one-armed cuddles. It had become a joke between them. Nick would throw his arm—singular—around Francie. She would tackle him in a full-frontal bear hug and then whine until he offered up his other arm. Was it technically a cuddle if you only used one arm? A joke, but another sign that told Francie, somewhere deep down, that he was keeping himself at a distance.

And then there was the way they walked. She'd thought about that on Saturday night. Nick never wanted to be in step with her. As if it showed that he had been tamed like a domestic animal. As if it said to the world 'we are together' and every avenue of escape was barricaded. But she had learned to live with the distance he put between them and figured that if she loved him hard enough he would come closer.

'Did you ever feel that you had to work hard to earn his love?'

Didn't she try to be perfect? Isn't that what her mother had told her to be? She had loved making a home for Nick and he had loved her back. She liked to please him. His pleasure made her feel loved. Her mother had also warned that they leave you anyway. But what was the alternative? To change her very nature? Francie would just do it better than her mother ever did.

'Did you mother him? Try to protect him from the world? Help him make his way?'

She had joked with Johnno that if Nick came back to her it would be because he wanted his washing done or to borrow some money. She had saved her wages and paid for most of their trips away together. But she hadn't resented it.

When he landed the role in the television soapie, Nick had brought home flowers and champagne. He was written out of the series after six months, but Francie had been happy to support him while he made the next round of auditions. She and Nick had a partnership. He was talented and acting was such a hazardous profession! Francie had never doubted that one day he would be really famous and she would be able to leave the newspaper, have a baby and maybe write a novel. It's just that they had broken up before it was her turn.

Francie was beginning to feel irritated by all these questions. Her answers didn't add up to a portrait of a neurotic relationship. She and Nick had been together for five years—longer than any of her friends. They'd loved each other. It had seemed a perfect arrangement. Right up to the last day, when it wasn't.

'As I say, Francie, a *clinger* and an *avoider*. It seems odd that you should choose each other, doesn't it?'

Francie had run out of things to say.

'See the pattern that started with your mother and father? Your father left and your mother held on to the idea that he would come home for years, didn't she?

'If you were with a man who was secure in himself, you would have driven him away by fussing over him and mothering him the way you did with Nick. It was only your intense neediness which got him across the starting line into a relationship. In some ways it's amazing that it lasted as long as it did.

'But in a way you two were suited to each other. You chased, he ran, and both of you were happy with that arrangement. He didn't ever believe anyone would want to catch him. You didn't believe anyone would want to be caught by you. It was perfect for a childhood game. You played it for five years. But it's no game for a grown-up woman.'

Francie was at last goaded into speaking. 'So what's this new relationship got that ours didn't? What sort of person is she? Another mother figure . . . what?'

Faith leaned forward and Francie noticed that the tissues were now positioned within reach.

'This is not about Nick anymore. This is about you. Why you were content to live the rest of your life—even have a baby—with a man who couldn't really love you the way you deserve to be loved. If I asked you the same question I asked you the day you walked in my door—"Tell me what you love about yourself"—what would you say now?'

I'm not ready for this. It's too much to ask of me. Leave me alone.

Francie hung her head and scrunched her skirt in her fists, willing herself not to start crying again. She knew Faith would keep on until she came up with something.

'I . . . I've got nice hair.'

Two teardrops made a run for it, but they only got halfway

down her face. Would it go on like this forever? Two steps forward and one step back?

☼

'Hmm, interesting theory.' Johnno fancied himself an amateur psychologist and was thrilled to have this notion on the bar for discussion tonight.

'You know, France, I'm sorry to say this, but I reckon she's got you nailed.'

'What?'

'Well it's pretty bloody obvious, really. Didn't you tell us your mum still puts an ornament on the Christmas tree which is supposed to represent the family—Mum, Dad, Joel, you—as it used to be . . . what? Back in the eighties?'

Francie fished a strawberry out of her champagne glass and sucked on it as she replied: 'It was a little blue glass house with snow on the roof. Joel smashed it last year. He said it was by accident but . . .'

'Ooh, Freudian, very Freudian. Or Jungian. I can never remember the difference.' Olga was not even an amateur psychologist. She was a Capricorn. A very contrite Capricorn who wasn't keen for a repeat of the embarrassing scene at Café e Cucina exactly a week ago.

'Do you ever see your father?' asked Jessie. She was sitting on a stool with her hand on Johnno's knee, just as his was on hers.

'A few times a year, here and there,' Francie replied casually. The truth was that they had come to a political arrangement where they met each other on neutral ground.

Their relationship was 'cordial'—that was the language of diplomacy, wasn't it? Where each side affected a willingness to listen, professed to understand, but was unable to comprehend the real heart of the matter.

'And what does your brother do?' Jessie continued with her interview.

'Joel? He's in technical support with computers. He's a genius geek, but he still lives at home with Mum. Twenty-eight, can you believe it?'

'Yeah, I can.' Johnno wasn't letting Francie off the therapy couch. 'He's a clinger too. Your mum probably projected all this stuff onto him and he's fucked.'

'Well, thank you, Doctor Purcell! Joel's not fucked, he's just . . .' Francie couldn't think of what Joel was, exactly. She felt guilty because she knew she was overdue for a visit home.

'Do you really think I mothered Nick?'

'Judging by the pile of washing in the laundry and the dishes in the sink at our joint, someone had to be looking after him or he'd have been dead from dysentery or cholera by now.'

Olga backed Johnno. 'Sorry, Francie, you did buy all his clothes for him. And in five years he never even gave you a ring. No jewellery at all. I mean, what does that say?'

'Probably that he's poor. Probably that he's a struggling actor. Probably that we decided that we had better things to spend our money on . . . like travelling the world together whenever we had the chance!'

'Probably that he thought if he gave you a ring, it would spell *couple*!' said Olga.

Francie had initiated this post-mortem therapy session at the Dog's Bar down the road in St Kilda, but now she was getting more than she'd bargained for. Especially from Olga, who peered at Francie over the top of her purple granny glasses and said stuff she'd never been game enough to say before tonight. Francie knew that Olga would still not have said it without the support of Johnno.

Then it was Jessie's turn to play at being self-help expert. 'Yeah, I mean even when I was fifteen I got friendship rings from boys. Even if it was the plastic ring off a packet of Whizz Fizz sherbet. I mean, it said *commitment*. You don't have to have money for that.'

At this point Johnno spied a white plastic ring from the top of a Coke bottle on the floor and bent down to retrieve it. He kneeled and offered it up.

'Jessie Pascoe . . . would you do me the honour of having sex with me tonight?'

'Oh yes, yes! I thought you'd never ask!' Jessie replied and laughed until she fell off her bar stool.

'Fabulous! Can I be voyeur of honour?' Olga jumped up and down with excitement.

Then they all laughed . . . except Francie.

'Hah bloody hah! Really, this "mothering" stuff. Does that mean he's found someone to mother him better than me?'

'Don't you mean *grandmother* him?' Ooh! That was a nice bitchy comment from Jessie. Francie smiled gratefully.

'Stop, stop! I'm not going to play your filthy girls' game,' declared Johnno as he banged his beer glass on the bar. 'The thing is, Poppy is much more . . . I dunno . . . distant, detached than you, France. They've actually got a lot in common, both being actors, and I think he's got more room to manoeuvre emotionally. She's older, she's less . . . Anyway, I can see why it works. They make a pretty good pair.'

Francie was wounded. Johnno was always trying to tell the absolute truth. Francie wished he wouldn't. She *was* trying to be grown up, but it still hurt. She downed the rest of her champagne and called for another.

Olga came to the rescue: 'They make a good pair because they're both cynical. He's finally found someone he can be a pretentious arty type with.'

'Come on, that's not fair! We're all pretentious arty types here. What are we?' Johnno pointed at each of them in turn: 'Stand-up comedian, scriptwriter, jewellery-maker, newspaper columnist. I don't want to bitch about Nick and Poppy tonight,' said Johnno definitively, and the topic was closed.

'Instead let's talk about Francie and Dave. What's the story there?'

Francie was defensive. 'Why do I always think that my life is going to end up in one of your scripts?'

'Well, pardon me, sweetheart, but *nothing* in your life is going to make it into the ABC kids' department. Of course when I write a black comedy . . .'

'Yeah, come on, Francie,' teased Jessie. 'I saw you and Dave the morning after the night before, and it all looked very cosy. You're not leaving it at a one-night stand, are you?'

Francie wanted to stop the conversation right there. 'Hello? I've just been telling you. I'm in therapy! I wouldn't wish me on anyone right now.'

Olga was thoughtful. 'It's going to be difficult living in the same house. I wonder what the form is? I'll bet there's nothing in the etiquette books about it.'

'Yeah,' said Jessie, with that distracted look in her eye Francie had seen before. 'Someone should write a book about the etiquette of one-night stands. I wonder if they already have?'

Francie knew immediately that Jessie had found her topic for the next episode of *Talkfest*.

'If you mention my love-life on national television . . . Jessie!'

'Come on!' Jessie was indignant. 'I won't mention you. Well, not by name. Not *specifically*.'

'Can you mention that I have a huge dick?' interjected Johnno.

'Hello? There is such a thing as *truth* in broadcasting,' laughed Francie.

'Yeah . . . don't want to be hauled before some sort of media regulation tribunal thingo,' added Jessie.

'Fuck! I'm going to have to take out an ad in the *Sunday Press* classifieds then.'

Olga had the last word: 'You can afford it, Johnno. They charge by the column inch!'

It was near 11 pm when they fell out of the crowded bar into the cool evening. The sea breeze from Port Phillip Bay hit Francie and she realised she'd drunk more than she intended. It had to be admitted it was a good feeling and, not for the first time, Francie wondered whether she was drinking more alcohol lately than was good for her. Then she thought that maybe thinking that way was what had made her life so safe and boring. Maybe all the drama with Nick was forging her, one way or another, into a more complex human being. A bitter, heartbroken alcoholic. Soon she'd be in a comedy club sharing the stage with Jessie!

Francie was in front as the friends threaded their way through the late night throng on Acland Street. Johnno caught her arm.

'I'm worried about you. You haven't told me what happened between you and Nick after you broke up. The thing that's worrying you.'

'Oh, nothing. I was just being a drama queen,' said Francie.

'Lemme guess,' said Johnno. 'You rang them.'

'Of course I did! Just to tell them how happy I was for them. At four o'clock in the morning, at ten-minute intervals, for the past six months.'

'I love you, Francie.'

'I know, Johnno, darling boy, I know. I love you too.'

As they walked arm in arm up the street Francie wondered whether Johnno would still love her if he ever found out exactly what she had done. She shivered to think about it and held his arm even more tightly.

Fifteen

From: elly@outPress.com.au
To: ssingle@SunPress.com
Subject: Recovery

Francie,

I am trying to recover from a broken heart and I have decided to take a holiday. I can't decide between a beach resort or a health spa in the mountains. Which would you recommend?

Elly XX

Francie was sure on this one. She typed:

Hey there, Elly!

From my experience, at mountains and beaches there are too many things to jump off. The last thing you need

160

is to sit and contemplate the infinite beauty of the universe . . . and your own personal ugliness.

You need mindless, cheap distractions. New high heels, cocktails, chocolates, bubble baths and gruesome crime novels (preferably where cadavers are dissected in intricate detail).

Seriously though . . . Run to the bosom of your friends and family. Find a new job. Join a sewing circle. Anything to keep you busy, girlfriend. This is one time when solitude really sucks!

Love from Francie XX

It was Friday afternoon. Francie was heading out of the office to the basement café for a coffee when she was accosted by Gabby Di Martino. Gabby clip-clopped down the concrete stairs in her high heels, prattling all the way.

'I've got the beauty editor blahs! I've spent all frigging day writing about the difference between lipo-hydroxy acid and glycolic acid. I tell you, one day women are going to have to supply a urine sample to buy a blusher. This is the hardest job I've ever had. It's one thing covering the war in Iraq, but sometimes it's just as hard trying to write four hundred words on fucking mud in a jar! That's Dead Sea mud worth three hundred bucks, mind you!'

'If anyone can do it, you can, Gabby.'

'Don't get me wrong, I know I have plenty of talent. I just don't give a fuck.'

They got their coffees and found an empty table in the little café. They were surrounded by a rumpled and bleary-eyed assortment of journos inhaling sandwiches and hot potato chips out of brown paper bags. Gabby caused the usual stir. Today she was wearing hipster jeans, a swinging diamanté belt and a pistachio green sequinned halter top. You could have played a game of handball on her hard stomach. She was used to the attention, however, and was checking out Francie. She approved.

'You look fab! I know you sneaked off at lunchtime to get your hair done.'

Francie was just about to make her excuses when Gabby cut in.

'Forget it. It was about time. Your hair was looking like crap.'

Thanks for noticing.

It was true that Francie was starting to take more care of herself. In the past couple of days since her therapy session she felt she was at last making some progress and had begun to rejoin the land of the living. Her first call was to her favourite beauty spa. She'd had her hair coloured five gorgeous shades of blonde and treated herself to a pedicure at the same time. Her dusky rose toenails were glossy perfection peeking out of white wedge sandals. She was wearing a pastel pink and white check cotton jacket with her jeans. She felt she was almost back to her attractive best.

A vision of Nick popped into her brain—*Look at you, you beautiful thing. Come here now and kiss me*—and just as quickly exited stage right.

Francie had to look twice to make sure, but she realised that she too was getting the once-over from the men. Looking back at her was a particularly handsome photographer she had been eyeing off before she and Nick had separated. She realised that she hadn't looked at him once in the past six months. He was, she saw, still particularly handsome.

Gabby followed her eye line. 'Oh Christ, not him! Married, and wouldn't go down if he was wearing concrete shoes. But this is a change for the better, Francie . . . actually looking at men!'

Francie could feel herself blushing. 'Yeah, I suppose it is.'

Gabby took a sip of coffee and regarded Francie over the rim of her cup. 'But you've sort of got it wrong. When the Prince kisses Sleeping Beauty she's supposed to wake up and fall in love with *him*, not start sleeping around. I mean, I assume you and Dave . . .'

Francie suddenly didn't fancy everyone at the *Sunday Press* knowing her business. Especially her boss.

'Maybe *this* Sleeping Beauty realises that she's missed out on a whole lot of possibilities while she's been having a nice lie-in.'

At that moment the afore-perved-upon photographer ambled up to the table. He had a couple of expensive cameras slung around his neck, which looked a whole lot more sexy than a diamond zodiac pendant, although the desired effect was probably the same.

'Hi. Hope I'm not interrupting a high-level editorial conference,' he said, extending his hand to Francie. Looking up, Francie saw him smiling. A blinding dawn broke over a mountain top.

'If I throw a stick, will you leave?' Gabby spat in his direction.

Francie stumbled over the nasty comment as she rushed to fill the embarrassing void.

'No, no . . . it's fine. We're just chatting. I'm Francie.'

Gabby sipped her coffee and pointedly stared into the distance.

'I know who you are. I'm Karl Johansson. I'm working in pictorial for the *Daily*. I'm having an exhibition soon. You might like to come?'

'Is your *wife* going to be there?' said Gabby with a sickly smile.

'Er . . . no . . . we've separated.' Karl fished in the back pocket of his jeans. 'I'd love you to come and have a look, Francie. Have a drink afterwards . . . ?'

Karl handed Francie an invitation. On the front was a black and white photograph of a soldier in some godforsaken war zone. The backdrop of a blasted village could have been from so many places on earth, the soldier from any number of armies. He cradled a bundle of dusty camouflage fabric and peeping out of it was the perfect face of a newborn baby. The power of the image hit Francie in the chest. She decided in an instant that the man who had taken this shot had a lot to recommend him.

'I'd love to,' she heard herself say. 'See you there.'

Karl broke into a huge grin, flooding the little corner table with more light, and walked away. Francie watched him go and couldn't help noting he was impressive from the rear as well.

'Oh God, how obvious!' Gabby took up the invitation in her painstakingly tended opalescent nails. 'The calling card of the metrosexual. I travel to war zones, I love babies, and there's no woman in the picture. Insert your name here.'

Francie snatched the invite back. 'Maybe I will go. I've been out of circulation a long time. I deserve a bit of meaningless fun.'

'Of course you do. And if you want *meaningless*, Karl's your man. So, you and Dave . . . ?'

'We had a one-night stand, that's all.'

'Well,' Gabby purred, leaning closer, 'good for you, Francie. It's all research for *Seriously Single*. Glad to hear you're back in business and trading.'

Francie took her purse from the table and stood to go upstairs. A final check of her work and she was finished for the week. But there was one last incendiary bomb from Gabby before she could get away. Francie could never tell whether these devices were artlessly thrown or aimed with premeditated precision. She knew she was a target Gabby couldn't miss.

'Oh, are you going to watch *Talkfest* tonight? Should be fascinating to hear what Nick and Poppy have to say for themselves. I've got a crowd coming over to watch. Of course, now they know the background—the way she stole him, you in analysis and everything—they're desperate to watch!'

The bomb landed and seemed to blow off Francie's limbs.

'Or you might spend the evening banging a four-inch nail into your head,' trilled Gabby. 'Anyway, I'll watch and report back. I'll ring you on your mobile. Byeee.'

Hope you trip on the stairs and break your neck. Byeee!

✳

Later that night Francie was sitting in her room idly perusing the pictures in *Vogue* magazine—not like she ever really read the articles.

She'd abandoned *Remembrance of Things Past* after reading the same paragraph for the fifteenth time. She didn't know why she was bothering to read it anyway. She was past measuring herself against Poppy Sommerville-Smith. Past torturing herself. Wasn't she?

Watching them on television tonight would be like lying down on the tracks and waiting for the train. And yet . . . She had never seen them together as a couple—except for small grainy black and white pictures in the social pages, and from a tram window. It had been the same with her father and his new wife after their wedding. She had never seen them together since. How would Nick and Poppy look? Would all the world see how mismatched they were? If she didn't watch, maybe she would always wonder.

And what would they say about their forthcoming production? She'd heard from Johnno that they were still going ahead with it. Her approval or otherwise hadn't meant anything in the end, as she'd suspected. How would they negotiate their appearance this evening? Would they refer to the way they had met? Would they own up to the fact that their liaison had started while she and Nick were together?

And then—Francie shuddered at the memory—there was *that night*. Surely that wouldn't get an airing on national television? But then again Francie was intelligent enough to realise that the sheer drama of it all could prove irresistible to an old luvvie like Poppy.

No, she wouldn't watch. Couldn't watch. And it didn't matter if she didn't. Everyone she knew would tell her what happened. She could bet that Olga, Amanda and Gabby would be on the phone in minutes with a review of their performance.

It was about 9 pm when she heard Robbie come home, then, she guessed, Dave. Francie would stay in her room and avoid the public spectacle. After all, she had better things to do than watch two people pick over her private tragedy for fun and profit. She climbed under the bedcovers, determined to stay behind her closed door.

Except she was starting to think about something to eat. She was having a recurring vision of grilled cheese on toast and a glass of icy white wine. Since she'd recently regained her appetite Francie was making up for lost meals. She would have been a liability at the Siege of Troy—standing on the ramparts begging for a snack within an hour and a half.

There was a knock on the bedroom door.

'Hey, Francie?' It was Robbie.

'Dave's brought some seafood Szechuan noodles home, and a bottle of chardy. There's plenty here. You want to join us?'

Damn! Forced from her fortress by a chilli prawn.

Francie could smell the food from halfway down the hall. She found Robbie and Dave setting up their feast in front of the television. Robbie was doling out steaming piles of noodles and stir-fried vegetables. Dave was pouring big glasses of white wine. It all looked delicious. There was no way she could take her food and drink back to her room. That would have been rude. The rout was complete. Francie would sit here with them and watch the program. Which wasn't a bad thing, she reflected. It would show the boys she was over the whole episode. Very grown up.

Francie gratefully took her noodles and wine and sat on the floor.

'Ooh . . . new toes. Very fetching,' said Robbie.

'End of the week treat.' Francie wiggled her rosy nails.

'Not going out tonight?' asked Dave cheerfully. Francie could sense that he was exercising the utmost diplomacy and she was grateful for his efforts.

'No, I'm pretty boring really. I don't think I'd know where to go. It's been so long since . . .' And here she could have kicked herself. It had only been a week since she and Dave had spent the night together. She had managed to avoid any situation in the house in which they might find themselves together again. For his part Dave had seemed relaxed in her presence. Her first instinct must have been correct then: *he's done this before.*

'Mmm, this is delicious,' she murmured, stuffing her mouth with noodles so she couldn't make an idiot of herself.

Robbie took up the challenge of manufacturing small talk.

'By the way, I've found something new for us, Francie—a Scottish salsa band playing at the Fitzroy Town Hall on Saturday!'

'Wha . . . ?' Francie sprayed Dave with half-chewed prawn. 'Oh . . . sorry.' She reached out and then quickly withdrew her hand as if his broad chest was a hotplate.

'It's OK. I'm getting used to you spitting on me.' He brushed the front of his white T-shirt, his eyes dancing with amusement. Francie was reminded again how lovely he was.

'It's Latin dancing with a whole bunch of blokes in kilts,' Robbie explained. 'And, as part of your re-education, I've signed us up for a demonstration class. Although you'll have to help me fake-tan my legs first.'

Dave laughed. 'What are you going to wear underneath your wee kilt?'

'Nothing, of course. It's traditional and I might get lucky!'

Dave and Francie were both laughing now.

'You ever been to Scotland, Francie?' asked Dave.

'With a name like McKenzie? We . . . I . . . spent Hogmanay with my relatives in Aberdeen once.'

Francie was instantly back there that New Year's Eve with Nick, standing in the snow watching fireworks cascade through the black and freezing sky. She slipped on the ice, looked up and was surprised to see that this time it was Dave holding out his hand to help her to her feet.

They talked about their working week over the rest of dinner, but the longer Francie sat there and looked at Dave, then looked at the television, the more she felt her courage desert her.

'Excuse me, I have to make a call.' She fled to her bedroom and her mobile phone. Johnno was with Jessie tonight, at the television studio. She could imagine the mounting excitement as the show counted down for the opening credits.

'Hey, France,' Johnno answered, 'you wouldn't believe who's sitting here in the Green Room—John Butler. You know, from the trio? So brilliant! I've been talking to him and—'

'Did you talk to Nick?' Francie hissed.

'About what?'

'Jesus, Johnno! You know . . . about what he's going to say tonight!'

'Yeah, yeah. I told him. Don't worry, Jessie's there, she'll look after you. Gotta go . . . it's starting. Talk later.'

He hung up. The thought that Jessie was there as her champion and protector made Francie's heart sink. Being indiscreet was part of her job description.

As Francie walked slowly back down the hall she could hear the opening music to *Talkfest*. It might as well have been a funeral march. Francie plodded into the room and curled up on the end of the squashy cream sofa. She cradled a faded fringed cushion in front of her for protection.

Before long Jessie was holding forth on this week's topic, which was (surprise, surprise) one-night stands. Francie wouldn't look at Dave, who she suspected was looking at her. And neither of them was looking at Robbie, who they suspected was checking out both of them.

'I mean, what's the etiquette of one-night stands?' Jessie was asking the rest of the male panel. They were momentarily lost for words.

'I dunno,' one of them spoke up. 'The last etiquette book I looked up was the rules for strip poker. How come a pair of jocks only counts as one item, but a pair of women's earrings counts as two. What's the deal there?'

There was laughter and when it died down Jessie was away.

'I found a book about the etiquette of a one-night stand by this American guy and he reckons rule one is—' and here Jessie read from a paperback—'You should wait at least a day after you meet someone to do the deed because the sex will be better if you've taken time to talk over your sexual habits.'

There was a groan of disbelief from the studio audience.

'Exactly! As if that's ever gunna work.' Jessie looked at the camera with raised eyebrows.

'Yeah,' one of the blokes interjected. 'Hey, babe, I like to thrash around for five minutes and then fall into a coma!'

Jessie fired back: 'Yeah, I like to lie there like a log and let someone else do all the work. Sounds good, let's do it tomorrow night.'

There was more laughter from the studio audience and a chuckle from Robbie in the lounge room. Francie and Dave were still not looking at each other.

'Actually,' Jessie continued, 'I'll bet you never knew that the topic was also covered in *Debrett's Etiquette* by Elsie Burch Donald. Of course, most of what Elsie says is stuff like how to take leave of royalty, or how to eat an artichoke with a knife and fork—'

'Or how to address a corgi and balance a beer at the same time!' Another interjection from one of the boys on the panel.

Jessie ploughed on: 'But to show how modern she is Elsie has also had a go at courtship and she says that before sex it

171

is considerate of each party to make sure that the other knows how much commitment is intended.'

'What?' General amazement from the panel.

'I know, I know!' exclaimed Jessie. 'With respect, Elsie, to be told by a bloke that he's intending to commit about five and a half hours to a relationship is a little more consideration than I can handle!'

Erk! This was the moment when Francie and Dave *did* catch each other's eye. How much time had they put in on their 'relationship'? From the initial chat-up in the Green Room, the dancing and flirting at the club to the sex and awkward brush-off next afternoon, it had been a very indecent amount of time indeed.

Francie squirmed with embarrassment and glued her eyes to the screen where Jessie was outlining her personal rules for a one-night stand: 'I reckon it's bad form to ring your girlfriends from his house to tell them that the Great Drought of 2004 has finally broken.

'And always try to keep a bit of an eye on where you are. Cos there's nothing worse than creeping out of bed in the dark, fumbling for your clothes, stumbling down the hall and closing the door quietly behind you to find you've locked yourself out of your own bloody house!'

Jessie sat back in her chair and beamed as the audience applauded.

Then the host announced that the *charming and talented* Poppy Sommerville-Smith and her *hot actor boyfriend* Nick Jamieson were up next after the ad break. Every instinct told

Francie that she should run away. The boys were quiet, waiting for her to do just that. When, after a minute's silence, she was, for some unaccountable reason, still in the room, Robbie turned to her.

'How's your drink, Francie?'

She held out her glass and he filled it to the brim. She took a mighty gulp and set it down on the coffee table.

'Are you sure you want to watch this?' Dave asked. The look on his face was too close to pity for Francie's liking. She sat up straight and squared her shoulders.

'Yeah . . . should be a laugh.'

No-one in the room thought anything about the next few minutes would be funny at all. They watched an advertisement for New Coca-Cola with a Hint of Cherry with unnatural fascination. And then the ad break was over. Nick and Poppy filled the television screen. Francie could feel the blood drain from her head and her hands start to sweat. She bit into the cushion she was holding.

It must have been the television lighting, but Nick and Poppy looked as if they were emanating a dewy aura. There were rays of light coming out of their heads. Nick's hair was shining blue-black and his brown eyes were sparkling. He was smiling hard, showing off a luminous set of teeth. Poppy was wearing a white jacket which made her look terrifyingly young—almost virginal. Her shoulder-length curls shone a lustrous amber. Her eyes were like a doll's—wide and bright—and her apricot lips were full and glossy.

It was weird, they were actually glowing! *Radiant* was the only word for it. Did they look mismatched? Horribly enough . . . no. They looked perfect together. They looked just like they had in her dreams. A golden couple. Francie wanted to hurl her glass at the screen. She bit down harder on her cushion. After a few minutes of banter the panel got down to business.

'So tell us about your new show, Poppy. A bit of a departure for you after Chekhov?' was the question.

Poppy answered in a breathy, marvellously theatrical voice which Francie found nauseating. Actually sickening. Prawns and noodles were writhing in her gut.

'Absolutely!' Poppy purred. 'It's entitled *Stupid Cupid* and it's a modest little cabaret outing which Nick and I have written ourselves—all the musical numbers and the dialogue. I've always *adored* cabaret—Kurt Weill, Bertolt Brecht and the French tradition Jacques Brel, Piaf . . . all that.'

Francie couldn't stop herself: 'No-one watching this show has ever head of them, you fucking wanker!' she spat at the screen. Somewhere outside her tunnel vision she heard Robbie splutter into his wine.

Poppy was now waving her delicate little paws as she spoke: 'Of course it's *wonderful* to be doing something very late night and *intimate* again—'

'I'll bet!' Francie muttered.

She looked over to see Dave's back heaving with a silent laugh.

'Sometimes one can get a little *caught up*, become *remote*, in the elaborate productions in the *big* theatres and I'm looking forward to breaking down that *fourth wall*—'

'Do us a favour, you old cow, and stay in your barn.'

'Shoosh, Francie, I want to hear,' Robbie said crossly.

Then it was Nick's turn to make a dickhead of himself.

'It's really *fabulous* to be doing something *original* with someone as *gifted* as Poppy—'

'Aaargh! Oh, pu-leese!' Francie threw her cushion on the floor. Then she was on her knees with her head buried in the sofa.

'She really does have the most *amazing* voice. I think people are going to be *blown away* when they see her—'

'SUCK MY DICK!'

'Francie, STOP IT!' Robbie was trying to be stern, but he was laughing too hard.

They were all having a wonderful time taking the piss out of Nick and Poppy when Jessie's voice halted them mid guffaw like a game of *Simon Says*.

'So, Nick, how does your ex girlfriend feel about the show?'

OH NO! JESSIE, SHUT UP, SHUT UP! Francie screamed silently as she threw herself back on the couch. Even from the lounge room they could see the high pink colour on Nick's olive cheeks.

'I . . . I think she's fine about it,' he stuttered.

'Cos if my boyfriend dumped me and then did a show about me with his new girlfriend, I would be devastated!'

Jessie sat back and folded her arms across her chest with satisfaction. She obviously thought she was grilling the Prime Minister over the War on Terror.

175

The walls of the lounge room seemed to become concave as Francie, Dave and Robbie sucked in all the available air and did not dare breathe out.

'It's not really about her . . . as such—' Nick started to say when Poppy's authoritative contralto voice sliced through the end of his sentence.

'The show is *also* about what it feels like to be *stalked*!' Poppy paused for theatrical effect and her deep blue eyes misted over with the tremendous pain of it all.

Francie's face was a still frame from a horror movie. The lounge room became as quiet as a crypt. The television studio had become dead silent as well.

'Stalked? What, you mean threatened?' Jessie asked.

'Well, imagine if you came home to find someone had cut all of your underwear to pieces. Ripped everything to shreds. Smashed up your bedroom. Torn up your precious possessions. It was *terrifying*! I mean, we all *joke* about revenge—seafood in the curtain rails and leaving the telephone off the hook to New York, and so forth. It's all *terribly* amusing. But think about what it's like to be on the *receiving* end. It's not pleasant *at all*. In fact, it was the most appalling thing that's ever happened to me *in my entire life*!'

The cameras came in closer. Was the poor woman to be spared nothing? Poppy turned down her mouth, her bottom lip wobbled attractively, her false eyelashes fluttered and there was not a person watching—from coast to coast—who didn't feel her intense personal suffering. There was a tidal wave of outrage from the viewing audience—and a desperate need for more information.

'Francie slashed your knickers?' Jessie's mouth hung open in astonishment.

Dave and Robbie turned to look at Francie, but she was already out the door. Just a warm imprint remained on the squashy sofa where her bottom had been.

The television ratings would later show that, in the whole of the country, not one set tuned into *Talkfest* switched to another channel for the next fifteen minutes.

Francie had just slammed her bedroom door behind her when her mobile phone rang for the first time. She switched it off and threw it on the floor. She could hear the telephone in the kitchen start to ring as well.

Minutes later the first knock came on Francie's door. By midnight Dave, Robbie, Johnno, Jessie, Olga and Amanda had all knocked on the locked bedroom door and been told loudly and rudely to go away.

Her brother, her therapist, her Pilates instructor and her Auntie Kath in Benalla (who just happened to be watching television and recognised Nick and put two and two together and couldn't believe her ears and got Francie's new phone number from her mother without letting on she knew anything) had all rung and been given the number of her mobile, which was now hurled in the bottom of her washing basket.

News of Francie's social demise travelled fast. She lay on the bed in the dark and wished that she was actually, in real life, dead.

Sixteen

It was Saturday night. Francie sat by the window in her childhood bedroom and looked out at the cloudy sky. The moon had disappeared.

She was back at the old house in the quiet leafy suburb of Blackburn with her mother and brother, but Francie had never felt more alone in her life. She closed the curtains, lay back on her bed and stared at the ghostly orb of the tattered rice paper light shade she had hung when she was a teenager.

There was not much left in the room from that time—her Pet Shop Boys and Bros posters had long gone. Her mother had claimed the room for her sewing and Francie's single bed was now jammed in one corner behind a dressmaker's mannequin and a clothes rack. Francie thought she just might stay in this hidey-hole forever. She didn't see how she could possibly show her face again. She had been revealed to the world as an unhinged housebreaker and there didn't seem to be any way back to the company of rational grown-up human beings after that.

Every time she closed her eyes she saw Poppy's downturned wobbly lip and Nick's hot, pink cheeks. It had been an award-winning performance. She had to congratulate Poppy on that.

Francie could see that this was a story which would run and run. She could imagine her competitors over at the *Sunday Star* jumping on it with glee. She could see tomorrow's front page with Poppy holding up a shredded pair of knickers, her face a perfect portrait of outrage. What had Francie said in her own *Seriously Single* column about revenge? That's right: *I don't actually believe in revenge. All the best ones have been done . . . leave it to a higher power to exact karmic retribution. As ye sow so shall ye reap . . .*

Sanctimonious crap! So she was a hypocrite and a liar along with everything else. After this she'd be lucky to get a job on a free TV guide. Everything was finished—her career, social life, her relationship—and she was back here in this house boarded up with painful memories. She might have known that the notion of living happily ever after with Nick was a mirage, that one day her past would come back to claim her. She felt that for the past five years she had been swimming on top of a lake and then, with the shore almost in sight, she had been pulled back under the surface. She didn't have the strength to fight anymore. She would just lie here on her old bed and let her lungs fill with tears until she drowned.

She buried her face in the pillow. She was instantly back there. Behind the wheel of her car, trying to resist the urge to drive towards 35 Everton Street, Parkville. The last time she'd driven there—three months ago now, a cool night in August—

she'd parked outside the house with its immaculately trimmed lavender bushes (to match Poppy's perfectly tended pubic hair?) and seen Nick's car in the driveway. His old Renault nudged up against Poppy's sleek little silver Honda. Jesus! Was there no end to this? Even their cars were kissing!

She had known they would be away in Sydney that weekend for the season launch of the Sydney Theatre Company. It was easy to track Poppy Sommerville-Smith's movements if you really wanted to. If you were, say, a kidnapper, a robber or a pervert. She was interstate for an arts festival one week or a play opening the next. She was routinely photographed here and there with an adoring Nick on her arm. He had been exchanged for the ageing theatre directors she was usually clutching at. Poppy's future engagements were apparently breathlessly anticipated by an adoring public.

The banality of their parking arrangements had blindsided Francie. Of course he would leave his car here so they could travel to the airport together. Then came the torturous questions. How often was his car here? Did he stay with her a night, a week, a month at a time? Were his clothes hanging in the wardrobe? Was his shaving kit in the vanity unit? His books, computer, CDs . . . what? Had he moved in with Poppy permanently and Johnno knew, everyone knew but her . . . Again?

So they were out of town, the house was silent and the back-door key was easy to find. It was inside a fake rock in a fake pot full of fake geraniums. Figured. Poppy Sommerville-Smith was a fake too.

A small click and Francie was inside the house. If she had been discovered that night she wouldn't have had an explanation for being inside the house with a torch. It was premeditated break and enter. She might have been able to plead mental instability. Imagining what Poppy and Nick's life together was like had driven her mad for months. She couldn't sleep, couldn't eat for trying to picture how it was.

As Francie stood there in the hallway in the dark she had a feeling she was drawing a thread through the fabric of her life from a long time ago. When she was a small girl she had lain awake night after night wondering what her father's new life was like. Her mother had never let her see Dad's new house with *that woman*. After a year, or however long it was, he had given up asking for Francie and Joel to come and visit. As a young girl she had endlessly pictured him in a kitchen, a bathroom, a hall, a garden. Did he have a new favourite chair in front of the television? Did he sleep on the side of the bed near the window like he did at home?

Sometimes she saw her father walking down a golden staircase in a tuxedo—he lived in a palace with white marble floors and stained-glass windows. Other times he was standing near a fireplace in a cottage which was all dark wood, like the home of the Seven Dwarves. She even saw him in a plastic Barbie condo. He was lying on a white sun lounge by a pink swimming pool holding a drink with an umbrella in it. So, you can understand why she had to see what the inside of Poppy's house looked like. She was grown up now. She could go wherever she liked.

Francie was surprised when she first saw Poppy's kitchen. She had predicted it would be a designer's dream of slick, expensive stainless-steel appliances with an aubergine feature wall. She had not expected to find it all so unpretentious and cosy— and yellow. Well, as cosy yellow as she could tell from the light of a small torch. It was altogether more . . . sensual . . . than Francie had imagined. Arty and bohemian. Perhaps if she had been able to switch on the light, the illusion of being in the back room of a café in Casablanca would have been shattered, but Francie didn't want to alert the neighbours that there was an intruder in the house.

She could see the two of them in this kitchen. They would sit around the restored butcher's bench on wooden stools, Poppy leaning towards Nick with an outstretched hand, waiting for him to kiss her fingers. He would walk around the bench and pull her amber curls to one side and kiss her bare neck. Maybe they would drink red wine as they waited for Turkish bread to come out of the old gas oven to accompany a platter of dips they'd bought from the Victoria Market. A cosy night in. Hot bread, hot . . . sex.

Francie discovered the lounge room next. She had carried an image with her of taupe linen sofas and a commanding oil painting of Poppy on the wall above. Again, as the small circle of light swooped over the room, she was surprised to find deep burgundy walls hung with tapestries. The long low couches were dark brown wool and strewn with cushions made from Moroccan carpets. Again she saw them lying here together.

Poppy was reading Proust aloud, in French, as Nick parted her silk robe and kissed his way up her bare thighs.

She groped along a dark hall through to the bedroom. She knew its configuration from the night in July when she had looked in through the window. Back then she had just stood on a plastic bucket and peered in. She was much more powerful now. A trespasser? Or just exercising her privilege as the third party in this sordid tale?

She crossed in front of the bed and entered an ensuite bathroom. She closed the door behind her and switched on the light. She was momentarily blinded by the brightness bouncing off the arctic white tiles. When Francie focused on herself in the mirror she saw someone she didn't recognise. She'd pulled a striped woollen beanie down over her head to her eyebrows. Her grey eyes were wide and bright, her skin was paler than she had ever seen it and her freckles were faded after the dull skies of winter. Her lips were set into a thin line spelling an emotion you couldn't quite read. She looked like the sort of person you would avoid sitting next to on the tram for fear of somehow being involved in a random act of violence.

Her heart was pounding faster than usual, her own breath a breeze in her ears. But her hands were steady and she was oddly calm. The house was empty. They were not coming here tonight. There was no need to hurry.

Francie was inside the inner sanctum where Poppy Sommerville-Smith groomed herself to face the world. It would take her a long time, she thought bitterly. At forty-three years old it had to be taking longer and longer.

Francie guessed that the vanity unit would be full of anti-wrinkle creams and vials of expensive youth serums. She opened the mirrored door and there they were—a row of expensive La Mer products. How much did that stuff cost? Three, four hundred dollars a jar? What else was in here which would give her a clue as to what she was dealing with?

Francie grimaced to find packets of Ural and a tube of Canesten cream. Thrush, cystitis? Disgusting. You could get them when your sex life took an unexpectedly vigorous turn. Francie wondered whether they fucked in the shower . . . or on the floor on the thick white mat in front of the bath. Or maybe Poppy liked to do it in the dark where Nick wouldn't see the latticework of wrinkles on her neck and be reminded of how old she was.

The one thing she didn't see was any evidence of birth control devices. At the age of forty-three Poppy probably didn't have to worry about all that. Had Nick given up on ever having a child? He was twenty-nine. One day, and it might take five years or it might take ten, but one day he would realise he was giving up the chance to be a father. If you went to the doctor and asked for a vasectomy when you were childless and twenty-nine, they wouldn't do it. But that's what Nick had chosen for himself, in effect. And then she wondered again what Nick's mother had said when he first walked through the door with a 43-year-old woman.

Poppy had stolen much more than her man. She had stolen her future. Her husband and the father of her children! She slammed the door of the vanity unit shut and looked into the mirror again.

'Fucking bitch! I hate you!' she spat at her reflection. She took up the torch and snapped off the bathroom light.

Francie stepped into the bedroom onto soft carpet. She could see it was grey from the moonlight slanting in through an old sash window.

She looked in the wardrobe next. The circle of torchlight played over a vast rack of clothes, mostly black. The labels were expensive—Dolce & Gabbana, Jean Paul Gaultier, Versace. Nothing Francie could afford. She tugged the bottom of her floral polyester top down over her midriff.

And then she saw them sitting next to a jumble of Poppy's shoes—Nick's boots. The good black Italian ones she'd found and bought for him from an outlet store in New York. She remembered she'd also found him a herringbone tweed Armani jacket on sale and triumphantly carted it back to their hotel room. The jacket wasn't here. Of course not. He'd need it with him in Sydney if he were to be carted around as Poppy's latest chic handbag.

She slid the mirrored door closed and turned her torch to a chest of drawers. The first drawer held Poppy's negligees—a swirl of pink and cream silk, a dessert of strawberries and cream. The second contained her underwear. Again, predictably, la Perla. A label Francie could only dream about. This stuff was mostly black with the occasional garish slash of scarlet—silk, netting, ribbons, bows. The sort of frilly shit which must have looked laughable on a middle-aged woman. The knickers were

Francie's size. The bras were a 'C' instead of a 'B', but close enough.

And then Francie did something she would never be able to explain. Lying on her bed here tonight in Blackburn, months later, thinking back on it all, she was still paralysed with shock trying to understand why. Why had she done it?

She had stripped off her clothes, kicked off her sandals, until she was standing naked in the gloomy bedroom. She rested the torch on the chest of drawers. The round button of light illuminated a photograph on the wall of Poppy in a crimson evening gown, curtseying on a stage, accepting a bouquet of red roses.

She slipped on a pair of Poppy's silky black knickers and a lacy, ribboned bra. She pulled back the bedcover to reveal white sheets and pillows and slid into the side of the bed she guessed would be Nick's. She was right. It was his side of the bed. She could smell him.

She lay there, closed her eyes and fell headfirst into a black abyss of misery. She thought she might never get up again as memories wrapped around her limbs like long trailing weeds, holding her down. Her voice swirled in her head, soundless. *Why did you go? I thought you loved me. I tried to be good. I tried to be perfect. Come back. Come back.*

So this is where it all happened? Where Nick took someone else in his arms, folded himself into her. Where all thoughts of Francie were gone. Gone to dust! Where memories of her were picked up by the four winds of love, togetherness, always and forever and scattered on a vast expanse of forgetfulness. It was an endless ocean where Francie disappeared and ceased to exist until she was swept back, some time later, large as life, on a vengeful tide.

Her pale limbs were illuminated by the full moon. Her body was picked out in the light, white and hard, a mannequin in a shop window. Stiff and dead like the bride doll in the corner of her grandmother's room. The warm blood in her veins slowed. Every pulse point in her body—her wrists, her neck, inside her elbows—chilled and fractured. Her eyes narrowed so she felt she was peering through a crack in a glacier.

The feeling was not unfamiliar to her. It was an emotion from a long time ago which had made her wrench the head off Joel's Batman action figure, bury it in the backyard and not tell him where it was. No matter how hard he cried. The same feeling which made her kick the back of Justine Smith's chair in Year 9, again and again, until Justine wept with frustration. The same feeling which had compelled her to crawl into her mother's bed in the middle of the night so that the man in the lounge room, drinking wine, laughing and dancing with her mother, would never, ever take her father's place.

Francie slipped out of the bed and groped in her handbag. She found her dressmaking scissors and held them up to the moonlight shining through the window. She'd carried the scissors for weeks. In those first days after Nick left she'd thought many times about cutting Poppy's heart out and had armed herself with the weapon in case she had the chance. This was her chance now. They felt cool and heavy in her hand. The blades sharp, precise, bright silver mirrors.

She upended Poppy's underwear and negligee drawers and felt the silky trifle slide cool and slippery over her bare feet. Then, sitting down on the floor in a slice of moonlight, she quietly and methodically cut the crotch out of every pair of la Perla undies in the pile. When she had finished with them she tore into the bras and negligees, stockings, corsets, suspenders.

With every cut a string to a memory was severed. This slash was for the night Francie had first had sex with Nick. When she had first traced the naked landscape of his body with her fingertips and knew it was a place she never wanted to leave.

This rip was for the afternoon on the beach when they were up to their necks in champagne surf at Aireys Inlet and he had carried her in his arms from the water and fallen beside her in the hot sand. He shouted to the white gulls skirting overhead that he loved her. Told her he would stay with her. Heal the hurt. Never leave.

Lies, lies, lies! All lies!

She went on like this, scything through satin, twisting wires, shredding straps and ribbons until everything in the drawers was ragged and unrecognisable.

Her hands ached from the effort of holding the scissors so tightly. Her fingers cramped with the pain of cutting through seams of folded satin. Severing one half of a pair of flimsy knickers from the other. Hacking a ribbon rose from a nightdress as soft as butter. Slitting a slip, from lacy hem to embroidered neckline. Renting the fabric, dismembering the sleeves of a feather-trimmed negligee as if she was slaughtering a small bird.

She uncurled her fingers and held the scissors in her palm like a dagger. This stab into the soft cup of a bra was for Poppy's right eye. Francie saw her on a stage, staggering along a cardboard parapet, a tragic Tosca screeching with pain and indignation.

This wound was for Poppy's left eye. Francie saw her blind and bleeding, in her death throes. Tragic, martyred, appealing to the heavens for mercy.

The final slash tore into Poppy's neck, from one side of her lovely white throat to the other, leaving her bleeding and mortally wounded centre stage. Then Francie tore down the theatre. She hoisted a chair and smashed it into the mirrored wardrobe doors. Shards of glass cleaved the room. Impaled themselves in the carpet, the bed. Each sharp splinter reflecting the moon as if she had broken the sky.

Her hand stung and she lifted it to see blood already making its way in a shiny black trail down her arm. She held her scissors high again—this time as if brandishing a mythical sword forged in righteous crusade—and then plunged into pillows and eiderdown. Feathery entrails haemorrhaged on the carpet.

Fuck him here, will you? Sleep with him here? Dream here?

She turned to the chest of drawers next and, with a sweep of her bloodied forearm, cleared the top of books, framed photographs, candles and keepsakes. Poppy's precious things arced and crashed into dark corners.

When the satisfying racket of destruction ceased, Francie saw one artefact remained. A heavy album, bound in red velvet, gold embossed. She took it down and sat on the floor, now white with feathered flakes. She found her torch and, in its eyeball of light, turned the pages. It was Poppy's scrapbook, lovingly and carefully cataloguing her stellar career.

Here, a review: *Once more Poppy Sommerville-Smith reminds us all why she is the doyenne of the Australian stage with a stunning performance as . . .* On the next page, a caption to a photograph: *Ms Sommerville-Smith graciously accepts her third Critics' Circle Award at a glittering night at the Sydney Opera House.* There were floral greeting cards from her fellow cast members: *ADORE working with you, precious Poppy! Here's to our opening night! Chookas!* And a collection of perfectly preserved theatrical programs: *She graduated from the National Institute of Dramatic Art in 1983 and has since been at the forefront of . . .*

Francie read all this through a crystalline prism of hatred. Poppy had everything—awards, public accolades, fame, money *and* a cache of la Perla underwear—but apparently it wasn't enough. She wanted Nick too. She had set out to steal him and then triumphantly set him as the prize jewel in her glittering diadem of privilege and success!

Francie's rage cast her fingers into solid, sharp claws of retribution. She ripped pages from their binding and then into pieces—smaller, and smaller again, until they were almost confetti. As she tore every membrane of paper and tissue from the spine of the album, Francie sang out loud. It wasn't a recognisable tune, but rather a discordant, shrieking aggregation of sounds emitted at the crescendo of an operatic murder.

And in Francie's mind, when the final page was ripped away, when the gold and velvet binding was at last limp, empty and useless, Poppy died too. All life left her. She was a stone cold dead diva.

Bbrring! Bbrring!

Francie spun her head to locate the sound. Was it the foyer bell ringing intermission? Was it a door chime heralding the return of Poppy and Nick? She realised it was an alarm clock making a piteous call for an end to the performance, and with that Francie knew she was done. The red velvet curtain came down on the melodrama.

If Francie was asked how she had left the house that night (through the door? The window?) or how she'd driven back to Richmond, she would not be able to say.

But she could tell you about the scene the next day, because every detail remained bright, vivid and unforgettable, like the spray of blood on a wall at the scene of a slaying which had soaked into the plaster and did not fade, no matter how many times it was scrubbed.

The morning after she had exacted her vengeance on Poppy, she was sleeping in the bedroom in Richmond and woke suddenly as the bedclothes were dragged off her. Nick was standing at the foot of the bed. The sheets were wrapped around his fists. His voice was low, cracking with menace.

'Get out of bed, Francie. Get out of bed right now and tell me why I shouldn't drag your arse down to the cops. This is an absolute fucking OUTRAGE!'

Francie had curled into a ball and whimpered into the mattress. Nick walked around the bed, still dragging the sheets, and stood over her.

'I know it was you. Don't tell me it wasn't. It's got your fucked-up, sad, vicious handprints all over it.

'I have spent the last two hours begging Poppy not to tell anyone about what you've done. Trying to protect you. And, believe me, there are plenty of people who'd like to know—the police, your friends, your family, the newspapers.

'Hah! What am I talking about? You write for a fucking newspaper! Is that where this stupid front page drama came from? WHY? Why'd you do it?'

What was Francie to say? I only did it because I love you? It was the same defence every screwed-up psychopath used when they shot presidents, stabbed their wives or gassed their children. But somewhere in there Francie recognised the truth of it. They were all saying the same thing: 'Look what you made me do! See how much you've hurt me! This is how much I love you!' And even as she thought this Francie also recognised the futility of it.

Once you were no longer loved, the meaning was just leached out of you. There was no care, empathy or comprehension of what you felt. And, why should there be? You were an ex. A former *something*, but in the present tense, *nothing*. The responsibility for your pain was yours and yours alone. Every cheapo self-help book told you that. *We all create our own reality*. That was easy to say if your heart hadn't been ripped out through your ribcage when you least expected it.

That morning, however, Francie knew her actions had stepped outside the boundaries of all civilised behaviour. She knew there was nothing to be salvaged. So she would have her say. She sat up and snarled.

'I'm sure your precious Poppy would love to tell the news-papers! What about the radio or the television, seeing she's so famous? I'm sure the whole country would love to know. Why don't you put out a fucking press release!'

Nick had wanted to hit her. She could see that. His fists clenched and unclenched as he struggled for composure. For one moment she hoped he would hit her. The pain would absolve her of guilt and, simultaneously, proclaim her the winner. But he gained control and this time his voice was as cold and even as a lake which had frozen over.

'You have no right to say that. None. I thought I owed you something, but from this moment on the debt is paid. We are finished. Even as friends. Forget you ever knew me.

'And if you thought this was a way of breaking up me and Poppy? Of punishing both of us? You are even more fucked-up than I thought you were.'

Nick dumped the bedsheets on the floor and turned to go.

Francie heard her voice come out as a screech. It was a thin, desperate noise she didn't even know she was capable of. As if she was a wild animal which had ventured onto the icy surface of the lake and fallen through. She was trapped there, freezing to death.

'Friends? You're a cheat, a sneak, a filthy fucking liar! Why would I want you as a friend?'

She grabbed a pillow and hurled it at Nick's retreating back. Then she gathered up the sheets and what remained of her dignity and wrapped them around herself. She sat on the bed and rocked, nursing her body for most of that dull August day.

And as she sat here tonight, three months later, on her narrow single bed watching the first raindrops landing hard and flat against the window of her childhood room, she wished her every atom could be scattered to the four winds.

Love, togetherness, always and forever.

Tonight there was no tempest fanning the wings of an avenging angel. No king tide sweeping her to victory. Francie saw she had been washed up on the shores of a place she knew all too well. The arid landscape of her past.

✳

There was a tap at the door.

'Frank?'

Her brother Joel's head appeared.

'Hey, are you coming out for dinner? Mum's made chicken Maryland.'

Francie sat up and wiped her eyes. 'I dunno. I'm not really hungry.'

'Come on. She's sacrificed an entire tin of fresh pineapple!'

Francie managed a twisted smile. Mum's cooking was always a joke between her and her little brother. The past twenty years of the multicultural revolution in cookery seemed to have passed her mother by. It was as if her cookbooks were themselves set in aspic.

She still cooked the same stodge they'd eaten as kids. Fish pie (tinned pink salmon and mashed potato); Toad in the Hole (lumps of sausage mince in Yorkshire pudding batter); Ki Si Min (mincemeat again, with cabbage, soy sauce and instant chicken noodles) and chicken Maryland (fried chicken in white sauce sweetened with chunks of tinned pineapple). Stir-fries, steamed vegetables and the world of spices were all exotic mysteries to Carol McKenzie, although she was a dab hand with puddings, slices, cakes and biscuits. It was a wonder Francie and Joel had escaped early onset diabetes. Although now Francie saw Joel had a pasty, puffy look about him which wasn't healthy.

'You can't stay here in this room forever, you know,' he said as he switched on the bedside lamp. 'This is Mum's paper pattern shrine to Simplicity, McCalls and Butterick. She's not gonna give it up for you! Sounds like a law firm, doesn't it? Simplicity, Butterick and McCalls. Attorneys at Dressmaking.'

Francie squinted against the light. Joel sat on the bed next to her. He was a big rumpled lump in his old sweatshirt and ripped jeans. His brown hair—the same dark shade as his father's—was a shaggy haystack. He peered at Francie from under his fringe and she saw her own soulful grey eyes looking back at her.

'You know she's still selling Barbie doll clothes? She knitted a Fair Isle ski jumper for a Barbie doll this morning. Can you believe it? And a pair of tights. I mean, what sort of a sick unit does that? Don't they mass manufacture Barbie doll clothes in China these days out of plastic and velcro shit? What sort of a fucked individual sits there, day after day, and actually knits Barbie doll clothes and even sews on buttons the size of pinheads? I tell you, she's mental. Anyway, if you don't come and eat the chicken Maryland she'll crochet you a doggie bag so you can take it home with you.'

Joel put his arm around his big sister's shoulders and whispered in her ear: 'Come on, Frank, come and have dinner with me! Rescue me for just one night.'

It was an invitation Francie was bound to accept. She would have liked to rescue Joel forever. It wasn't right, an almost thirty-year-old man stuck here in this house in Blackburn with his sixty-year-old mother. There was something creepy about it. Johnno had hit the mark. Joel was a *clinger* too. He was collateral damage from Mum and Dad's break-up way back in 1982.

Francie knew that Joel had never been the same since Dad left. He was six then. She remembered him standing on the front lawn one wintry afternoon in his yellow and brown Hawthorn football jumper waiting for Dad to come by and take him to the match. He stood there until after dark, until the temperature was almost zero, and Dad hadn't come.

After that, Joel never put the jumper on again. Instead he read *The Hobbit*, then *The Lord of the Rings* and retreated into Middle Earth. It was almost as if Gandalf the Grey had become his long lost father. And now here he was—Joel, the hobbit who never left the Shire, the pineapple ring bearer. Francie kissed his forehead and tried to reach her arms around him, and when it all became a bit embarrassing for them both they heaved themselves off the bed. Joel clomped down the almost soundproof, carpeted hallway, leading the way to dinner.

'Hello there!' her mother sang cheerily. 'You're up and about. Good to see. I've made your favourite! Chicken Maryland.'

Francie couldn't be bothered to tell her that since the age of fourteen she'd been scraping the sickly white pineapple-flavoured sauce off the chicken and hiding it under a pile of peas.

Francie sat at the dinner table and watched her mother take her place, still wearing her blue floral apron. Carol always wore an apron around the house, as though the letters M-O-T-H-E-R were emblazoned on the front so there could be no confusion as to who she was. As long as she was wearing her apron, she had a purpose in life.

Her mother had a plump face, strangely unmarked by time for someone who was sixty years of age. But then she didn't smoke, didn't drink and hardly left the house other than to walk to the end of the street where she had been the receptionist at the doctor's surgery for the past twenty years. She was almost unused. She had an emotional snap-lid like a Tupperware container.

Doug walked out on Carol when she was thirty-nine. For a few years after that she still saw herself as a sexual human being, and there had been attempts at romance. She had been to dinner with a couple of men. Even cooked here at home for them and danced in the lounge room, but none of it had come to much. Francie had played her own small part in that. And then at some stage in her early forties, Francie couldn't be sure exactly when, Carol had packed away her notion of herself as a woman and become just a person. It was as if she'd seen enough of romantic life and decided it really wasn't for her.

She kept herself and her house neat and tidy. Tonight she was the same as she had been for the past fifteen years. Smooth, mousey brown bobbed hair, small pearl earrings, navy trousers, white pintucked blouse and the inevitable apron. If she was going on a social outing she would wear a navy skirt, the white blouse would be silk instead of cotton, and a pair of black court shoes would be matched with a black handbag. She would take her delicate diamond watch from the jewellery case and a modest pair of diamond stud earrings and hum a little tune as she put them on. A spray of Estée Lauder's White Linen, a light application of plum lipstick and she was set to go.

Everything was in order, from the little patch of gay annuals in the garden outside the front door, to the ornaments in the polished crystal cabinet in the lounge room and the swept and weeded path between the back door and the clothesline.

But there was something so desperate and fragile about it all. There was sometimes a far-off look in Carol's eyes, a catch in her voice that made Francie think that just one accidental knock would send the whole elaborate construction smashing down. Francie thought that her mother was an emotional addict who was on a lifelong twelve-step program. If she took even one draught from the cup of despair she would be off on a bender of fury. Maybe that's what Joel understood too, and why he couldn't bring himself to leave her.

Joel slumped in his chair at the round table. Francie always suspected that the table was round so no-one was reminded there was no father up one end of it. The table covering was floral plastic with an elasticised hem which tucked neatly underneath. No point in using a good linen tablecloth when it was just the family!

Each place setting had its own salt and pepper shaker. It was a family tradition to use a different set of shakers for every person at every meal. It was a way of giving Carol's vast collection an airing. Francie had a pair of handpainted china toadstools in front of her plate, Joel a pair of silver robins perched in a little silver branch and Carol a fish and seahorse in a clump of ceramic seaweed. Carol placed the dinner plates, decorated with Irish shamrocks, in front of both of her children and then took her own place with a grateful smile.

'Well, isn't this a nice surprise?'

Francie looked at her plate and was not surprised at all. It looked like the same inedible mass it always was. Dinner tonight would be an endurance test. She needed alcohol.

'Thanks, Mum. It looks delicious. Um, could I have a bread roll, please?'

'Well, we haven't got rolls, we're not a restaurant, after all, but I might have some wholemeal slices . . .'

Her mother headed for the pantry and, as soon as she was out of earshot, Francie turned to Joel.

'I need a drink, JoJo! What have you got stashed?'

Joel reached down under his chair and retrieved a can of rum and Coke. She might have known that his innocent tumbler of soft drink contained something a lot harder. After all, he'd been smoking dope since he was thirteen.

They were both furnished with orange tumblers decorated with daisies and filled with Dutch courage when their mother returned.

'So . . .' Her mother beamed with satisfaction as she dumped the plastic bag of bread on the table. 'Here we all are. I might just say, it's lovely to see you, Francie. Although she does look quite thin, doesn't she, Joel? Still, at the end of the day it's lovely to have you home . . . it's where the heart is, after all.'

What was her mother—fucking cliché woman? Francie trawled her mind for one original thing her mother had ever said. She drew a blank. Joel took up his tumbler and drained half of it. Carol was obviously not expecting a reply to anything she ever said to him.

'You do look peaky, Francie, so I'm expecting a clean plate from you tonight. I've made your favourite, lemon meringue pie.'

Carol watched with pride as Joel ploughed through the glutinous pile on his plate. Francie thought she could see the beginnings of tears in her mother's eyes.

'They were the best days of my life when you were both little and we were . . .'

Together with Dad. A perfect family.

'Come on, Francie, you've hardly started yours,' she admonished.

Francie took a bite but couldn't manage to swallow. She washed it down with rum and Coke. It was all so depressing. Francie and Joel were children again and Carol was a sad suburban single mum. How different it all could have been. Francie imagined a parallel universe where she and Joel sat drinking a glass of wine and picking over a plate of French cheeses with their parents, who were just back from a trip to Europe. They would be talking about the Picassos in the Pompidou Centre or the Velasquez portraits in the Prado Museum in Madrid.

'Your Auntie Kath's had her eyebrows tattooed,' said Carol. 'You know she had alopecia and all her hair fell out? Well, she wears a wig now, but her eyebrows have always been a worry, so she came down to Melbourne from Benalla on the bus and she had them done by a cosmetic tattoo artist. Have you ever heard of such a thing? Wonders will never cease.

'She rang me last night wanting your new phone number, Francie. Was Nick on television last night?'

'Drop it, Mum,' Joel said tersely through a mouthful of peas. 'Where's the pie?'

Later in the evening, when Joel had retreated to his room and his computer, Francie sat with her mother in the lounge room. They were at either end of the couch. Its knobbly teal synthetic covering scratched the back of Francie's knees and she pulled at her denim skirt. Carol was proud of the fact that the lounge-room setting was not arranged around the television—that was gauche and suburban—so instead they looked at a featureless drop of beige synthetic curtains and a knick-knack shelf crowded with gleaming, handpainted china plates and figurines.

Carol was knitting the tiniest item Francie had ever seen— a white woollen handbag for a Barbie doll, the size of a ten-cent piece. Francie was flipping through a *Woman's Day* magazine from last October. When she realised she had read the same item on Paris Hilton three times, she finally laid the magazine on her lap.

'Mum . . . how long did it take you to get over Dad leaving?'

'Oh!' Carol looked up from her handiwork, startled. 'Do you really want to talk about all that, dear? It's so long ago now. Water under the bridge.'

'Yeah, I think I do. I haven't told you but I'm seeing a counsellor and it's bringing up a whole lot of stuff I have to—'

'A counsellor? Like a psychiatrist? Are you alright?'

Carol finally put her knitting down and looked closely at her daughter. Francie could see furrows of concern where her mother's forehead was usually a blank, bland space. She suddenly looked all of her sixty years.

'No, I'm not really. It's not really going all that well since Nick left . . .' And then her promise to herself not to cry in front of her mother dissolved in a salty deluge.

Carol was across the couch in an instant and took her daughter in her arms. Francie buried her face in the flowery blue apron and gave way to heaving sobs. Carol smoothed her blonde hair.

'There, there. Come on now. I know it's been a difficult time for you. The thing is, darling, that I think you never do get over it when he leaves. But that's not something to worry about, because you're just not the same person you were when you were with him. That person's gone.'

She took Francie's face in both her hands. 'And hopefully, there's an older and wiser woman in her place.'

'It hurts so much, Mum.'

'I know. I know, sweetheart. But time will heal all, you'll see.'

It was the cliché which snapped Francie out of the tender moment. What was next? *You'll get over it, there's plenty more fish in the sea, you should be glad it happened now, it'll all be for the best in the long run.*

Francie sat back and wiped her face with her sleeve.

Carol went on with quiet determination: 'I've got no use for passion, Francie. It was something my mother said to me and she was right. It took me a long while to understand that passion is a degrading emotion. It leads you down all sorts of paths you don't want to go down.'

Francie sniffed and saw that her mother's face had settled back into its soft contours in the same way a quilt can be pulled over rumpled bedsheets. Could she really mean that a life without passion was something to strive for?

'But you're a Christian. What about Christ's passion?'

'Goodness me! We're Anglican! We leave all that nonsense to the Catholics. I think you'll find that quiet forbearance will be of greater use to you. I think the secret of life is to be resigned to your fate. That's the way to achieve real peace of mind.'

Forbearance and resignation. They were the twinned emotions which had enabled Carol to endure twenty years of loneliness and despair and lead her to this place. Which was . . . nowhere.

'And what *is* my fate?'

'It's the fate of all women, Francie. To never be truly loved in the way you would imagine. That's what happens when you put your faith and your fate in the hands of men.'

If this was actually true, and so far it was what Francie had experienced for the first thirty-two years of her life, then it was a terrifying prospect. But what had her counsellor Faith hinted at? That it *was* possible to be truly loved, and that all Francie's life she hadn't dared to imagine it.

Looking at her mother, who was now rummaging through her knitting basket, Francie could see very clearly that Carol's disappointment had been handed down as a tangible object by her mother before her. It was a family keepsake, like a precious gold locket or a diamond ring. Francie, in her turn, had probably been given it, along with her first training bra, when she was thirteen.

'You know, Francis—' Carol's needles clicked methodically as she spoke—'there are only two men in this life who will not let you down. Jesus and Our Heavenly Father. That's the place to put your faith. Faith, hope and charity are what's left when the illusion of romantic love falls away. You might not see it now, but you will. And with faith, hope and charity comes real contentment.'

It was then that Francie knew she couldn't stay here. Everywhere she looked she was reminded that this was a house of unfulfilled promise. Francie and Joel had lived their whole lives in a quiet suburban street knowing that either side of them there were houses where love was so abundant it spilled out the windows and into the front yard. They would watch fathers washing the car, mowing the lawn or up on the roof at Christmas time, stringing up lights and cardboard Santas while mothers impatiently called them in for dinner. They had watched as children reluctantly straggled to cars piled high with suitcases for annual beach holidays while parents squabbled in the driveway. There was enough love in those houses that it could be taken for granted.

But in Francie and Joel's house, love was something you treated as a precious, fragile commodity. If you were careless it might dissolve or evaporate. The only way to be loved was to be good and kind and quiet and compliant. And even though Francie had been all that, love remained elusive. It was like quicksilver, running through your fingers whenever you tried to take hold of it.

She stood and tugged at her shirt, patted down her skirt. 'I'd better get going, Mum. I'll just go and say goodbye to Joel.'

'Are you going already?' It was her mum's standard query. She would even say it to the postman if she had the chance. Francie felt guilty saying goodbye so soon, but she also knew that it wouldn't matter if she stayed here for eternity. Nothing would change.

'Yeah, I should get back. I've got a lot on . . .' *Like getting my hands on enough prescription drugs so I can kill myself.*

Francie tapped at Joel's door and, getting no reply, tiptoed into his room. His bulky frame was silhouetted against the glow of his computer.

'Whacha doin', bro?' She bent to peer over his shoulder when he suddenly swivelled in his chair, blocking her view of the screen.

'Hi! Nothing! Just stuff, you know, nothing interesting,' he stammered as he pushed the hair from his eyes.

'Come on! What? What are you up to?' Francie teased as she attempted to duck under his arm. It was their old game of curious big sister and secretive little brother. They'd played it all their lives. Joel knew how it went. But tonight he was having none of it.

'Hey! You can't just walk in here like you own the place!' he protested. He reached behind him and shut down the machine.

'Joel . . .'

'You think nothing happens in this house when you aren't here. You imagine everything's the same from when you moved out. Well, it's not, and if you came here more often . . .'

'What?'

Joel shifted in his chair and folded his arms across his chest. 'Nothing.'

Francie sat on Joel's bed and tucked her hands under her thighs. She shook her head to bring him into focus in the shadows. Even through the fog of her own misery she could tell this was a moment when she needed to be clear.

'Tell me. What?'

'You're fucking kidding me! What's the point? Telling *you* anything right now would be like chucking a rock into a mine shaft. We could sit here for a year and still not hear it hit the bottom. Go home, Francie, you're not much use to anyone the way you are.'

Seventeen

Later that night Francie was sitting in the car outside the St Kilda 7-Eleven. For company she had a plastic container of cold chicken Maryland and a tray of caramel slice on the back seat. She turned on her mobile phone. There were twelve messages on Francie's voicemail, signalling a rising crescendo of concern.

Francie . . . it's Johnno, Olga, Amanda, Johnno, Olga, Gabby, Dave, Amanda, Robbie, Auntie Kath from Benalla . . . where are you? Are you OK? Do you want me to come over? Do you want to talk about it? Don't worry, it's no big deal, everyone's done it, no-one takes that stuff seriously, it'll all be over by tomorrow. I'm sorry, we're sorry, he'll be sorry, she'll be sorry. Sorry, sorry, sorry. Are you sure you'll be OK? Call me back. In the morning, now, immediately!

But there was one message which was genuine cause for alarm: 'Hello, Francie McKenzie? This is Sheridan Waters from the *Sunday Star*. We are running an interview with Poppy Sommerville-Smith for tomorrow's paper about the stalking and vandalism allegations she made against you on *Talkfest* last night. I would like to hear your side of the story. It's Saturday morning and my deadline is midday, so if I don't hear from you I will be going with "declined to comment". Please call me as soon as you get this message. I'm at the *Star* on extension 1723. Thank you.'

Midday. That was twelve hours ago and in one minute it would be tomorrow. Francie watched as people walked from the dark car park into the fluorescent light of the shop. She saw them stop near the paper stand, pay up and then walk past her car with the *Sunday Star* tucked under their arm.

She felt sick and considered opening the window to vomit up the remains of her pineapple chicken and lemon meringue. Taking a deep breath, she got out of the car and walked to the shop door. Was it the blinding brightness which made Francie fumble for her sunglasses? Or an attempt to go incognito? She didn't know, but standing there looking at the front page of the *Sunday Star* she knew that any attempt at disguise was futile. There was a red banner right across the top of page one. At either end of the headline PAYING BACK POPPY were two full-colour head shots. On the left was Ms Sommerville-Smith looking like an adorable wounded faun, and on the other was Francie's portrait from her column in the *Sunday Press*— unbearably smug and self-congratulatory.

There wouldn't be one person who picked up the paper who could resist turning directly to page three for the full story. Well, maybe one person, and that was Francie.

Her hands were shaking as she took both the *Star* and a copy of the *Sunday Press*. She knew what would be in her *Seriously Single* column in the *P.S.* liftout. A collection of marvellously witty, carefully constructed replies to the lovelorn. Nothing in there (go figure) about a vicious act of vandalism on your rival's knickers with a pair of scissors.

Francie's mind and body were numb with shock. Now she did feel she was going to vomit, right here in front of the cash register. She turned and stumbled towards the fridge. She needed a bottle of water, fast.

As she turned around the end of the aisle the colours of the packets of chips and chocolates began to swirl. She lurched and reached blindly to push the man standing in front of her out of the way. She clutched a handful of black leather and looked up to see—Dave. It was the final shove her stomach needed to bring up a boiling mess of dinner, shame and humiliation. She bent over and heaved all over Dave's Cuban-heeled boots. And while she was down there, the acidic bile burning the back of her throat and bringing tears to her eyes, she noticed another pair of feet dancing out of the path of the noxious tide. They were, unmistakeably, the ten French-manicured toes of Gabby Di Martino.

Dave was soon beside Francie with his arm around her waist and holding back her hair as she kept heaving until there was nothing left. The shop attendant was soon on the scene with a mop and bucket, complaining loudly about weekend drunks. Dave helped Francie to the front door, Gabby paid for the bundle of newspapers and the bottle of water and then, mercifully, they were out in the night air.

'How do you feel now?' asked Dave. 'Are you OK?'

Francie wasn't looking at him, she was leaning against her car, pressing her face into the cool metal of the scratched roof.

'Yeah, yeah. Thanks . . . I'll be fine,' she replied shakily as she unfurled her fist and her car keys clattered onto the concrete.

'Give 'em to me. I'll drive you home.'

'No, I'm OK, really. You and Gabby go . . .' And then she wondered where exactly they were going at midnight. Back to her place? His bedroom? If they were in the middle of some romantic assignation Francie had certainly wrecked that. But then, Francie wrecked everything. Even Joel had told her she was useless.

Dave took Francie firmly by the waist and deposited her in the passenger seat of her car. She watched in the rear-vision mirror as he had an earnest discussion with Gabby about the direction the rest of the night would take. Again she was reduced to a problem being discussed. Francie guessed correctly that Gabby was keen to come along for the ride, but that Dave was pulling the pin on their night together.

Gabby knocked on the car window and Francie reluctantly wound it down.

'Look, Francie, this . . .' she said, waving the *Star* in front of Francie's eyes in case she hadn't seen it, 'is a piece of shit. It's so badly written. Sheridan Waters is a total fucking hack!'

Oh good! So not only was Francie portrayed as a maniacal stalking vandal, but they hadn't even put a decent writer on the job. Who would Gabby have preferred the story to have been written by? JK Rowling?

'It's all . . . well, it's all . . .' Gabby was struggling for words.

A complete and utter appalling disaster.

'Call me tomorrow morning. We have to talk about this. From my point of—'

Dave leaned across Francie and called out the window. 'Thanks, Gabby. She'll call you tomorrow morning. Goodnight.' He backed the car and almost squashed Gabby's perfectly tanned toes. Francie watched her stomp with annoyance to her smart pale green Peugeot.

Francie wound the window up and was hit by the disgusting smell of her own vomit on Dave's shoes. She quickly wound it down again. They didn't speak on the three-minute drive to *Elysium*. Francie swigged from her water bottle. Neither of them had the slightest idea what could possibly be said.

Inside the house Francie was heading determinedly for her own bedroom when Dave took hold of her again.

'At least let me make you a cup of tea. I know you're not going to get to sleep any time soon. Come on.' He tugged her towards the kitchen.

He was right, Francie was looking down the tunnel of a long, sleepless night. She might as well have a cup of tea with Dave. He knew everything now. Everyone did. No amount of sitting in her room by herself was going to change things. Francie was surprisingly calm—she supposed it was from sheer physical exhaustion—when she walked into the kitchen to find Jessie and

Johnno and Robbie all standing around the table with the *Sunday Star* open to page three.

There was a profound silence as all five of them regarded each other. The first to break rank was Dave: 'Evening all.' He crossed to the sink and found a dishcloth to clean his shoes.

The second to speak was Jessie: 'Oh Jesus, Francie, this is all my fault! I am *so* sorry. I can't begin to tell you how sorry I am.' She slumped into a chair with her head in her hands.

The third was Johnno: 'Fucking hell, Francie! Why didn't you tell me about this? Fuck!' He turned from Francie, picked up the newspaper and threw it into a corner of the room.

The fourth was Robbie: 'Well . . . all I can say is the bitch had it coming to her. She deserved it. And that was just for murdering Chekhov. She was shithouse in *The Seagull*!' It was a decent attempt at a joke, but no-one laughed.

Dave wrenched open the door of the freezer and retrieved a bottle of frozen vodka. Cranberry juice and three beers followed from the fridge. It was the signal that the *Elysium* discussion group was now in session.

In the first instance the group came up with the expected platitudes: *Don't worry. Today's newspaper is tomorrow's fish and chip wrapping. No-one reads this rag anyway.* But none of them believed a word of it. The fact was, this was a public humiliation on a scale no-one could have imagined. Francie's reputation, both on a personal and professional level, was toast.

And that this should happen to Francie—of all people? Nice, quiet, friendly Francie! And that she should do it to Poppy

Sommerville-Smith—of all people? The gifted, intelligent, intuitive Poppy!

No-one could think of a strategy that would get her out of this any time soon. Francie, for her own part, just sat there, figuring that she was like a fish on a hook and that if she didn't wriggle it wouldn't hurt as much. But then, as the alcohol kicked in and midnight gave way to early morning, something interesting happened. Francie realised that, beyond the caring platitudes, her four companions were utterly *fascinated* by what she'd done. They interrogated her about every minute detail of that bizarre evening back in August.

'Did you plan it, or did it just happen?'

'How did you get in?'

'What were you wearing?'

'Were you worried about the neighbours?'

'What did you cut up . . . exactly?'

'What sort of scissors did you use? Hairdressing? Dressmaking?'

'What sort of underwear does she have?'

'Where did you cut it? Crotch? Nipples?'

'What else did you destroy?'

'How did it feel when you were doing it?'

'How did you feel when you finished?'

'Have you ever done anything like that before?'

'Would you do it again?'

'How did they know it was you?'

'What did Nick say?'

'What did she say?'

'Why didn't she go to the cops?'

As Francie downed one drink after another she offered a full confession. She knew why Poppy hadn't gone to the police. Nick had intervened on her behalf and, anyway, it was all highly embarrassing for everyone. As Francie told the tale, even she had to admit that it was compelling. It had everything—heartache, grief, rage, celebrity and very expensive underwear. Her heart sank some more as she realised the story would be repeated endlessly around the country for a long time to come.

In fact the story was *so* compelling that everyone at the table felt they had to contribute their own tale on the topic: the most shameful thing you've done in the name of love.

'OK, I'll go first,' Johnno volunteered. It was the least he could do. After all, he'd known Francie the longest. He'd been there the night she met Nick.

He sat back in his chair, smoothed his Greenpeace T-shirt over his chest, pushed the hair from his eyes and was about to begin. Then he stopped.

'I'm not sure I can tell you this in front of Jessie.'

'Confess!' cried Jessie. 'I want to know everything! We all do. Full disclosure. If Francie can do it, we can too.'

Jessie, Dave and Robbie started banging their glasses on the table. 'Confess, confess, confess!' they chanted.

'Alright, alright.' Johnno held his hands up. 'Here it is. I was seeing this chick for about six months—'

'Who was it? Anyone we know?' said Francie, who was glad to be asking the questions for a change.

'Yeah. You remember her, France—Elinor. You know that Polish chick I met at film school?'

'Oh yeah, that sociopath goth with the long black plaits. She was a weirdo,' Francie muttered.

'*She* was a weirdo? Thank you, Francie Scissorhand!'

It was the first time anyone had dared make a joke at Francie's expense and when everyone laughed she managed a rueful smile.

'We'd been going out for about six months when I found out she was screwing this bloke behind my back. Some fat hairy drummer out of a heavy metal band. And I just . . . lost it.'

Here Johnno coughed, ran his fingers through his hair, drained his beer and saw that four people had now leaned forward to hear more.

'So, one afternoon I went over to her place and I filled her bed with food.'

'You did *what*? What do you mean?' came the chorus.

'I pulled back the covers and piled in baked beans, jam, chutney, eggs, sugar, flour—everything I could find in the kitchen. Then I remade the bed and left.'

There was a wave of disbelief which broke into squeals of laughter.

'I wanted her to come home and jump into bed with him and make some sort of disgusting infidelity omelette,' Johnno raised his voice over the hubbub. 'But—' and here he paused like the experienced scriptwriter he was—'she was at his place and didn't come home for four days. In the end she smelt it as soon as she walked in the door and she came straight around to my flat and punched me in the face.'

Amid the laughter Francie smiled gratefully at Johnno. She knew the story was told for her benefit—to make her feel more normal—and she mouthed a silent 'thank you' to him.

Johnno smiled back and said: 'Although I really did care about her. It's funny how you sometimes miss your chance and have to wait ages for the next one.'

He looked at Jessie and Dave looked at Francie, who looked at her drink. Jessie took up the thought.

'Yeah, like playing "skippy" in the schoolyard when you had to find a moment to run in between the ropes. Sometimes you could run in and be in the moment straight away and jump for ages. Some days you'd stand there and never find the rhythm. Other days you'd run in and get whacked in the face by the rope. Being good at the game was about blind faith and courage in the end.'

'And,' said Johnno, looking at her with blind faith and courage, 'about never giving up, no matter how many times you're whacked in the face.'

'Uh-huh.' She reached for his hand.

'So,' said Jessie, 'I don't think I can beat that, but when Henry and I broke up there was a *minor incident* with a chainsaw.'

Nicely done. Jessie also had a talent for picking her moment and immediately had everyone's rapt attention.

'When we started living together Henry found this love seat in an antique shop in the country. It was the classic red velvet number. Something you'd imagine Elizabeth and Mr Darcy sitting in. Pretty shabby, but he loved it. He used to insist that

216

we sit in it all the time to drink champagne, and read poetry to each other.'

'Sounds very romantic,' said Johnno, who was fascinated to hear anything of Jessie's past.

'But the thing about sitting in this stinking chair night after night was that it came to be, as far as I could see, a substitute for real sex. I mean, we'd sit there until midnight and then in bed . . . the big fat zero. Anyway, when I moved out I rented a chainsaw and cut that piece of red velvet junk in half.' Jessie sat back with a satisfied smile at the quartet of astonished faces.

'Well,' said Robbie, 'nothing says "it's over" like a chainsawed love seat. Sure beats a text message.'

'And,' continued Jessie, 'you'd think Henry *would* have got the message, but he's still a problem.' Her cheerful smile slipped.

'But he's not your problem anymore, beautiful, he's mine,' said Johnno emphatically. He leaned over the table and kissed Jessie hard on the mouth.

Francie knew that for Johnno and Jessie the searching was over. She was pleased that she had been the reason they'd met. And as she thought that, she knew the flame of romantic hope flickered within her still.

'The word was "shameful" right?' Dave took a deep breath. His voice was low. His words were measured and precise.

'So, you're in your twenties and you are betrayed in business by a middle-aged man preoccupied with his success and career. He's a record producer—a smarmy smart-arse, a complete prick. He rips you off.'

It was odd that Dave was telling this story as if it had happened to someone else. But the way he was looking at a spot on the wall above everyone's heads made it clear he was telling this story at some personal cost.

'You remember this, Robbie?'

Robbie provided corroborating evidence for the audience: 'Your band was brilliant, could have gone anywhere. I know the bastard you're talking about.'

'As I said, he betrays you—the "how" and "why" are unimportant now—but he has this assistant. Very beautiful . . . a princess. Big hair, short skirts, very sexy-girlie, and she bounces around his office. You can see he's utterly infatuated with her. Protective, obsessed in that way middle-aged men can be. When the fantasy of something they can't have becomes more real than what they already have—a wife and kids.

'It's clear he's got no hope with her. And it's killing him. So . . . you take her to bed. And the next time you see them, you completely ignore her. This is your way of saying: "I can take anything I want from you and it means nothing to me".'

The men were silent, savouring the revelation. The women were shocked and needed more details.

'What was it like with her?' Jessie asked.

'OK, good enough. Doesn't matter really.' The men nodded.

'Did he ever know what happened?' Francie asked.

'I never bothered to find out. I'm sure he did.' The men understood.

'Impressive,' said Johnno. 'Very impressive.' He raised his drink in salutation.

Francie and Jessie sat back in amazement and Dave, seeing them, was quick to mount a defence.

'I know, I know, it was evil! But it was in a former life. I would never do that again.'

Francie wasn't so sure. Of course, as a revenge it was perfect. It was certainly shameful, but done in the name of love? In the name of business, perhaps. Francie thought of the anonymous sexy-girlie. She would have fallen for Dave. Francie imagined them in bed, Dave lying across her naked back. He was taking a handful of her long hair. He was crooning in her ear.

You hair is so . . .

Now let me see if we can just get rid of this . . .

And these . . .

Can I turn on the light?

Oh God . . . perfect . . . just perfect . . .

He would have been impossible to resist.

'Now, Robbie, it's your turn, I think,' Jessie broke into Francie's thoughts.

Robbie was silent for a long moment. He put his beer down on the table and turned over both wrists. He held them under the light so everyone could see the raised white ridges of two scars. He traced the lines with his fingers as he spoke.

'What was the topic? The most shameful thing you've ever done in the name of love?'

Everyone nodded.

'How about when you're sixteen and the first boy you love tells you he hates poofs so you slash your wrists with your dad's fishing knife?'

✿

It was almost 3 am when Francie finally crawled into bed.

The alcohol, friendship and shared stories had all done their part and she was physically and emotionally anaesthetised.

She dreamed that she was sitting in the very back seat of an aeroplane. She was squashed right up against the window amongst dozens of people she half recognised but couldn't put a name to. They were all weeping. Some were howling into handkerchiefs, others were silent as tears dripped from their chins.

The airliner and its grief-stricken cargo were flying over lands Francie didn't recognise. She flattened her face against the glass and looked out at endless swamps roiling with noxious yellow slime. Acrid fumes were seeping through the floor of the plane, adding to the burden of misery on board. They flew on over plains jagged with rocks as sharp as glass, then over mountains of obsidian. Bare black ridges pierced through dense grey smoke. Charred bones in the ash of a campfire.

The plane banked steeply and the passengers cried out. Francie was thrown harder against the window and could now see they were heading for the mouth of a volcano. Looking into its stony maw she could see a livid porridge of lava and she knew that if the plane didn't change its course everyone on board would die.

Francie clambered over the poor tortured souls next to her and lurched down the aisle to the front. Hands clawed at her clothes, clutched at her legs and arms. Now she was at the door of the cockpit and struggling to open it against the terrifying forces of gravity as the aircraft dived earthwards. With all her strength she wrenched it open.

There they were. Captain Poppy and her copilot Nick at the controls. They turned, smiling and waving a cheery hello, and offered her a plastic container of orange juice.

On the control panel Francie could see a glowing red button labelled 'eject'. She pushed past Poppy and Nick and pressed down hard.

Beep, beep, beep.

The floor of the cockpit opened and Francie was falling, falling through storm clouds. Was it true, as they say, that if she hit the ground she would be dead?

Beep, beep, beep.

She woke suddenly with her arms flailing and saw that Nick and Poppy were in the driver's seat of this story. If she didn't get out fast they were all headed for a crash-landing. There had to be a way to escape before they took her with them to oblivion.

Beep, beep, beep.

It was Francie's mobile phone. She must have turned it on before she went to sleep. The digital clock showed 7.30 am, which was hideously early for a phone call on a Sunday. And then, as the fog of her dream cleared, Francie remembered with horrifying clarity that the whole of Melbourne, if not the whole nation, would be now consuming the Poppy Sommerville-Smith and Agony Aunt saga with their bacon and eggs this morning. She felt another wave of nausea. So she had already crash-landed and now had to clamber out of the wreckage.

By 10 am Francie had turned down requests for interviews with two television current affairs programs, three radio shows and one women's magazine which was offering the fair sum of five thousand dollars for the story and photograph. (They had kindly offered to supply the underwear and scissors for the shot.)

She had also received calls from Olga and Amanda in varying states of indignation and alarm, and she'd screened calls from Auntie Kath from Benalla and her mother—both of whom were going to take more emotional energy than she could muster this morning. But there was one call which finally forced Francie out of bed.

'It's Gabby Di Martino. I've had a visit from the managing editor and I want you here in the office within the hour.'

Eighteen

The *Daily Press* newsroom was already busy with staff putting together the next day's edition of the paper.

Copies of the *Sunday Star*, many of them open to the page-three story, were on most desks. The journos nursing their third cups of coffee for the morning were most surprised to see Francie hurrying through the open-plan office. The noisy hum of the room stopped and Francie thought it was as if there was news that someone had died. And then she remembered: she had. She could feel all eyes on her back and hear the excited whispers when it was estimated she was out of earshot. Only she wasn't quite, and she could hear the whispers turn into stifled giggles.

Francie had decided to muster what dignity she could and held her head high. She had scraped her hair back into a ponytail and pulled on jeans, T-shirt and sneakers, knowing that she wasn't going to be here long.

Gabby wasn't in her office, so Francie went to her shabby desk in the deserted *P.S.* corner—no-one would be working here until Monday afternoon—and began packing up her pens, notebooks and postcards, and emptying her drawers of lipstick and perfume samples into a calico bag.

She would miss working at *P.S.* and certainly miss her column, although it was probably time she moved on anyway. Four years working at the *Press* and the last two at *P.S.* were probably enough for anyone. She would land another job at a women's magazine. Writing blurb for knitting patterns . . . Maybe.

How did she feel about it all? Francie was in shock and couldn't feel anything much. She decided it was probably like being savaged by a white pointer. You look down to see a limb missing and your own blood turning the water bright pink and you can't feel anything at all.

She looked up to see Gabby Di Martino stride up the corridor resplendent in a powder blue jogging suit and white high-heeled sandals. *Here comes Nurse Ratched. Hide the electrodes.* She'd never been sacked before, but there was no way this could hurt. What's a paper cut when you're already an amputee?

'Brilliant, you're here!' announced Gabby. Her face was flushed pink, she was breathy, excited. This was exactly the sort of drama Gabby loved. Francie reflected that she couldn't have been more excited if the staff photographer had presented her with photos of Elton and Jacko in a clandestine clinch.

Gabby threw a pile of papers on the desk. 'Look at these. I think there're about eighty emails here and it's not even lunchtime—on a Sunday! You're a genius, Francis McKenzie! A full-on, fabulous genius!'

Francie stared at her. Her mind could not form one coherent thought.

'Poppy Sommerville-Smith, of all people! How long has she had this coming? She's a serial offender. We've got two ex wives as well as you. She is absolutely *stuffed*.'

Gabby was hopping on the spot and clapping her hands, her bracelets jangling in celebration.

'You're a dark horse, Francie. I would never have thought this was your style, but I love it! How many times do I wish I'd had the balls? What did it feel like? Did you do the crotch and the nipples, or—? Well anyway, sit down and start writing. The *Daily*'s holding open the middle pages and they want your side of the story, the whole thing, by three.'

It was at this point that Francie could have walked away. She could have taken her calico bag full of sample cosmetics, her free books and notepads and left the office. She could have driven off into exile and maintained a dignified silence. That would have been the grown-up thing to do. But that would also have signalled defeat. The world would see that she was vanquished. She could envisage Poppy riding onto the battlefield like Boadicea in a winged chariot claiming dominion over all.

So Francie didn't leave. Instead she sat at her desk and spilled her guts. She wrote everything. How much she had loved Nick. How she believed he had been stolen from her. How the lovers had conspired behind her back. The devastation when he left. The uncontrollable passion which drove her to a filthy act of vandalism. What it felt like to be in the grip of a rage beyond rationality. Francie felt she wasn't just doing it for herself. She was doing it for every woman who had had her man stolen from her—every husband, every father who had been lured from his home. She wrote to avenge her mother, who had endured twenty years of loneliness. She wrote to avenge herself for the act of female capriciousness and vanity which had stolen her childhood. She wrote because she had nothing left to lose.

Two hours later Francie was sitting on a white swivel chair in Gabby's fragrant office. Gabby was bent over, reading her computer screen, her pert blue velour bottom on the edge of her seat.

'Oh—my—God! This is wild! Just . . . amazing! It's so honest. I mean, I'd almost cry if I wasn't going out for drinks later.'

She turned to Francie and flapped her hands in front of her face by way of explanation. 'Cos, you know what I mean, my eyes totally puff up and look hideous.'

She swivelled back to the screen and read more.

'I adore this part about *griefe* being a notifiable disease back in London in the 1600s and that people actually died of broken hearts. How did you know that? I mean, it makes the whole undie-slashing thing so understandable, even rational. Like self-defence. Someone should have written this stuff years ago. I love it, love it, love it! Of course it's a bit long and a bit melodramatic in places, but we can fix that.'

Francie was about to say that she'd rather it wasn't 'fixed'—that it was her life, after all—when Gabby hit 'send' and the screen went blank.

'There. Gone to the subeditors at the *Daily*. I've seen the pages they're laying out. They look amazing. They've got your bit and dozens of emails from readers, which, by the way, are all *totally* supportive, and two of the ex wives of men she's run off with have given us interviews which are cringe-making.

'And . . . you should see the pics they've chosen of Poppy! Cruella De Vil? She should look that good! And they've got a hilarious one of Nick the Dick.'

'They're putting a photo of Nick in there?' Francie squirmed in her seat.

'Yeah, they found some hammy shot of him from that TV soapie he was in. What a loser!'

'He's not a loser, he's . . .' Francie faltered. 'I did love him, you know. We were together five years. I dunno, maybe I . . .'

Gabby got up from her seat and walked around her desk and took Francie's shoulders in both hands.

'Listen, honey, don't lose your nerve now. What you're doing here is great! It's a war, Francie. All women know it. We all know how hard it is to find a man and keep him. Men are essentially weak. They're vulnerable and there are any number of vixens out there ready to pounce. At the moment they've got the upper hand.

'But you, you're fighting back! You're saying *Take my man at your peril, you bitch!* And judging by the number of emails we're getting, a lot of women feel the same. You're a moral hero, Francie. You don't know it yet, but you'll see.'

This rousing speech was delivered with great conviction and passion, but there was one puzzling detail which didn't add up. Francie had to ask.

'But didn't you have an affair with a married man?'

Gabby let go of Francie and turned to get her handbag.

'Oh, that was different. We really loved each other.'

❈

That Monday, 6 December 2004, was what those in the media call a 'slow news day'. In fact even a story about a family who paid $5000 to give their Jack Russell dog a pacemaker made the newspapers. So the further details of the Francie–Poppy fracas in the *Daily Press* came as a godsend.

'THE WAR OF THE POSEURS' was the headline. As Gabby promised, it made fabulous reading. The agony aunt, the soapie star and the actress made excellent leading players and the character roles taken by the ex wives were likewise perfectly cast. One was a mother addicted to painkillers with three kids at primary school and the other was a minor celebrity spokesmodel now known for her herbal skincare range. There were so many angles to this saga that it was a diamond-faceted opportunity.

The radio talkback shows went ballistic. There was no end to the number of aggrieved wives and lovelorn mistresses who were put on hold that day, all patiently waiting for their chance to be heard and understood.

There were plenty of talking heads willing to wade into the debate. Opportunistic politicians: 'This is the tip of the iceberg. What we are looking at here is the erosion of family values. If more of our young people married within the church, then they would find that the sanctity of their union would be respected by others. In fact the statistics on the break-up of de-facto relationships are startling! They clearly demonstrate . . .'

Fame-seeking psychologists: 'Of course rage is just another facet of passion, and in some cases it can have dire consequences. If anyone, be they male, female, married, single or de-facto, feels they are the target of undue attention in these circumstances, there are any number of professional people who are trained to deal with . . .'

Even the odd policeman: 'Look, emotion aside, at the end of the day what everyone should be focusing on here is the wilful damage to private property. A serious crime often begins with petty vandalism, but of course, in many respects we have our hands tied. I think we would all agree that if the courts started to take seriously . . .'

Actual husbands, boyfriends and fathers seemed to be rather thin on the ground. But, as everyone knows, when the elephants go to war, the ants get trampled.

For her part Francie was appalled to read the coverage, which was surprising since she'd been working at a tabloid newspaper for some years. Factually the story was correct, but what was missing was the *nuance*. After all, Francie had written that she regretted what she'd done. Hadn't she?

She was listening to her car radio on the way to work and heard herself labelled a 'moral heroine' (as Gabby had predicted), a 'crusader on behalf of decent women everywhere' (it had a certain ring to it), a 'criminal' (which was technically true), and a 'publicity-seeking mediocrity who was probably bad in bed' (ow, that hurt!).

Poppy fared much worse. A 'serial man-eater'; an 'over-the-hill actress with no family of her own', a 'trollop'. 'Really awful in that Chekhov thing, but I loved her in *Twelfth Night*' was the best she got. Even Francie had to admit she was copping an absolute belting.

Nick was barely mentioned, being, apparently, just a bit player. Third spear carrier from the left.

This time when Francie walked through the *Daily Press* office at midday she noticed quite a change in attitude from her colleagues. There were a couple of nods in her direction, a couple of 'nice one, Francie' comments and even a high five from the editor of the gossip column. Although Francie did reflect that admiration from the denizens of *Pssst!* was a sign that things were not at all well.

Sitting on her desk was a large pair of scissors tied with a pink ribbon and a bottle of French champagne—a 'thank you' from Gabby. Within minutes the woman herself had landed on her usual perch on Francie's desk.

'You've done it!' she announced with a triumphant toss of her tawny locks. 'An absolute Houdini. You've taken a totally fucked situation and turned it around to your advantage. Poppy Sommerville-Smith will be lucky to get a carpet-cleaning ad after this. How does it feel?'

It was too much to take in. But Francie did know that she felt better than she had twenty-four hours ago. Her brain was still on cruise control, but at least she was starting to regain some feeling in the ends of her fingers and toes. Gabby waved a sheet of paper in Francie's face. *You're always doing that. What am I? Blind?*

'I've got a million media requests here—magazines, radio, television—but I've turned them all down on your behalf. What we have to do is build on this and make this week's edition a killer!'

Francie dropped her head into her hands and groaned. 'No, no. Can't it just finish here? Can't this be the end?'

Gabby threw her head back. Francie was eyeing a well-toned set of stomach muscles heaving with laughter.

'Francie, Francie, Francie! Here you are, you've endured six months of pain and heartache and now, just days away from the payoff, you wanna bail. You really are a classic, you know that?'

'What payoff? What do you mean?'

'I mean, Dear One, the payoff when the Powers-That-Be see next week's circulation go through the roof. I mean, who knows what's in it for us exactly, but you've got to say that every man in this building is sitting up and paying us a lot more attention than he was last week!'

Francie was about to say that she'd had enough attention to last her a lifetime when Gabby reached over and clamped her hand over her mouth. Francie winced as a heavy gold and aquamarine dress ring banged her front tooth.

'Now, shoosh up! I have two things to tell you. First, we have tons of emails here for you to deal with. Pick the most brilliant ones for next Sunday's column. Christ knows we've got some real nutters in there! Take as much room as you need.

'And second, I'm taking you for lunch at Jacques Reymond. It's on the company so I've already rung through and told them to put the French on ice.

'By the way, I've arranged make-up and hair in my office, cos we're going to need a couple of shots. So shift yourself and I'll see you downstairs in an hour, OK? Byeee.'

Francie was really starting to hate that 'Byeee'. Instead of 'shifting herself', she decided on a small act of insurrection, and opened up her computer. The in-box was full. She picked up her phone. The voicemail was jammed. On second thoughts, having her hair done and going to lunch seemed like an excellent idea.

Francie was sitting in the perfumed sanctuary of Gabby's office with a head full of hot rollers and Gemma the make-up artist flitting about her face like a damsel fly. She could sense that Gemma—spiky blonde hair, pierced lip, maybe in her late twenties—wanted to talk. She hesitated a couple of times and then, while plucking a few stray hairs from Francie's eyebrows, couldn't hold her tongue a minute longer.

'I just wanna say that I thought what you wrote was cool. I mean, the thing is, we've all had those revenge fantasies when some slut nicks your boyfriend, but you actually did it. And then you owned up to it, which is even more cool. I would never have had the guts.

'I hope your bastard ex boyfriend is sorry for what he did and I hope he never forgets it. I wanted to smash in my sister's car window with a brick when she slept with my fiancé. But I . . . I dunno . . . I just couldn't. Anyway, I just had to say it, that's all. I hope you don't mind.'

Why should Francie mind? Apparently the entire population was now sitting in judgement on her actions. Why should the make-up girl be any different?

'Your sister slept with your fiancé?' asked Francie. Not that she really cared. The question was more a polite reflex action.

'Yeah. How about that? But you know, I got over it. Never look back, just go forwards. That's my motto. In the end she did me a favour. I'm married now and four months pregnant.'

'Congratulations,' Francie croaked.

Gemma's story was starting to push all sorts of buttons Francie didn't want pushed. She looked at this girl who had just been an anonymous person a couple of minutes ago but had now come into focus as being everything Francie wasn't. How Francie wished she had never looked back, just gone forwards. How she wished there was a button marked 'eject' in front of her right now. There was one question that needed to be asked and Francie didn't want to know the answer. Gemma filled in the blank space.

'And if you're wondering whether they stayed together? Yeah, five years now. Just goes to show, huh?'

✺

Francie was sitting in the back seat of a company car next to Gabby. Two very fashionable women off to enjoy a chichi lunch. Only Francie would rather have been heading right out of town to lose herself in the Great Sandy Desert. She had nothing to say for herself and looked out at the sky, which was appropriately overcast.

Gabby was relentlessly primping in a hand mirror. She must have checked her lip gloss fifteen times on the short drive from the city to Windsor. What was the point? She always looked perfect. And not only was she doing her lips, but she was checking her teeth, fluffing her hair, adjusting her jewellery. If Francie didn't know better she would have sworn Gabby was expecting a red carpet on the footpath.

When the car pulled up outside Jacques Reymond, Gabby sprang out the door and held it open. This was odd because normally she did not move a muscle until her driver did the honours. Francie clambered out and was suddenly aware of people running at her from all directions. Flashes of bright light turned the grey day brilliant. Calls of 'here, Francie, over here' and 'this way, Francie' should have been a clue that she was the star attraction, but even so she looked around wildly hoping Cate Blanchett was getting out of the car behind. No such luck.

Francie at least knew enough to compose her features in a calm mask and smile for the cameras. The last thing she needed was footage of her bolting down the street and hiding in a bush. However, in a minute the lights were turned off, the scrum dissipated as fast as it had gathered, and the street resumed its grey overcoat.

Gabby grabbed Francie's hand and led her inside the restaurant. 'Well done,' she muttered. 'You looked gorgeous.'

The door was opened and one last lone paparazzi jumped out for a quick shot before sprinting away.

Francie turned on Gabby: 'What the hell was that? You knew—'

'*Shhh!*' Gabby commanded through gritted teeth. 'Smiling, smiling . . . Let's just get to our table.'

As they walked through the room all eyes were on them. There had obviously been some public and unpleasant exchange between the waiter and the photographer because the waiter was apologising profusely.

'I'm so sorry, Mademoiselle Di Martino. I asked if he would wait outside *mais* . . .'

'It's all fine, fine,' said Gabby airily. 'Divine table. We'll have champagne straight away. *Merci.*' The waiter was dismissed and they sat down.

'I cannot believe you did that! You told them I was going to be here!' Francie hissed.

Gabby checked her lip gloss again, as if the twenty-five paces from the car to the table had somehow weathered her careful facade. She smiled radiantly at the other diners, who then resumed their meals assuming (incorrectly) that calm had been restored.

'Relax! You should be grateful. It took me absolutely hours to set that up. They all wanted to send reporters, but I told them to fuck off. I said they could get their shots, but there would be no actual interviews—take it or leave it.

'So . . . the current affairs shows will have their little rehashes of the story on television tonight. The papers and mags will have a go. But they won't have *you*. I don't want you talking to anyone until *P.S.* comes out on Sunday. *You* have got to be exclusive to *us*.'

Two glasses of champagne were poured at the table and the bottle of Moët et Chandon 1995 Brut Impérial was slipped back into its ice bucket. Francie almost inhaled the contents of her glass and immediately wanted a refill.

'Gabby,' she said with all the measured determination she could muster, 'you are NOT my agent. I am NOT a celebrity. I am a hack on a crummy liftout in a Sunday paper. We are not working on *Hello* magazine, in case you hadn't noticed. This whole . . . circus . . . has got to stop!'

Gabby took a sip of champagne and eyed Francie steadily. 'You can't just make it stop. You know that. You can't get off the merry-go-round until it stops and lets you off. But I will make you a promise. We just need one more column with all the emails. One final wrap-up on how you've been overwhelmed by the support . . . blah-blah-blah . . . and then it will be over.'

Francie shook her head. 'No.'

Gabby sighed. *You'll hardly feel it. Here we go. Just a little sting.*

'Francie, it's like this. The column is going to happen with or without you. Now, you can do your readers the courtesy of answering their emails—God knows they seem to love you, even if you are a *hack* on a *crummy liftout*—or you can refuse and I will put together the column myself and use your by-line. It's your choice.'

Francie was sure Gabby would do exactly that. It would be outright fraud, but who was Francie going to complain to? She was considering her options when a familiar shape loomed over the table. It was the managing director, Mr Kevin Jenkins, landlord of the vast mahogany desk Francie sometimes found herself at the wrong end of. She clutched her champagne flute tightly and would have liked to slide to the floor.

'Well well, ladies, good afternoon. You certainly seem to be enjoying some celebrity today, Miss McKenzie,' he said with amusement.

Francie grimaced and ducked her head. She could see him from the waist down. Too-big belt buckle, shiny black trousers, nasty shoes.

'Kevin, helloooo! Yes there was an exciting little media scrum out there,' Gabby simpered. 'You know, now that I think of it, what we have here is a classic Princess Di versus Camilla Parker Bowles scenario. And we all know where the public support went on that one!'

Kevin chuckled appreciatively and replied, 'Mmm, but I could always see the sense in Charlie and Camilla. They look like they belong together. And we all know how Di met her end—hounded down in a tunnel by paparazzi.'

'Well, that's true, of course,' Gabby immediately agreed.

'Well, enjoy your lunch. I assume the champagne is on us. You've earned it and I imagine you've got the next thrilling instalment for us in *P.S.* on Sunday. Good stuff!' He gave Francie a hearty pat on the back.

'Would you like to join us for a glass of champagne?' Gabby cooed.

'Ah, love to, but I've got a table of clients over there who have me hostage this afternoon.'

'Oh, what a pity.' Gabby stuck out her bottom lip, which just looked ludicrous at her age.

'Perhaps for a coffee later, at the office. And if you're driving back to the city, don't go down any tunnels, Princess,' he boomed, amused by his own wit, and headed back to his table.

It wasn't until Francie estimated that Kevin Jenkins was out of sight that she raised her head. Come to think of it, she did feel a bit like Princess Diana ducking under her blonde fringe. She reached down and collected her handbag.

'I don't want lunch. I will do the column. Not for you, not for him, but for the readers and then that's the end of it—the column, everything. And I won't be in for the rest of the week. I'll see you on Friday.'

Gabby reached out to grab her sleeve and missed.

'Francie!'

She would have liked to have run from the restaurant, but instead affected a casual stroll from the room with her chin held high. Even so, she did notice that at least a couple of diners recognised her and almost gagged on their *asperges au beurre blanc*. She didn't turn back to look at Gabby. Francie stood on the kerb and hailed a taxi. Inside, Gabby had already hailed another table.

She wished she *was* Princess Di so she could go home and throw herself down a monumental staircase. She also recalled that Princess Diana had tried to top herself by taking to her wrists with a lemon slicer. As if she could somehow peel herself to death. There was a lemon slicer in the kitchen drawer at *Elysium*. She decided to go home and see if she could make a better job of it than Di had ever managed.

Nineteen

As Francie reluctantly walked up the stairs to Amanda's flat that same Monday night she could hear the sound of the television coming through the French doors which opened onto the balcony.

She guessed at once what Amanda and Olga would be watching—what Gabby had called a rehash of her pathetic story on the nightly current affairs shows. She hesitated before rapping on the glass door. She would rather have climbed back into her car and driven away. But she was expected for dinner and with new resolve had decided to go forwards—her new direction after the conversation with Gemma the make-up artist. She pushed the brass button by the front door and heard the chime inside the hallway followed by a flurry of activity in which the television was switched off. Amanda opened the door with a flourish.

'Hi, hi, come in. We were just—'

'So how did I look?' asked Francie, attempting to be a facsimile of herself at her cheerful best.

'Oh . . . good, good, good. Fabulous hair. It was all . . .' Amanda faltered.

'Hideous,' piped up Olga from behind her.

'Thanks, Olga,' said Francie tartly, and pushed past them into the lounge room.

'What I meant was, that it's just tabloid crap! Why that was on a current affairs show, I don't know. They should stick to chasing dodgy electricians down the street. Not my friends.' Olga was trying to put things right but should really just shut the fuck up.

Francie turned to face her. 'Nick was on there too?'

'It was just a bit of old stuff from *Talkfest*. They didn't have anything *new*. I mean, there isn't anything new, is there?' Olga asked nervously.

Francie wondered whether she would be disappointed to learn there wasn't.

'No,' Francie sighed. 'Just the same old disaster.'

'Oh God, you poor thing.' Amanda gave her a hug. 'You must be a wreck. Come on, I'll get you a drink.'

Francie felt that at last she had found some sort of sanctuary. About an hour after she arrived, the events of the past few days had been laid out in chronological order. The second bottle of white wine was opened. Francie realised she'd drunk most of the first bottle by herself. Amanda was sitting on the couch nursing a glass of orange juice and rubbing her stomach, although Francie couldn't see any sign of a bulge under her loose white linen shirt.

Olga had occupied about six chairs around the room, smoothing her expansive rose-printed skirt each time she sat down. She was always nervy, but seemed especially stressed out tonight. Francie thought that there was something else on her mind.

Amanda put down her orange juice and clasped her hands underneath her belly in that way pregnant women have of using their new hard tummies as a comforter and shield. Francie could see Amanda was mustering her courage for a deep-and-meaningful.

'Look, I think there's something here that you're not really facing, Francie. And I don't think you're going to like it, but I'm going to say it anyway.'

Francie sat back in the overstuffed chair and gripped an armrest with one hand. She took a gulp of wine and listened. She knew Amanda could not do any more damage. She'd already beaten herself to a bloody pulp.

Amanda tucked her sleek, dark, bobbed hair behind her ears, which she always did when she was nervous.

'You know, and I know, that if *she* hadn't come along you and Nick would have broken up anyway. I think we all saw it coming and so did you, if you're honest. You remember that weekend we all went away to Aireys Inlet? You were complaining *then* how distant Nick was. You were wondering *then* whether he was really the man you wanted to spend the rest of your life with. And that was a couple of weeks before he'd even met *her*.'

The name *Poppy* was mercifully never mentioned in this company. Francie's silent forbearance encouraged Amanda to keep going.

'I remember that weekend because I was ovulating and Lachlan and I had started trying for this baby. There was a lot of talk about babies and every time the subject was raised Nick would get up and go for a walk on the beach. You were wondering way back then whether you two were going to last. You were putting a lot of pressure on him to make a commitment—which was fair enough after five years—but you had come to a sort of crossroads. Don't you think?'

Francie was now looking around the room, avoiding Amanda's eyes.

'Francie, we have been trying to tell you this for months, but you haven't listened. You've been too angry and upset, but you're going to have to accept the reality. You and Nick were over even before *she* came on the scene.'

Olga felt it was an opportune time for her contribution: 'You'd started looking at other men too. There was that photographer from work.'

Another dose of reality Francie had to take.

Amanda continued: 'You would have left anyway . . . that's if he hadn't got in first. I know the way he left was bloody hopeless and that he owed you something better than that, but we all love Nick and you've got to stop punishing him.'

'He started it. He punished me first,' said Francie, and as soon as the words were out of her mouth she heard how childish they sounded.

'Oh come on, Francie!' Amanda was exasperated. "Where's this going to lead to? It just—'

'I know, I know. That was stupid.' Francie finally looked at her friends.

'Everything I've done has been stupid. I wish I could take it all back. You're right. The truth is I should have left Nick years ago. I know. I promise I'm trying to work it out. I'm really sorry. I'm sorry that I've bored you all shitless for the past six months. I really have tried not to. I'm sorry.'

There was silence as Amanda considered her plea, but Olga had one last charge: 'All that stuff in the paper about married men and husband-stealers—where did *that* come from?' Her tone was surprisingly sharp.

'I don't know. I just saw *her* on television and I wanted to punish her too. And then there was this opportunity at work and I got pressured. I know it's no excuse, but I—'

'Well it didn't just punish *her*, it hurt a lot of other people,' said Olga emphatically.

Francie and Amanda turned to Olga, who was compulsively rearranging her skirt again. She looked up and blurted, 'I'm in love with a married man.'

Francie and Amanda glanced at each other—yes, they were both stunned—then looked back at Olga, who had leapt from her chair and started circling the room, her white wine sloshing from her glass onto the floor rug.

'And it's not how you think it is, Francie! I didn't *steal* him. I mean, can any man really be stolen? You make it sound like a man is some sort of inanimate object, like a VCR. Like I'm some sort of cat-burglar who cased his house and then stole him from his wife and kids in the night. That's not how it was at all!'

'Well, how was it?' asked Amanda.

'How long has this been going on?' asked Francie.

'A year.'

'A year?!' they chorused.

'And there's something else. I just found out yesterday that I'm pregnant. Four months, Amanda—just a week ahead of you.'

Olga plopped down on her chair again, her skirt billowing out like a pink toadstool.

There could not have been a greater difference between the two pregnancy announcements. Where Amanda and Lachlan's news had been greeted with cheers and champagne, Olga's was met with open-mouthed amazement. She looked at her two friends and burst into tears.

'I couldn't have another abortion—I've already had two,' she wailed. 'I'm thirty-five! And anyway, I love him and I want to have a baby with him. And I am. So that's that.'

The details of Olga's affair were haltingly recounted. She had met her married man, whose name was Dominic, at a weekend jewellery trade fair. She was manning her booth, selling her handmade beaded necklaces, and he was next door flogging his silver rings and pendants. They had extravagantly admired each other's handiwork and then, as these things happen, each other. It was a meeting of artistic minds—although she was also taken with his dreadlocks and silver toe ring and he with her cat's eye glasses and elegant long neck.

Olga told her friends how she and Dominic had spent a scintillating afternoon drinking in the local country pub and then been treated to a tarot reading together by Mistress Merriweather—one of the weekend mystics who also had a booth at the fair. His cards had turned up The Lovers, The Sun and The World, which meant *relationship*, *enlightenment* and *fulfilment*; and she had selected The Hanged Man, The Fool and The Empress, which told her to *let go*, it was the *beginning* of *abundance*. If they had instead revealed the six cards of The High Priestess, The Devil, Justice, The Tower, The Moon and Strength—which would have meant *non-action*, *hopelessness*, *cause and effect*, *downfall*, *illusion* and *willpower*, it was doubtful their conclusion would have been any different.

They were handmade for each other. They were joined body and soul that night at a motel down the road. It wasn't until a few months later that Olga discovered Dominic had already turned his capable hands towards fashioning himself a family—a wife and three-year-old twin daughters. But by then it was too late. Olga and Dominic's relationship had been forged in the hot furnace of passion and deception and, according to Olga, couldn't be undone. They would go wherever it led them. Only it didn't seem to be headed towards a divorce court—from what Francie and Amanda could divine—any time soon.

'He's going to ask his wife for a separation,' said Olga.

'*Ask* her? They're still living together then? Jeez, Olga, what about his kids? How old are they again?' Amanda demanded.

'At pre-school probably . . . I don't know. I didn't ask to fall in love with a married man. I didn't know he was married.

245

I met him and fell in love the same way you and Lachlan did. The same way Francie and Nick did. You don't pick who you fall in love with! The heart wants what it wants!'

'But you could have stopped it when you found out he was married,' added Francie.

'Oh yeah? The same way you could have stopped before you slashed Poppy's things with a pair of scissors? Don't give me your sanctimonious bullshit about self-control, Francie.'

Olga had a dangerous and determined look in her eye which her friends had rarely seen. Her remark hit the bullseye. Francie breathed deeply and took it. She tried a more sympathetic tack.

'Why didn't you tell me? Maybe I could have helped.'

'Hah! Like you've had a teaspoon of emotional energy for anyone but yourself for the past six months. If you had, you would have seen that Nick has been going through hell too. Poppy says it's been a nightmare watching him so tormented by you falling apart the way you have.'

Amanda groaned and put a cushion over her face. She didn't want to watch the next bit.

'Oh?' said Francie sardonically. 'Poppy is your new best friend, is she? It occurs to me, Olga, that you are on her side because you and she have a lot in common.'

Olga threw her wineglass at the wall. It smashed and sprayed the room with glass. Amanda ducked behind her cushion and uttered a muffled 'Oh shit.'

'DO YOU HAVE ANY IDEA OF THE AGONY YOU'VE CAUSED?' Olga was shouting now. 'Agony Aunt—that's the perfect name for you. Nick stopped loving you. Is that a fucking crime? Why shouldn't they put on a show together? What's it got to do with you? Do you think they would bother to mention you and your sordid little deeds? Just how big is your ego?

'You advising people about their love-lives is the biggest joke ever. You don't know anything about love. You've never had it and you wouldn't know it if . . . what was your charming phrase? *If it bit you on the arse.* Get fucked, Francie! Goodnight.'

Olga snatched her little beaded bag from the coffee table and ran from the room. Her high-heeled lace-up boots crunched on broken glass.

When she heard the front door slam Amanda took the cushion from her face. She eyed Francie carefully.

'Don't worry,' Francie said wearily. 'I had it coming. All of it.'

Amanda tried to make it better. 'If she is pregnant . . . I mean, she is if she says she is, it's just such a shock! Anyway, being pregnant, she'll be teary and tired. I know what that feels like. She'll come around.'

'Yeah, she will. But a baby . . . bloody hell!' said Francie. 'I think we'll have to be there for her. I don't like the sound of this Dominic thing.'

'God, Francie!' Now it was Amanda's turn to be up on her feet and walking on broken glass. 'Why does it all have to be so complicated? Sometimes I get this foreboding about me and Lachlan. It feels like it's been so easy. I can't help feeling that somewhere down the track we're going to pay the price. The fact that it's been so, I dunno, *normal* feels almost *abnormal*.'

'Don't start thinking like that, Amanda. It's supposed to be easy. We're just living in a moment when people have too much time to think about all this shit. Once, you got married when you were a teenager, got pregnant and the responsibility of raising kids and just surviving made you grow up too. You didn't have a choice.

'But now . . . It's like when you go into the supermarket and you look at a hundred different brands of shampoo. It's the same stuff, just different packaging, but having the choice can send you mad. If we went into the supermarket and there was just one bottle with "shampoo" on the label you wouldn't always be wondering whether there was something better you could have bought. It's the same with love. Doesn't matter what brand it is. If you find it, buy it. Be happy. And if it runs out, I dunno, buy a new bottle.'

Francie had no idea where this bizarre analogy had come from. What if the shampoo hurt your eyes? What if someone nicked your bottle? What if there was no more on the shelf? But she just sat with it and thought it was as good as any other banal self-help pronouncement she had come up with in her life.

She decided she would go home, sit in the bath and wash her hair.

Twenty

'Why is all this happening to me?' Francie looked at Faith Treloar without a tear in her eye. It was time for Francie's Wednesday night confessional. The box of tissues sat on Faith's shelf behind her desk and that's where they would stay. Francie's crying had stopped and she doubted whether she would cry again as long as she lived.

'And what *is* happening to you, Francie?' Faith asked. She was leaning back in her red velvet thinking chair with her hands folded across her embroidered bosom in their usual manner. Her fingers wove a jewelled prayer mat.

Francie mirrored her and leaned back in the blue chair and regarded the ceiling. *Where do I start? With my professional ruin? My friendships blasted to rubble? My family a relic I can't identify anymore? My own feelings a foreign land I don't know how to navigate?*

Francie still resented being psychoanalysed by Faith Treloar, which was stupid. After all, she was the one who drove here. She was the one paying for it.

'I know you are going to say that this has all been sent to me for a reason and, honestly, if you tell me that the Chinese words for "crisis" and "opportunity" are the same, I think I'll throw up.'

Faith smiled. 'Why did you think of that particular proverb?'

Francie shifted in her seat with irritation. Why did she have to do all the work? She could add 'poverty' to her list of problems if she had to pay Faith when she could have come up with these glib questions herself.

'Because,' she sighed, 'I know that the standard self-help crap is that you can't form a new pattern of thinking until the old one is broken. That the journey of a thousand miles begins with one step . . . blah, blah, blah.'

Faith smiled. 'So you've been giving this a bit of thought then? In what way would you say your old pattern of thinking has outlived its usefulness?'

'You're the therapist. You tell me.'

'OK, time to earn my fee.' Faith sat up and leaned over the desk.

She took her lavender-rimmed glasses from the top of her head and perched them halfway down her nose. It occurred to Francie that she'd never seen Faith actually look through her glasses. She had to be about sixty, the same age as Francie's mother. But her dangly hippie earrings and elaborate kurta said she was still young at heart. The dozens of positive affirmations stuck on the walls of her consultation room were signposts on a journey of personal growth. If Francie told her mother she was doing some 'personal growth work', Carol would have assumed she was talking about a pot of parsley for the kitchen.

'I would say,' Faith said in her professional calming tone, 'that, as we identified last week, you have certain ideas which have been patterned in childhood. I think your life is driven by fear. The fear that you are not good enough. That you don't measure up. That any person you love is bound to leave you, to run away. Now, while most of us have these fears from time to time, you are crippled by them.

'You chose Nick because he was emotionally unavailable and then came to believe that the feeling of insecurity you had with him was love.'

'But I did love him,' Francie ventured.

'Yes, but the question is, Francie, did you feel safe in his love? Did you feel he'd love you no matter what? Or did you feel that unless you were perfect he'd leave?'

Faith and Francie already knew the answers to those questions.

'And then he *did* leave. Your worst nightmare came true. Everything that has played out in your life since has come from a place of fear and anger. And if you don't deal with it, it will become worse.

'Looking at you as you are now, I'd say you've got no hope of forming a decent, grown-up, loving relationship unless you go back and resolve some of the grief you felt when your father left home. We've started the process here, but we've got to keep going until you "get" it, until your behaviour actually changes.

Who could you talk to about that, Francie? Where could you gain some insight into your past?'

Francie thought for a moment. 'Well . . . I suppose I could go and talk to Nick . . .'

She still didn't get it.

When the time for her session was up, Faith walked Francie to the front door of the old terrace house. Francie sneaked a look back down the hall into a small room where a young woman, about the same age as her, sat huddled in a chair waiting for her appointment. Francie saw she was just another unit on an assembly line of grief.

Faith held out a small box wrapped in silver paper and tied with ribbon. 'Open it.'

Under the hall light Francie could see it was a pack of cards. They were bright blue, edged with gold and had 'The Journey' written on them in white.

'I do try to operate in the realm of human logic. But who knows what's real and what's not? A little divine guidance never goes astray. When you have some time to contemplate, take a card and just sit with it for a while and think on the message. See what comes up.'

✿

Later that evening Francie was sitting and toying with the ribbon of apple peel in her martini as Joel polished off the last of his veal cutlets. He sopped up the meaty juices with a chunk of bread and stuffed it in his mouth. Francie reflected that she seemed to have been doing this a lot lately—watching people eat as she drank. The waistband of her size-ten jeans was loose.

They were sitting in Becco's, just around the corner from Joel's favourite bookshop in Bourke Street. A few tables were occupied. It was a quiet Wednesday night and it had been a happy coincidence to find that Joel was in the city, just out from a movie, and able to meet Francie, just out of therapy, for a meal.

She wasn't sure that Joel would be able to give her much insight into her childhood but, of course, Dad had left him too. How much did Joel remember? How much did he care? It was odd, Francie realised, that she had never asked him directly. The circumstances of their family had been endured and coped with, but never really talked about. She knew that her mother's twenty-year ban on discussion of the topic had been total and effective. Even now, Francie felt that she was betraying her mother by seeking out Joel to talk about it.

And then there was the strange encounter in his bedroom to be negotiated. Joel had said that Francie didn't know things had changed. How had they changed? Francie took another sip of her drink and considered where to begin.

Joel sat back and wiped his mouth with a napkin. He reached for his beer.

'I've been to Dad's house in Albert Park, you know. Three storeys. Cathedral ceilings. Swanky neighbourhood. All old Victorian buildings,' he said. His voice was flat, matter of fact, but it was clearly a statement delivered with intent.

'They've got a great place—if you can find your way through all the wind chimes and Tibetan prayer flag junk. Denise paints.

All sorts of New Age crap—goddesses, fairies, dragons—shit like that, but she's not too bad actually. She's even got Dad picking up a paintbrush. Hah! They'd piss themselves at the bank if they knew.'

Francie put down her glass and stared at her brother.

'Yeah. Thought you'd be surprised. You should come with me. The next time Dad calls and says he wants to take you to some expensive joint for your birthday, why don't you say you'll go to his place? He'd like it and I'll bet you'd get on with Denise.'

At the mention of this name Francie's mouth fell open and it was a moment before she could form a sentence.

'You think I'd like . . . *Denise*?' Even saying her name felt like treason.

'Yeah, you would. She's great. I know Mum doesn't get it, but Dad's happy. And Stella's cool. She's a violinist with some orchestra in Sweden.'

Stella? The surly seven year old with the buckteeth? Cool? Francie tried to reconcile this pronouncement with the image of the hostile stepsister in a bridal wear shop from twenty years ago. And Denise? Every time Francie thought of her she was hosting a sex-aids party. Picking up edible g-strings with orange nails.

'Why haven't you told me any of this?'

Joel sighed and pushed the hair from his forehead. He was trying to be patient. *Alright then, we'll take it slowly. How many fingers am I holding up?*

'Look, Frank, that's the way you and Mum have wanted to play it, and that's fine. It's just that at the beginning of this year

I decided that it was all bullshit. What was the point? I just thought that even if you and Mum couldn't move on, it wasn't what I wanted. I thought, what if I ever get married and have kids? What if they want to go to Christmas at Grandpa's or Grandma's? What am I gunna say? So I just picked up the phone and . . . well, I'm glad I did, that's all.'

Joel was comfortably seated in a sunny clearing on the moral high-ground. Francie was still groping along a dark tunnel, trying to adjust her eyes to the light.

'You've been going all this year? You should have told me. I would have come too!'

Francie's tears were instantaneous. They took her by surprise.

'Aaargh! Jesus, fuck, Jesus, JOEL!'

She grabbed a table napkin, scraped her face. Her voice took on a childish tone of *not fair*. Baby talk you could only get away with in front of your family.

'Do you *really* think that Mum and I are the same? Do you think I've enjoyed creeping around this whole thing for my entire life? I saw you standing in the yard waiting for Dad to come and take you to the footy. I know how hard it has been on you. I just figured that maybe Mum was right, that if we all just got on with—'

Joel raised his voice, just slightly, enough to stop his sister in her well-worn tracks: 'Got on with WHAT, exactly? The dumb fairytale where the handsome prince is put under a spell by the evil witch and the good princess waits her whole life for him to come back to the palace? And then . . . guess what, boys and girls? HE NEVER FUCKING COMES BACK!'

Francie adopted an attitude that was familiar to her brother—
not looking at him, not wanting to hear.

Joel's voice took on a desperate tone. He gripped the edge
of the table. 'GROW UP, FRANCIE! Is it any wonder you're
seeing a shrink? Is it any wonder you're all over the newspapers
and the TV—let's not forget that—for being some sort of mad
psycho bitch?'

Francie hid her face in her napkin.

'And you can STOP CRYING! I'm sick of you crying.
Everyone is.'

He reached out and tore the fabric from her hands.

'Come on, think about it! You go off and try to recreate some
stupid domestic "happy ever after" with Nick, pretend it's real,
and you're surprised at the way he left you? And the way you've
fallen apart? It was always going to happen, Francie. He was
always going to dump you like Dad dumped Mum. Your
relationship with Nick wasn't real! Anyone with half a brain
could see that! Oh sure, he visited on weekends, but he wasn't
really *here*. He was just going through the motions.' Joel leaned
forward and muttered, 'I've hated him for it for years. And if
he was here now, I'd punch his fucking lights out!'

Francie, stupidly, took Nick's side. 'You can't say that—'
she began.

Joel shook his head in exasperation. 'No! You can't go on
being so hurt. Some innocent victim of circumstance. At some
point you are going to have to actually get over it.'

Francie wiped her eyes again. Get over what? Who she was?
Her life? If everything was going to be laid on the table, there

were things she wanted to say too, and since Joel was saying exactly what was on *his* mind . . .

'Well, I could say the same thing about you!' she charged. 'You're almost thirty, still living at home with Mum.'

Joel took up his beer and drained the glass. He set it on the table. 'Not for long, I'm not. I've met this girl on the net and we've been together for four months. She's from Sydney and she's coming down here.'

So this must have been what he had hinted at the other night. Francie said what most people she knew would say under the circumstances: 'What? On the internet? Are you kidding?'

Joel was calm, defiant. He was expecting a fight. 'We talk every night, sometimes three, four hours. Like last Sunday we were together for the whole day and I think she knows me better than anyone I've ever met.'

'But you *haven't* met—' Francie began.

'If you haven't ever done it before, Francie, you wouldn't know! You can get to know someone properly, without all the superficial shit. Anyway, her name's Vanessa and we're engaged.'

Engaged? To be married? Francie tried to make sense of it all. She clutched at her familiar persona of Big Sister/Agony Aunt.

'Joel, this is mental! Can't you see what living with Mum, the emotional vacuum cleaner, has done to you?'

'No, I can't. Why don't you tell me? Seeing *your* personal life is going *so* well.'

It was another sardonic remark which hit its mark. Francie had always feared Joel's psychoanalysis—one of the other reasons she didn't visit as often as she should have. She scrambled to defend herself.

'Look, I know my life is shit at the moment! OK, everyone knows, but this is bizarre! The reason you're in love with someone you've never even met is that it's a fantasy! You spent five years being in love with Galadriel from *The Lord of the Rings*—and you say *my* relationship wasn't real?'

Silence. Like the silence in the aftermath of a terrible crash, when all you can hear is the dying hiss of a punctured radiator or the echo of a hub cap spinning on bitumen. Francie and Joel lay in the wreckage and were still for a moment. They then tentatively checked for injuries. Wiggled toes, shifted limbs and put their hands on their faces to feel for blood. They were brother and sister still strapped in the back seat of a car out of control. Still being punished by a failed love affair from two decades ago. Divided and conquered by an argument that was never theirs to have or understand.

Eventually Francie became aware of the sounds of the outside world. Conversations of people walking past in the laneway next to the restaurant. The clatter of plates being carried to the kitchen. The clink of glassware.

She looked at her little brother. She remembered him sitting in front of the television. Eating cornflakes. Watching cartoons. Unaware of the carnage just around the corner . . .

'God, Joel,' she whispered, 'how fucked-up are we?'

Twenty-One

It was about 11 pm when Francie walked through the front door of *Elysium*. She checked all the rooms in the house and there was no-one home. She was glad for the emptiness. There was so much to think about. Then again, she reflected, none of it bore thinking about at all.

She was standing in the kitchen boiling the kettle on the stove top and idly thinking about killing herself. How did you do it with an oven anyway? Stick your head inside? Then what? Did you light a match in the hope it would explode? Or did you sit at the table and wait until the whole room filled with gas and you were asphyxiated? That wouldn't work. The ceiling was too high.

Looking closely at the oven Francie figured that, because it was just a domestic appliance, it could probably only blow your hair off and burn your face. That would be a great look—a bald, burnt, heartbroken stalker. That had to be the definition of a complete loser—someone who couldn't even pull off their own suicide.

And that's what Francie figured she was, just an everyday common or garden variety loser. She knew she wouldn't kill herself. That would require even more drama and theatrics. If there was one thing Francie knew after her well-publicised Night of the Scissors, it was that dramatic and theatrical acts often inspired anger, laughter or worse: indifference. Unless the audience really cared. And no-one cared about Francie. Why would they? She didn't even care about herself.

She would leave suicide to the professionals. Francie picked up her cup of tea and plodded to her bedroom.

She was propped up in bed against her embroidered red pillows with the 'Journey' pack of cards Faith had given her. Everyone she had talked to in the past few days had told her she did not understand, that she was missing something. Didn't get it. That she had to keep thinking.

She drew a card at random and turned it over.

The card was 'Mind'. The text read: *Your mind does not exist, except in your imagination. Poonjaji.*

So, here was a concept to think about. *Your mind does not exist, except in your imagination?* Doesn't your imagination exist in your mind? Francie was puzzled. Or is your imagination in your . . . er . . . big toe? What do you think with if your mind doesn't exist? What can your imagination imagine, if not your mind? And who was this *Poonjaji* anyway?

The nature of the thinking mind is fear, doubt and judgement—a stream of imagined words, sounds and pictures passing through Consciousness. The only meaning it has is the meaning we invest in it. It is not real.

Francie knew what this meant. She'd read enough of the aphorisms on Faith's walls to know this was a gold standard of the self-help industry. It meant that the events in her life could only affect her negatively if she let them. That she had to, as she herself had observed, be more detached. Let go. Well, this had been the mantra of every guru since time began and surely only gurus could achieve a thought process without fear, doubt and judgement? If she lost those three thoughtful companions, Francie's mind would be a blank. Then it wouldn't exist. Then she would have nothing. Except her imagination. Damn! She was going around in a circle.

She read on: *Have you been entertaining thoughts recently? Have you been analysing, interpreting, dissecting, revisiting them until you're tired of them?*

Oh yes! Francie had been doing that alright! But she hadn't been 'entertaining' thoughts. Her thoughts were gatecrashers who kicked down the doors of her mind and imagination at all times of the night and day. And was she tired? Yes! She glanced at her bedside clock—she was utterly exhausted.

The card went on to suggest that Francie should stop trying to barricade her mind against negative thoughts, but just let them all in and attach no meaning to them. *Let them be none of your business. Let them come and let them go, and then discover what remains untouched by any thoughts.*

Attach no meaning to anything and see what's left?

The brief moments of clarity she had experienced while sitting with Faith suggested that there *was* hope. And just as suddenly they had clouded over and these Elysian fields had gone from view.

Elysian . . . now there was a thought. She realised she had been thinking lately that *Elysium* was hell. A place of eternal torment. But it was supposed to mean—Francie leafed through the dictionary she kept on her bedside table—'a blessed abode'. Paradise at the end of the world.

So was she, even now, in paradise?

❋

That night in her dreams Francie died and went to heaven.

She was walking across Swanston Street mall on a sunny afternoon to meet her mother and didn't hear the tram. She didn't see it either, until it was only an arm's length away. This was surprising because it was an old green and gold rattler. It bore down on her with all the bells clanging.

She saw the big round light on the front and estimated that it would smash her right in the solar plexus, crush her ribcage and flatten her heart and internal organs. They would end up like a stack of pancakes on a serving platter.

At this point, it was like every near-death experience she had ever read about. Time stood still. She called to her mother standing on the footpath. 'Bye, Mum, bye,' and waved. Her mother waved back. 'Goodbye, darling. It was lovely to see you. Take care of yourself. Have you got a warm cardigan?'

Looking down she saw she had made a slight miscalculation because it was the tram's front bumper which hit her first, breaking both her legs and then pitching her body slightly forward so that her face took the next blow. The light did crash into her chest after that and shards of glass sliced through her clothes and skin. And then Francie was dead.

She found herself floating and watching the scene in the street below in the same way a snorkeller observes the activity in a coral reef. The sounds down there were muffled, but she could clearly see the human drama unfolding.

Her mother ran to the scene and was restrained by the tram driver. The passengers peered from the windows.

Francie smiled to see everyone she had ever known in her whole life on board. There was her third-grade teacher, Mrs Bevan. The Carmichael twins who had lived next door when she was seven. Joel was sitting up the back in between her father and Denise. Denise gripped the handrail in front of her with orange fingernails. Amanda, Olga and Johnno queued patiently in the aisle behind Auntie Kath and Kevin Jenkins. Gabby Di Martino was checking tickets.

They were all keen to view her body, which was lying on the tram tracks. Her old Mohair cat, Wellington, pushed through the legs of the crowd to lick her lifeless hand. She spied Nick and Poppy in the throng. They had just come from the market and still held a basket full of fruit and vegetables, one handle each.

'I'm fine,' Francie called. 'I'm up here. I love you.' But no-one on earth heard her.

She just hovered above it all and watched as the emergency vehicles arrived and her body was covered with a blanket and then loaded into the back of an ambulance. Her mother was helped into a police car.

She wasn't sad to see her body taken away. It was of no use to her anymore, but she did think it had been an attractive body and she was glad to have had the loan of it for more than thirty years.

Her death really was an inconvenience. She was sorry for that. She looked back down Swanston Street and saw the trams backed up and blocking traffic in all directions through the city. It wasn't until the firemen had hosed her blood off the road that Francie felt she could finally take her leave.

She rolled onto her back and looked up. There it was, the bright light everyone talked about. A cloud of luminous intensity. Francie could feel herself being drawn towards it. She spread her palms as if to warm herself by a fire. The light shone through her flesh, turning it translucent pink and illuminating the bones in her fingers. *I'm touching heaven. I'm taking handfuls of heaven.*

Francie's eyes opened to a dense blackness. She knew she was dead. She felt something she had not experienced in a long time. Maybe even in her whole life. Absolute peace. She didn't think anything at all. All was calm and merciful peace. She lay in the dark like this for a while, just enjoying being dead, until she observed the first thought creep across the horizon. *If I am really dead and in heaven, why is it so black? Shouldn't it be . . . white . . . and fluffy?*

She looked around her and saw a sliver of pale light appear through the . . . They must be curtains. This must be her room.

Then she saw the numbers on her alarm clock glowing green and could make out her bedside lamp. She wasn't dead and gone after all. She held out her hands and stretched her fingers. She was still alive.

At first Francie was disappointed. Especially if being dead was going to be as comforting as the feeling she had just experienced. But then, she reasoned, it was good to be alive and to have had a little visit to the afterlife.

So she had only dreamed she had been killed. Why had she dreamed that? Could it be a real near-death experience if it was just a dream? Maybe that card was right. Maybe life and death were all in your imagination.

Twenty-Two

Francie got into the *Sunday Press* office after lunch on Friday. She had calculated that this would give her enough time to finish her very last *Seriously Single* column. It was also calculated to be the very least amount of time she would have to spend in the presence of Gabby Di Martino.

From where Francie was sitting she could see Gabby behind the glass wall of her office. She was wearing a short black skirt and matching fitted jacket and was rattling around like a blowfly in a bottle. Francie saw that Gabby was trying to look important and busy so she wouldn't have to come and talk. She guessed that Gabby was still royally pissed off.

For her own part, Francie felt oddly detached, as anyone would be if they had just died and gone to heaven. Why was she still here? She could only imagine it was like everyone who has died says: *I was sent back because I had unfinished business on earth.* Francie was doing that now. Finishing her business.

"Uh . . . thought you might like this.'

Francie looked up to see Gus, the designer, scratching his neck and holding out a cup of coffee.

'Thanks, Gus.' Francie gratefully accepted his offering. 'Look, I'm sorry about not being here this week.' She knew that without her *P.S.* was woefully understaffed. Gabby would have tortured Gus and he would have had precious little time for his favourite online pursuits.

'Forget it. Doesn't matter. Shit happens,' he shrugged.

'Well,' Francie went on, 'I also want to say that I hope you can trust me, because a whole lot more shit is going to happen.'

Francie looked up at Gus with his iPod plugged in his ears and wasn't completely sure he had heard anything she said, but then he surprised her.

'Yeah, well, whatever. I always trusted you. I'm sorry you're leaving. We all are. You should have got the editor's job. We all know that. Everyone likes you. You should remember that. So good luck. One day you'll look back on all this and see it was all a fuckin' joke.'

Gus turned to shuffle back to his desk and Francie knew she'd had a farewell speech containing more heartfelt sentiment than any executive on mahogany row could ever manage. His punchline, however, wasn't quite so gracious.

'And, hey! Way to go with the scissors! I always fuckin' hated that slag.'

Francie began sorting through the hundreds of emails, letters and faxes which had been sent to her during the past week.

She estimated that about eighty percent of them were from wronged women who were supportive of her stand and another fifteen percent were from women on the other side of the debate—accused husband-stealers and home-wreckers who were defiant and wanted to throttle her.

Francie's admission of wanton vandalism had also encouraged every unbalanced nutcase in the world to come out and confess. The itemised list of damage was astonishing—cars, clothes and CDs were the main targets of rage. They had been scratched, smashed, slashed and bashed, melted, burned and, in one alarming case, dropped into a river by crane. And it seemed that most of this had gone unreported to the police. The victims had taken the attacks on their property as just and rough punishment for their crimes in love. Francie saw she was now the poster girl for destructive revenge.

And then there were the paybacks which didn't involve crude destruction of property but were even more hair-raising. The possibilities of the internet had inspired a whole new level of shameful behaviour. Nude photographs, intimate details from diaries and love letters had all been circulated for a keen international audience. Some hapless individuals had been bombarded with information from websites touting Viagra, explicit pornography, penis enlargements, hair replacement and all manner of cosmetic surgery. Others had been signed up to gay and lesbian dating agencies and, in one particularly venal instance, a Kenny G fan club. It seemed that the world wide web was a new war zone where transgressors in love were blogged and bagged, blamed and shamed. What was it Jessie had said? *How much human wreckage has been created in the name of love? It's a battlefield out there, baby.* And so it was.

This outpouring of anger, resentment and outright cruelty was just another campaign in a war which would never end. It was fiercely and relentlessly waged despite the fact that none of the combatants knew what the outcome was supposed to be.

Francie was reminded of a message she'd once read on a noticeboard outside her mother's church in Blackburn: *The person who plans revenge should dig two graves.* That's what she'd done—dug two big holes. She was lying in the bottom of one and Nick and Poppy were in the other, just their arms and legs sticking out from a pile of dirt.

Francie continued to trawl through the debris. The men who wanted to tell their stories were a grab bag of adulterous or abandoned husbands. There were also three marriage proposals and a couple of nasty polaroids of anonymous genitals. Yikes! She trashed those and the ones which began: 'I think if we could all just be less judgemental . . .' Those, as any journo would tell you, were death to a lively letters page.

She chose the letters carefully. She decided the best way to handle this was to give both sides an equal hearing. The spokeswoman on behalf of the wronged wives and mothers said:

From: Jasmine@hotkey.com
To: ssingle@SunPress.com
Subject: Infidelity

Dear Francie,

I cannot adequately express to you my thanks for sharing your heartbreaking story in this week's paper. All the pain, grief and rage was there for everyone to see, and while you didn't actually say it, I know you regret what you did.

But what you said about women who prey on other women's men is true, true, true!!

I had nine-month-old twin girls when my husband was stolen. I know she stalked him. I could see, even when I was pregnant, that she had marked him out. I can't help feeling that what happened was no better than the primitive law of the jungle.

I would have fought like a tiger for my man if I wasn't weighed down with my two precious babies. She was a younger and fitter tigress and waited until she could see I couldn't defend my family and hunted him down.

Why can't women see that robbing two children of their father is wrong, utterly wrong? No better than an animal act.

Well, now my girls are in school and this tiger is back to her old ferocious self. I will raise my cubs to be stronger than I was. They will be wary and watchful. And woe betide the lone huntress who tries to take what is ours.

Roooaaar!!

Love from Jasmine

To head up the opposing camp, she chose an equally heartfelt letter:

From: D.Montgomery@Pressall.com

To: ssingle@SunPress.com

Subject: Mistress

Dear Francie,

I am sorry that you are so upset, but what you wrote this week doesn't do you any credit at all.

You make out like women steal men, but the truth is that men leave and often there is a woman driving them out the door.

I met John at work and could see straight away he was a very unhappy man. We got talking and he told me his story. His wife gave up on him after she had her third child. He said he didn't feel like a husband anymore. He felt like a sperm donor who had done his job and wasn't wanted.

In the six years after his first child was born, she put on fifteen kilos and they only ever had sex when she wanted another baby. The rest of the time she slept with the kids.

When I met John they hadn't been out to dinner or to the pictures in three years. They didn't talk anymore unless it was about picking the kids up from school or driving them to sport. We started to have lunch together and one thing led to another. We fell in love.

Do you know what it's like to be the 'mistress'? Well, it's hard, really hard!!! After years of sneaking around, being alone for Christmas and birthdays and feeling so damn guilty, we have finally been able to move in together.

The hard work has just started. We have his kids with us every other weekend. His wife hates me, his family hates me and so do the kids. I get no thanks at all for running around after them all weekend. It takes me two weeks to recover and then they are back with us again.

But through all this I know that it's worth it. John is my soul mate. We are destined to be together. I will make our relationship work if it's the last thing I do.

You could break into my house and cut up my clothes, smash everything I own and it wouldn't stop me loving him.

You should learn a few facts about life. Love doesn't obey the rules we make for it. It's a force of nature and will always find a way.

Di

Francie also considered one of the proposals she'd received. Although this one fell far short of marriage.

From: Darryl.M@uhu.com.au
To: ssingle@SunPress.com
Subject: Slaveboy

Mistress Francie,

i am waiting here 4 U. Cum and cut me with yr scissors. i have been bad. i deserve pain. i must be taught a leson.

Yr servent Darryl.

Ahem! Francie hit 'delete', then dropped a letter from a single woman into her page:

From: Kerryn@blah.com.au
To: ssingle@SunPress.com
Subject: Revenge

Dear Francie,

I think you are really brave to tell everyone what you did. I don't think people talk enough about the trauma that can happen when a relationship breaks up. People tend to think that listening to some soppy love song can make you better!

In my case I was so devastated when he left me for my best friend that I couldn't face the world for months. I lost my job, crashed my car and got evicted from my flat. My world fell apart.

People kept telling me that I should get over it, but I couldn't. In the end what friends I had left just gave up on me.

I really did want to kill myself and I even got hold of some pills to try. In the end my mother dragged me along to a doctor who said I was clinically depressed. I did get better but it took me years and even now I am frightened to get involved again.

Maybe we should learn about this stuff in school. Maybe the subject of mental health should be as much a part of our education as geography or maths.

The topic of lover's revenge is always treated as if it is funny, but it's really about tragedy. If your story helps people realise that the brokenhearted need serious care and attention then it's a good thing.

I wish we could all take more care in matters of the heart and realise the pain we can cause each other.

I hope you now realise that you are not alone. I hope this gives you the strength to go on and love again one day.

Best wishes,
Kerryn

And then, because Francie was determined to be fair, she selected this one as well:

From: Sophie.S@mindgames.com.au
To: ssingle@SunPress.com
Subject: Stalking

Francie,

What you have done is a criminal offence! Do you have any idea at all what it feels like to have someone creepy like you hanging around?

When I started going out with my new boyfriend, his ex made our life hell. She rang at all hours of the night and day and broke into our house and left disgusting notes in our bed. In the end we had to change our phone numbers and the door locks.

She sat in front of our place in her car and every time we went outside she shouted obscene things at us. She called his mother and stole my underwear off the clothesline!!

She threatened to kill me and I was too scared to go out by myself. In the end we had to get a restraining order put on her.

How can you try to justify what you have done? You are only encouraging people to do the same and making people's lives a misery!

I hope Poppy Sommerville-Smith does report you to the police. Stalking is a crime. You have a sick mind and you need professional help.

I hope any woman out there who is thinking of doing what you did thinks twice about it when she reads your pathetic whingeing. Shame on you, Francie McKenzie! I will not read your page ever again!

Sophie S

PS None of her tactics worked and we are getting married. If we survived all this, we can survive anything.

By late afternoon Francie had assembled all the letters and forwarded them to Gabby. She watched as Gabby scanned her computer screen and then, not unexpectedly, marched from her office to Francie's desk. She didn't take up her usual roost, but instead stood tap-tapping her spiked heels in annoyance. She narrowed her brown eyes, folded her arms across her black bosom and gave Francie the fiercest look she could muster. Francie was supposed to be terrified, but instead found Gabby's stagy pose quite comical. Gabby tossed her hair and looked about as terrifying as a yappy Pomeranian. *If I throw a stick will you leave?*

'Yes, yes, well it's fine as far as it goes!' Gabby barked. 'But where's the rest of it?'

'What "rest of it"?' Francie played dumb.

Gabby huffed with annoyance and waved her claws. 'The *rest of it*! The bit where you say how heartened you have been by the response. The bit about how you feel, and that you had no idea feelings were so strong on the subject. How you've had a hard time, but you'd do it all again. Blah, blah, blah!'

Francie dropped her head into her hands and pushed her fingers into her temples as she spoke. 'Well, I wouldn't do it all again. I wish no-one had ever found out and it's been the worst experience of my life.'

'So?'

Francie looked up. 'So . . . what?'

'So, you're a journalist, for fuck's sake, make it up!'

'The letters say it all. There's nothing else to say.'

'Francie, there are thousands and thousands of women waiting for closure on this. You can't just light a bonfire and walk away from it. They need to hear from you . . . God knows why!

'If I have to write it myself, I will. You know I will. So put your blonde bird brain in gear and get on with it. And I don't want any *mea culpa*, *woe is me* crap. We're here to write a

newspaper, not to provide you with a private therapy session!
I want it in an hour, I have to get away early.'

Francie watched Gabby totter away on her high heels, pausing
only to hand a bollocking to Gus, who was unlucky enough to
be in her path. *Just once! Fall off your fuck-me shoes just once!*

Turning back to her screen, Francie read all the letters again.
It was quite obvious what had to be done. She sat and wrote
her copy exactly as Gabby had ordered. Her opening paragraph
was vintage tabloid fodder: *A memo to all you would-be home-
wreckers, husband-stealers, man-eaters and mistresses out there.
We're mad as hell and we're not going to take it anymore!*

The piece went on in this scintillating fashion at some length.
Francie knew what to write to get Gabby excited—a lively
collage of personal revelation, opinion, half-truths and spurious
statistics finished off with an outrageous conclusion. It was not
unlike baking a spicy casserole with a crunchy, cheesy topping.
It was all aimed at generating *water-cooler talk*. A wanky term
the esteemed national editor of *P.S.* liked to throw around to
show she was media savvy. Would Francie's article become a
subject of discussion by office workers standing around a water
dispenser, paper cups in hand? Francie thought that the *P.S.*
liftout was more likely to be used to soak up the mess from a
leaky tap.

As Francie had predicted, the article hit the mark with her boss.

'Yes, yes, oh yes! It's perfect. Just perfect. Couldn't be better.
Too good!' Gabby was almost salivating on her keyboard. Francie
wondered if she was this voluble during sex.

'I'll sign off on this exactly as it is. I won't change a thing.' Gabby was about to hit 'send' when Francie shouted.

'WAIT!'

'What?'

Gabby was impatient to get away to her vitally important appointment which, Francie had been informed earlier, had been made two months ago. Gabby was heading off for two fun-filled, free nights at a luxury spa. Somewhere, even as they spoke, some perfumed slave was mixing a herbal scrub for her bony arse.

'Um,' said Francie with studied casualness, 'there's something I'd like to change in that last sentence. Would you mind if I just jumped on your screen and did it?'

'OK, fine, but send it across as soon as you can. I've gotta run!'

Gabby slid off her chair, collecting her honey coloured suede coat and matching squashy handbag on her way out.

When Francie could see that Gabby was all but gone—her Chanel perfume still lingering in the air—she locked the office door and sank into the soft hide of Gabby's chair, still warm from her tiny designer-clad derrière. She wondered, not for the first time, what it would have been like to sit in it on a more permanent basis. It was such a luxurious little corner, surrounded by bottles of free champagne, perfume and scented candles, and lorded over by a pinboard covered with glossy A-list invitations.

Alas! Francie would never know. After the escapade she was planning came to light, her security pass would be confiscated. The only place she'd be plonking her backside would be in the middle of the street outside the revolving glass doors of the *Press* offices.

She hit 'control + A' to select all her copy on Gabby's screen, and then 'delete'. The pages went blank. Her story was consigned to a toxic-waste dump in cyberspace. This time Francie would write the truth. Not a fanciful concoction which came from a confused place of fear and anger—the place from where Faith had said most of Francie's thoughts had emanated for a good part of her life. Instead, these words would come from a place in her heart which she felt she was only just discovering. A place where Francie felt calm and in control. Francie bent over Gabby's keyboard and typed: *A Letter of Apology to Miss Poppy Sommerville-Smith.*

The truth was, Francie owed a lot of people an explanation. She could have written Poppy a private note, but in the end she had to acknowledge something Gabby had said—that she was responsible for igniting this public conflagration and she had a duty to put it out. (She also had a sneaking suspicion that any private missive to Poppy would end up in the papers anyway.) And then, call it her journalist's instinct, or her own ego, she knew what she had to say deserved an audience. The words came surprisingly easily and Francie knew it was because somewhere in the back of her mind, while her fury had raged out of control, she understood she would have to say them, one day.

She re-read her message in a bottle three times and then, with a click on the 'send' button, threw it into the ocean.

Twenty-Three

Francie had decided she wouldn't watch tonight's *Talkfest*. She was lying back in milk-and-honey scented water observing plumes of steam drift lazily towards the cavernous ceiling of the bathroom in *Elysium*. She should have been feeling like the Queen of the Nile; instead she was anxiously wondering on which shores her message would wash up.

It was all very public and the thought of that made her put her head under the water. Although, how could her reputation be any worse than it already was? She decided she would just lie low for a while and her eyes broke the surface of the bathwater as she played crocodile.

She hadn't been officially sacked yet. That call would come early Sunday morning. Gabby would be screaming blue murder from a steam room in a five-star spa. Francie tried to care and couldn't. She was inspecting her toenails propped up at the end of the tub when there was a knock at the bathroom door.

'Francie, can I come in?'

There was no reason why Francie should have been shocked to hear Dave's voice—after all, he lived in this house, his bedroom was next to hers and she had already spent the night with him. But the sound of his voice was indeed shocking, so she scrambled for a washcloth to cover her breasts and slid under the bubbles.

'Sure, sure, come in,' she called.

Dave poked his head around the door and was careful to keep his eyes on Francie's.

'Look, I know this is an extraordinary request because I haven't talked to you—in fact, I haven't seen you—for days. But would you come to dinner with me tonight? My treat. I want to take you somewhere fabulous. You've had a hard week and you deserve it. So, *please* say yes.'

Francie was so surprised that she did say yes, and she added 'that would be wonderful' and then 'thanks'.

'Great! I'll pick you up at your room at seven-thirty.' He gently closed the door.

Francie's bath languor evaporated. She sat up and considered her situation. She could feel that things had changed for her. She was no longer an ex girlfriend. She was now single. Not suddenly single. Not sadly single. Just plain by-herself single.

When she had been lost in the fog of heartache she'd had no control of her emotions. Her driving force had been just to get through the day, one foot in front of the other, trying to climb out of a crevasse of pain and exhaustion. But she felt that she had finally clawed her way up that slippery slope only to find that the landscape in front of her was an endless plain of singledom. Of course it was a relief to regain her footing, but what would propel her forwards now? This was a whole new world to navigate and she didn't have a map. There was so much to learn—the culture, the etiquette, the language of being single.

For a start, who would she hang out with? With Amanda and Olga pregnant (Olga pregnant? It didn't seem possible), and Johnno in a relationship, she would be the odd one out at the dinner table. Not to mention the baby change table. How would she cope when her best friends were knee-deep in nappies and plastic toys? Where would she go?

She supposed she would find herself standing on the darkened edge of nightclub dance floors again, or in pubs like she did when she was in her twenties. She knew which clubs and pubs to go to, but how could she walk in the door by herself? Would there be any single men there? Were there any left? Judging by the complaints of most women her age, she was facing years of trawling the town for a partner of any kind.

And what kind of man was she looking for? Did she want another relationship so soon after Nick? She had known instantly that she wanted to be with him. Did she wait until she was struck by lightning again? Maybe she couldn't trust that feeling anymore. Maybe it had nothing to do with love. She was so out of practice.

What about sex? What was reasonable here? She knew enough to know that a woman no longer had to wait to be asked for sex, but then again, she wasn't sure how she, Francie, would go about it. And how many times would she be able to ask just for sex before she had to make a commitment to something more?

She sighed with the weight of it all. She had endured a long walk through a stormy night after her break-up with Nick, there was a new dawn coming and she could see her problems were just beginning. It was all very well to talk with Faith about 'breaking old patterns' but finding a new one wasn't going to be easy.

Francie sat in the bath and mused on all this until the water went cold.

✯

Dinner with Dave that night turned out to be a more fascinating experience than Francie could have imagined. They were sitting at a cosy corner table in the Flower Drum, Melbourne's most celebrated Chinese restaurant. It was a place she had never been able to afford to go to, but had always been curious about. The dining room was all plush carpet and dark wood with red and gold oriental flourishes. The subdued lighting and waiters in tuxedos quietly going about their business gave it a luxurious feel.

Francie was feeling deluxe too, in a classic little black velvet dress with a lace wrap over her shoulders. Dave? Well, he was always beautifully put together. Francie had never seen him look scruffy, even around the house. She was nervous at being out with him. Was this an actual date? She reasoned that she was going to have to do more of this, and being with Dave was as good a place as any to start.

The meal had been a procession of delicious dishes—divine steamed prawns delicately flavoured with ginger, sweet spring onion cakes and Peking duck—accompanied by a very good

Margaret River sauvignon blanc. Dave's discourse on the new architecture in Shanghai, the latest in genetic research and the rise of the fundamental right in American politics was likewise substantial and satisfying. He was so bright, brilliantly opinionated, witty!

Once more Francie felt like an uneducated ingenue, but it wasn't an altogether unpleasant sensation. She exercised her brain to keep up and was rewarded for her efforts. Dave laughed at her jokes and seemed impressed with some of the nuggets of information she managed to unearth and add to the conversation. However, Francie knew that no matter how much she was enjoying the exchange, sooner or later they would have to get down to her exploits as a depraved night stalker. She fidgeted as the last of the dishes was cleared away.

'I can't believe you want to be seen with me after everything that's happened.'

Dave threw his head back and laughed. 'Yeah. My reputation will be in tatters!'

'Don't laugh at me, Dave, it's not funny.' Anyone could see that it wasn't funny. Not at all.

'You're not *still* worried about that?'

Francie looked at Dave, astonished. *Still* worried? It was only a week ago that she'd been exposed on television as a total barking nutter! She could very well be the subject of discussion on *Talkfest* right this minute. Francie was still staring at him, unable to believe he was smiling. His dark green eyes were wide, trying to engage hers.

'You don't get it, do you?' he said.

Not again! No, she didn't *get* it. Apparently she didn't *get* a lot of things.

Dave folded his hands neatly on the table. 'From the first moment I met you, Francie, I thought you were lovely. Of course I could see you were wounded. A bit wobbly on your feet. But then we spent the night together. You were unbelievably sexy. It felt like you started to open up to the possibility of . . . something. I could sense there was all this stuff there underneath. Then this *incident* came up. I read all of your rage and passion in the newspaper and I started to see what drove you to it. I will admit, it was an extraordinary thing to do! Wild!'

Dave seemed to find it amusing on some level, as if it was extreme performance art. For Francie it was embarrassing on every level. She ducked her head again, Princess Di style.

'I thought, *she must have really loved this guy*, and it was then I realised that I wanted someone to feel that way about me. I wanted a passionate person in my life.'

Dave reached across the table and put his hands on top of Francie's. She remembered how expert they had been in bringing her sublime pleasure. She raised her eyes to see him leaning as far forward as the table would allow.

'You're beautiful and alive and passionate. You're smart and sexy and . . .' Here Dave paused and took a deep breath. 'I want you to be in my life.'

This was weird. Three hours ago Francie was sitting in the bath contemplating the lonely marathon she would have to run before she found a new man. Now, after a 100-metre sprint, she'd fallen over the finish line without working up a sweat. It didn't seem right. It wasn't right. She knew that instinctively. There was no doubt Dave was desirable. The sex had been good, the conversation better. He was handsome. He had excellent professional prospects. But there was something so bloodless about his offer. As if he had made an intellectual decision to add Francie to his life like a new extension—a sunroom or an extra bedroom.

Francie was silent for so long she became aware of the sound of someone three tables away cracking the shell of a King Island crab.

'I can see you weren't expecting this.'

Francie reached for a drink to lubricate her throat, which seemed to have her voice stuck about halfway down it.

'I wasn't really . . . I'm sorry, Dave, I don't know what you mean, because I *am* in your life. I'm in the bedroom next door.'

Dave reached for his wine too, gulped and found the courage to go on.

'It's time I made a commitment to someone. I know it's the right time in my life. And it feels right with you.'

'But, Dave, don't you hear what you're saying? You said a commitment to *someone*. Not me especially. You're probably right, it is time for you to settle down. What are you, thirty-three?'

'Thirty-four.'

'It makes sense that you want to be with one person, but you can't just make a decision and ask the girl standing next to you. Or the one sleeping in the room next to you!'

Dave inspected a carving of an oriental dragon on the wall.

'So I'll take that as a "no".'

'I haven't said that,' said Francie. 'I will say that I am unbelievably flattered. But you know that I'm still climbing out of the wreckage of my last relationship and I'm not sure I have anything to offer anyone right now. I've already told you that. I've told everyone that. I don't think it's the right time in *my* life.'

Dave elected not to hear Francie decline his offer and continued with his sales pitch.

'Francie, there's a notion here that the worlds have to collide, the heavens have to fall, and that the planets have to be in alignment for love to happen, but, equally well, there's another way to go about things. There's logic to what I'm offering. We are a great match. I've thought about this. We could spend years trying to find a match that made as much sense.

'Now, I know that you will instantly reject what I'm saying. You'll think it's all too calculated. But think some more. It's well documented that—what's the saying? *Our need for love precedes our love for anyone in particular*. 'So I've made a decision that I need love. But, so what? What's wrong with that? By the laws of probability, we won't find anything better.

'Let me tell you—now that you're single, you'll find the world is made up of two kinds of people. People who like you more than you like them. People who you like more than they like you. And all the rest are relatives.

'I'm out here, I'm single, I'm living it and it's not easy. Mindless distraction is what most people are doing while they wait for their next hit of the love drug. They're addicts. I don't want to do it anymore and, believe me, neither do you. We can both save ourselves years of disappointment and pain.'

Dave's presentation was falling on fallow ground. He could see that.

'And besides, I think we could be great together. I really think we're a great match. I promise to give it all the energy and commitment I've got.'

His closing argument wasn't working either. It sounded as if Dave was pouring a concrete slab, not entering a relationship.

'At least tell me you'll think about it.'

Francie nodded and, mercifully, at that moment a waiter approached the table with a silver tray. Francie and Dave took such an interest in his offerings you'd have thought they'd never seen coffee and biscuits in their entire lives.

✲

They somehow got through the ride home in his old black Porsche from the city and to the front gate of *Elysium*. The quartz gravel of the driveway was picked out ghostly white in the moonlight. It was a calm evening and the scent of the last of the spring roses was in the air. Dave stood back as Francie put her key in the lock of the towering wooden front door.

'Are you coming in?' She turned and saw the silhouette of his head against the streetlights.

'I'm not tired. I think I might kick on.'

'Dave, I don't want this to be difficult between us. You know I love living here with all of you. I feel as if I've found a new family . . .'

'So, you love me like a brother?'

Francie kissed him on the cheek and felt a surge of desire as she smelt his warm neck. 'There was nothing "brotherly" about the night we spent together.'

'Should we do it again?'

Francie touched his arm and said softly: 'I don't think so. Maybe in a while . . .'

'So I guess I'll see you round . . . probably in the kitchen.'

'Don't . . . Wait . . .' Francie didn't know what she could possibly say, but there was no point anyway. Dave was already halfway down the driveway and she could hear the crunch-crunch of his boots on the gravel. She listened as the car growled into life and roared up the street.

It had started. This whole 'single' thing had started in earnest and Francie had already found that it was going to be every bit as tricky as she had predicted.

She stood on the front terrace in the dark and breathed in the remains of the roses. She thought of Nick. He'd be with Poppy. Perhaps they'd be curled up against each other, asleep. She wondered if he ever woke in the night and thought of her, or if he'd managed to obliterate the memories of the years they'd spent together.

At least the pain of being alone was making her over into a new person. She was different already. When she and Nick met again, would they even recognise each other?

Twenty-Four

It was mid morning the next day and Francie was driving to her mother's house for lunch. She had been summoned home by an early phone call from Joel. He was agitated, excited.

'She's coming, Frank! Vanessa's coming. I'm picking her up from the airport now and taking her to Blackburn. You have to come. You can't leave me with Mum. I need tech support.'

Francie had rolled out of bed, showered, pulled on jeans and T-shirt and jumped into her dented Mazda. Despite her earlier misgivings, she was determined to keep an open mind on Joel's internet romance. After all, she didn't have any answers. There were so many paths to finding love and so many ways to stumble out of it again. Joel's cyberspace quest for love seemed to be as valid as any other. What had he said about Vanessa? She knew him better than anyone he'd ever met. Well, she'd just watch and see. Like a good big sister should.

It was a warm, sunny morning and the drive out east into the suburbs allowed Francie time to think. Dave hadn't come home last night. This had proved to her the difficulty of trying to negotiate a relationship with someone who lived in the same house. They would move from 'one-night stand' to 'live-in lover' within one conversation. All the delicious uncertainty, the thrill of the chase and capture, the yearning and hesitancy, the drama of commitment, would never happen. Dave's relationship of convenience was doomed to failure. Then again, maybe he *was* right. In India marriages were arranged and everyone had the good sense to avoid the entire soap opera.

Francie was stopped at traffic lights watching couples load their Saturday morning shopping into the back of cars. Strapping toddlers in seats. Talking about nothing in particular. They were taking their love, their little families, for granted, as they should. There was all the time in the world for grieving when there was no happy ending. Falling in love remained the only game in town—no matter what the psychological ruin or financial fallout.

Dave Matthews was on the radio singing about ants marching or some such. For the first time in ages Francie was listening to the music without thinking that she was missing some vital part of the experience because Nick wasn't there. In the middle of all this, Francie had a revolutionary and unexpected thought. She was happy. That's if happy could be merely an absence of pain.

She was sitting in the calm, sunny eye of a storm. There had been only a couple of letters to the editor this morning in the *Daily Press*. One from a man who'd had his car vandalised by an ex (she had taken to the duco with a cheese grater), and another asking the very good question—*don't you people have some actual news to report on instead of the ins and outs of people's private lives?*—and that had been it. She assumed she hadn't been mentioned on *Talkfest* last night because there were no messages on her phone.

No doubt the rough weather would begin again tomorrow when her piece in the paper became public. What would everyone think of it? There was no point worrying. For now she wasn't hurting and that was enough to be going on with. She reached down and turned up the music.

It was the second week in December and Francie was keeping an eye out for Christmas decorations. She was back in her childhood when she would spend hours walking all the dark streets in Blackburn. She loved the fake snow, the wire reindeer wound with flashing bulbs, the plastic icicles, spray-on frost on the windows and stuffed Santas hoisted onto roofs. She remembered that when she finally made her way back to her own house she was always disappointed to see the front yard just as bare as it had been all year round.

'We don't want to make a spectacle of ourselves,' was her mother's reply when Francie had begged for a string of lights to thread through the front fence. 'Besides, think of the electricity bill.'

With just two weeks until Christmas now, Francie knew she would have to get organised. Where would she spend Christmas Day? For the past five Christmas days she and Nick, faced with the equally gruesome prospects of a long trip to see his family at Bairnsdale or overcooked turkey and boiled brussels sprouts at her mother's place, had dodged festive celebrations. Last year they had picnicked in the Botanic Gardens and the year before that it was lunch in the grand dining room of a city hotel. All at Nick's insistence. Looking back, Francie wondered whether this had been another way he had pretended they weren't a couple. They'd never had to field the questions from her Auntie Kath from Benalla, or his mother: 'So when's the Big Day?' 'When can we expect the grandkiddies?'

This Christmas Day Francie imagined she'd be sitting on her bed with a bag of potato chips and a bottle of champagne, getting blind drunk. It seemed as good an option as any.

✵

Francie sat at her mother's kitchen table looking at her salt and pepper shakers wrought in the likeness of a rooster, hen and yellow baby chicks in a plaster nest. Carol had taken complete leave of her senses and made pizza with fetta cheese, smoked salmon and capers!

'I saw it on a cooking show,' she said bashfully as she put the serving plate on the table. You can put all sorts of things on pizzas nowadays. Although you've got to draw the line at tandoori chicken. The base is Italian and the topping is Indian, and I don't believe there's any point in mixing them up. It just leaves all your guests confused.'

And thanks for that, Martha Stewart.

Joel and Vanessa were actually a very nicely matched couple. Joel was wearing a clean long-sleeved sweatshirt which hid his tattoos, and Vanessa sported a nose-ring. It was the first time Francie had ever met a psychiatric nurse with piercings. It was a first for Carol too. Francie entertained herself watching her mother desperately trying to avoid looking at Vanessa's left nostril . . . and right eyebrow. Joel's arm was at exactly the right height to drape over Vanessa's shoulders. They looked good together, whatever that meant. Their hair was the same colour, they were both wearing jeans, they both . . . oh, what the hell! Who knew anything about how couples were made?

Maybe Dave was right. Our need for love precedes our love for anyone in particular. No, that couldn't be it. It just didn't explain the legion of single women in their thirties who were dissatisfied and still searching for The One. And it certainly didn't explain why she had rejected Dave.

Joel had spent four months online getting to know Vanessa, and here they were now, sitting in the family kitchen, holding hands and beaming at each other under the watchful gaze of older sister and mother. It really was a very old-fashioned way to make a love match. If they'd been sitting around a table in Bombay, would it have been much different?

They hadn't even had sex. At least, Francie was presuming they hadn't. Not unless they'd pulled over on the freeway on the way back from the airport and done it in the car. Francie observed them both carefully. What Joel had said was true, they did seem to know each other very well.

'Mum, you'll have to scrape the capers off for Vanessa. They make her feel sick.'

'And this photo must be from when JoJo went on the student exchange to Japan in 1995.'

Of course it was no surprise to Francie when Joel and Vanessa announced their engagement. But Carol! She got such a shock she hoiked up a caper which bounced off the plastic tablecloth and rolled across the carpet tiles and under a plant stand.

'Oh my goodness! Pardon me!'

Carol jumped to her feet and straightened her apron. She dabbed at her mouth with a paper serviette. 'Engaged! Well, I have to say . . .'

Uh-oh, here we go!

'I'm thrilled for you both. Congratulations!'

Francie was astonished by her mother's reaction, and then she saw that Carol was almost paralysed with emotion. After the obligatory hugs and kisses all round, it took the three of them in the room to wrestle her back into her chair. When she was finally sitting in front of a celebratory glass of warmish champagne, which had been unearthed from the crystal cabinet and cooled with ice cubes, she regained some of her senses.

'A wedding!' Carol breathed.

Francie knew that her mother's mind was whirring with the possibilities. Flowers, frocks, tablecloths, gift registries, menus, crockery, cutlery, lights, camera, action! Francie knew her mother was thinking about all this because she was doing the same. She was her mother's daughter, after all. And then mother and daughter alighted, simultaneously, on the one contentious issue— the guest list.

'Dad and Denise will have to come,' exclaimed Joel, thrilled with the notion. Thrilled with himself. 'And Stella.'

As soon as the words were out of his mouth Francie felt something crack. For twenty years the inhabitants of this house had never uttered the 'D' word. It was as if Joel had thrown a rock through the panel of a glasshouse and the cold air had come rushing in. In the ensuing silence—as they sat picking sharp splinters from their clothes; as Joel looked at his mother; as Vanessa looked uncomprehending; as Carol took a long look at the wall clock and registered that it needed dusting—Francie summoned up her courage.

'Yes. Denise. Joel's been to their place. It's great, isn't it?' she said cheerily.

Carol turned on Francie, her cheeks flushed an angry red. 'I cannot believe you can sit here in this house and bring her name up as if it means nothing at all.'

'Mum, it's so long ago . . .' Francie began.

'It might be to *you*, Francie. It might mean nothing to *you*. But if you knew what that woman has done to this family.'

'For fuck's sake, Mum, can you stop calling her *that woman*!'

'Don't swear, Francis. I don't like it.'

It was obvious that it wasn't the swearing her mother objected to so much as the mention of Denise's name. Francie could feel her own cheeks grow hot.

'Her name is Denise McKenzie, Mum. She's been married to your ex husband, our father, for two decades. She is my stepmother and Joel's. And as for not knowing what she's done to this family . . .'

Carol was on her feet, hastily stacking dishes complete with uneaten pizza, and gathering knives and forks in a clattering heap.

'Not in front of visitors,' she huffed, and turned to march to the kitchen sink.

Francie was duly admonished. Yes, of course, manners.

'I'm sorry, Joel. I didn't want it to be like this. Sorry, Vanessa . . .'

Joel drew Vanessa closer to him to protect her from the gathering thunderclouds. 'It doesn't matter. I've told her about all of it anyway,' he said.

Vanessa dealt with the families of psychiatric patients all the time. She had the good sense to vacate the kitchen.

'Is it OK if I go and check my emails in your room, Joel?'

There was a polite moment as Vanessa collected her backpack, kissed Joel on the cheek and headed down the hall. Francie watched her go and reflected that she liked Vanessa. She liked her a lot.

When it was clear she was out of hearing range, Francie took another deep breath. This conversation had been a long time coming. She stood behind her mother and watched her back bent over the sink, the bow of her apron neatly tied. Carol began her familiar, soothing ritual of squirting dishwashing liquid into the running water. It all said, *go away, I've heard enough.*

'Mum, you have made it very clear, every single day since Dad left, what Denise is supposed to have done to this family. But maybe she hasn't done anything. Maybe it's all in your head. What are we going to say if Joel and Vanessa ever have a family? Here's Grandma, Grandpa and *that woman*? It's long enough now. *Time heals all*, you said. Christ! How much time do you want?'

Francie saw her mother's shoulders hunch at the taking of the Lord's name in vain. A plate was ferociously banged in the dish rack as a rebuke. Francie was startled, but kept on.

'Joel and I have known, every day of our lives, how hurt you were when Dad left. But we can't pass your anger on to another generation. It can't be this hereditary thing. I won't let it be.'

Carol hurled her yellow-handled dish mop into the soapy water and spun on her heels to face her daughter. Her face was a contour map of rage. She was in a place Francie hadn't seen her venture for many years.

'You don't know, Francie! You don't know what it felt like! You were both just children! How could you know?'

Francie and Joel rolled their eyes at each other. Francie was nominated to continue.

'He left me and Joel too, didn't he? It wasn't just you.'

Carol grabbed a tea towel from its blue hook and pushed past Francie. She was at the table now, brushing crumbs off the floral plastic cover into her trembling hand.

'You don't know what it's like to have people pointing at you. "Oh, there's Carol McKenzie, the woman whose husband ran off with his young blonde secretary. What's wrong with her?" And what chance did I have to make a new life with two little children? NONE.'

Francie couldn't believe what she was hearing. 'You cannot be serious. You can't still be blaming us for the fact that you're single. You also said you're supposed to become wiser. Listen to yourself! You haven't learned anything. What's wise about you?'

Carol clenched her fist full of crumbs and fought to regain control of her emotions. It didn't take long. She was an expert.

'I've learned enough to know that romance is just a fantasy. I've told you. It's just a silly illusion. It's some modern invention which doesn't actually work. Look at all the broken marriages out there. What's the point of it all? Just rely on yourself. You'll be a lot better off.'

It was at this point that Joel at last chose to speak: 'So what are you saying, Mum? That Vanessa and I *shouldn't* get married?'

'I'm saying . . .'

He looked up at his mother and brushed the hair from his eyes. 'Are you saying that I should stay here living with you? Watch you knit doll's clothes, clean the house, watch bloody quiz shows on TV for the rest of my life? At least Francie's out there taking a chance. Look at what you've built here! A fucking coffin for yourself. Full of pieces of SHIT!'

Joel stood and snatched up the salt-and-pepper perfect poultry family and dashed it against a cupboard.

'STUPID FUCKING KNICK-KNACKS AND PAINTED PLATES AND DOILIES AND VASES AND PIECES OF SHIT!'

Carol darted for the dustpan and brush and when Joel blocked her way, stood instead and buried her face in her apron. Francie and Joel could hear her sobbing through the gingham. Francie moved to comfort her mother, but Joel caught her by the arm and held her back.

'Joel . . .' Francie was panicked. This was all her fault. Everything was getting out of control.

'No, Frank, you're right. It's long enough. Dad left and I'm leaving too. I can't do this anymore. I'm not bringing Vanessa into some weirdo eighties time warp. The two of you should talk. You know what I think.' With that Joel stomped from the kitchen and down the hall to where Vanessa had taken shelter from the storm.

Francie stood behind Carol and circled her arms around her mother's heaving shoulders. She lay her face on her neat bobbed cap of hair.

'Mum . . . it's alright. We didn't mean . . .'

Carol lifted her head and Francie felt her mother's body become rigid.

'Goodness,' she sniffed. 'I really should clean up this mess.'

Twenty-Five

Francie's mobile phone was ringing. She checked the time on her bedside clock. It was 7.30 am. Gabby was right on cue.

'Thank you, Oprah, for this morning's little sermon! At least it means I won't have to go to church today. You know, I can forgive you for being a little sneak and going behind my back, but there's one thing I can't forgive you for, and that's for depriving me of the pleasure of kicking your arse out the front door. You and I both know that changing an editor's copy is a sackable offence, you—'

'Fuck off, Gabby.'

There! Francie had said it out loud at last. She snapped the phone shut, turned it off and threw it into the laundry basket.

So there was at least one shore on which her message had washed up and then exploded like a stepped-on landmine. She was propelled from her bed, down the hall to the front door. She collected copies of the *Sunday Press* and the *Sunday Star* lying on the tiled terrace and darted back to her room.

Francie retrieved the *P.S.* supplement and the rest of the papers followed her phone. After all, she didn't work at the *Press* anymore and would never have to read the rags again.

Her modest *Seriously Single* column was now a bloated beast disporting itself across a double-page spread. All the letters were in there. That was no surprise, since Francie had signed off on the pages herself. And then—Francie steeled herself to read it—there was her own letter.

A Letter of Apology to Miss Poppy Sommerville-Smith.

Dear Miss Sommerville-Smith,

Although you have occupied my every waking thought and haunted my dreams for the past six months, we have never met. Like so many, I have admired your dedication to excellence in your chosen craft. I have watched you on the stage and on television and seen that you are a tremendously gifted woman. A person of substance and integrity.

When my relationship of five years ended earlier this year and it came to light that you had taken up with my ex partner, I cast you as the villain in my private tragedy. I could only think of my situation as being a devastating loss. I felt that there had been a crime committed against me and that you were the perpetrator. You were the criminal and deserved to be punished.

Driven by jealousy and anger I, in turn, committed a crime against you. I wilfully destroyed your property and in doing so caused you a great deal of distress. Even when faced with the consequences of my actions, seeing for myself the pain I had put you through, I still refused to take responsibility, and for that I am truly, truly sorry.

The truth is that this has never been about you. How could it be? As I said, we have never met. It has been, it is now, all about how my life is unfolding, and what I need to learn to be a more loving and complete person.

I have known, since I was a small girl, that falling in love comes with no guarantees. People change, they fall out of love, they die, they leave. What I have learned now is that we have to take our circumstances and have the courage to look deeply into them and see what can be learned.

I have now had the chance to walk on the dark side of love. I feel that I have descended from the surface of the physical world into the underground of the soul. While this has been at times a frightening and lonely journey, I can see that in this shadow world there are many things to be discovered. It is as if I had entered a cave and ignited a small flame only to see jewels sparkling in the walls of rock in front of me.

Where there was separation there is now independence. Where there was certainty there is surprise. Where there was invincibility there is vulnerability. Where there was the grief of death there is now the joy of resurrection. What was lost will be found. While none of us can ever know the unique path another soul is destined to take, you, Poppy, have become part of my journey. I feel as if you have been sent to me as a guide, to challenge me to reach a deeper understanding of my own nature.

My life is a story of my own making. Whether it turns out to be a cautionary tale or a heroic myth is up to me. This letter is my way of absolving you of any responsibility for where my story leads me. As I said, I deeply regret any pain I have caused you and I ask your forgiveness.

This is my last 'Seriously Single' column. Thank you to all my readers and correspondents for your indulgence during the past two years. I have had a brilliant time talking to all of you. You have constantly amazed, inspired and amused me.

I hope every one of you finds happiness, with or without a person to share it.

Love and goodbye, from Francie McKenzie

Francie put a pillow over her head and tried to get back to sleep. In vain. By 9 am she had read her letter seven times and was reading it again when Johnno's head appeared around the door.

'Morning . . .'

'Johnno! Hi, come in, come in.' She sat up against her pillows and affected a breezy air. Johnno shuffled in the door and Francie smiled to see him. He was his usual dishevelled self in a holey grey Planet Ark sweatshirt and an old purple sarong. His hair looked as if it had been tortured with a cattle prod. Francie saw he was holding a copy of *P.S.*

'I stayed the night here with Jess and just went out to get croissants and the papers,' he explained. 'I see you have yours. Mind if I sit down?'

'Sure. Sure.' Francie smoothed a spot on the bed for him.

Johnno sat down, barely rumpling the sheets. His frame was small, wiry, but it vibrated with an energy which couldn't be ignored. It was almost electrical and disturbed the grid of every room he entered. While she didn't always agree with everything he said, Johnno's passion was unimpeachable. Francie could never recall him telling a lie. Or pulling a punch. No wonder he and Jessie had found each other. Each was searching for the truth in their own way.

Francie breathed in. Stuck her chin out. *So tell me, Doc. How'm I doin'?*

'I read it. You did a good thing . . . at last.' Johnno saw Francie's contrite face and was encouraged to go on and say the rest.

'I've been so fucking mad at you! You cannot know the damage you caused. You can count yourself lucky I didn't catch up with you in the last week because, honestly, Francie, I wanted to kill you!'

Francie started fiddling with the edge of the sheet. 'I know, I know,' she murmured. 'Was it, you know, really bad?'

'YES! It was really, really bad! Nick has been out of his mind. Poppy has been almost suicidal. Not only did she have you trashing her stuff, but then she gets the blame for it! And whatever you think about her, you have exacted cruel and

305

unusual punishment. You've asked for her forgiveness, but don't expect that you'll get it.'

'I'm not expecting anything,' said Francie. And this was true.

'And you better get used to the idea that they're going to be together, because . . .' Johnno paused to clear his throat as if the next words had lodged there, 'Nick's moving in to her place. He's bought her a ring and I think they're engaged or something . . . If people still do that shit anymore.'

This news came like a punch in the stomach. Francie threw her head back, her hands clenching and unclenching. She was breathing hard. 'Oh, God!'

'I know, I can't believe it myself.'

Johnno fell back on the bed alongside Francie. She rolled over into his bony arms. What was that about never crying again? She was blotting her face on Johnno's raggy shirtfront.

'Ah, Francie girl! When you do something, you really do it well!'

'I'm sorry, Johnno,' she managed to gasp between sobs. 'It's all I seem to say lately . . . sorry, sorry.'

'Well you can stop now, baby girl. No more "sorrys". Your apology in the paper today is enough to last anyone a lifetime.'

When Francie's sobs eventually subsided, Johnno spoke softly into her hair. 'We all love you, France. We love your kindness, your generosity, your sweetness. It's been hard for us to watch you go through all this after Nick, but in a way you were sort of an accident waiting to happen. I guess we could all see the fragile little girl underneath.'

Francie's chest heaved again. She had always thought of herself as being so grown up. So in control.

'Of course, we're all too scared to leave you in case you hack up our undies . . .'

Francie snorted into Johnno's chest and punched him in the arm.

'But the fact that you can love so fiercely? We love that about you too. And don't you worry, there'll be someone else for you. You know my mother's old Dutch saying . . .'

Francie had heard him say it a hundred times and finished the sentence for him: 'For every pot, there is a lid.'

'That's the one! There's a happy ending waiting there for you. I know it.'

No wonder Francie loved Johnno so much. He wore his heart on his sleeve. The same sleeve Francie was at this moment wiping her nose on.

'So Poppy Pot and Nick the Lid—when's the wedding?'

'Easy, girl, easy. I think there's a long way to go before we see them walk down the aisle. I wouldn't be putting my name on the gift list for the fondue set just yet!'

Francie nestled into Johnno's neck. He held her tight for as long as she needed to be held.

☼

Sunday morning passed quietly enough at *Elysium*. Dave still hadn't made an appearance. Robbie was in the study laying down tracks for a music project. Johnno and Jessie headed out for lunch. Francie mooched about in her room, read a book, slept some more.

It was late afternoon when Robbie found her sitting on the back veranda in the sun painting her nails. He held a glass of white wine in each hand and a bag of potato chips between his clenched teeth. Francie was glad of the company. He handed over her drink and eased himself onto the wooden steps. The setting sun turned his hair a startling shade of platinum.

'Nice colour,' he commented, looking at her bottle of nail polish. 'What is it today? Revenge Red? Payback Pink? Mea Culpa Maroon?'

'Uh-huh,' Francie winced, 'take your pick.'

'What is it they say about nature? *Red in tooth and claw.* Jeez, Francie, there hasn't been a dull moment since you moved in.'

He held his glass aloft, waiting for a friendly clink which did not materialise.

'I'm sorry if . . .' she began, and then remembered that she had told Johnno *no more apologies.*

'No, no, forget it,' said Robbie cheerily. 'It's all been hugely entertaining.'

Francie rummaged in the bag of chips. Robbie could see that his casual banter was wasted this fine December afternoon. He thought he might get to the heart of the matter.

'I read you've quit your job. Can't say I blame you. Working with Gabby Di Martino every day would be a punish! Having the Italian princess around here commandeering the bathroom on Sunday mornings has been bad enough. She used my whole bottle of Annick Goutal Eau D'Hadrien in her bath once.'

Gabby here on Sunday mornings? That could only mean . . . Francie stopped mid crunch and raised her eyebrows at him.

'I thought you knew,' he said.

'Knew what?'

'Gabby and Dave, they've been on together for years. It's no big deal. I think in common parlance they're *bonk buddies*.'

Francie had suspected, of course, but hadn't known for sure. Her face must have registered surprise, disappointment, distaste or something similar, because Robbie was compelled to keep talking before any one of these emotions took root.

'It's nothing to worry about. Nothing that hasn't been going on for centuries! Do you remember *Dangerous Liaisons*?'

'Remind me,' said Francie, eyeing Robbie over the rim of her glass.

Robbie was pleased to have a chance to air his erudition on all things cultural. He leaned back on the wooden boards of the veranda and shielded his eyes from the last, intense afternoon rays.

'The book, *Les Liaisons dangereuses*, was written in the 1700s by Pierre Choderlos de Laclos. It was scandalous, absolutely scandalous, in its day. Apparently Queen Marie Antoinette kept a copy for herself bound in a blank cover.'

Francie sipped at her wine as he continued. More damned French classics! She really had to—

'Anyway, the best-known movie—there have been three—was in 1988. As I recall, the Vicomte de Valmont and the Marquise de Merteuil (John Malkovich and Glenn Close to you and me), arrange a seduction of a virtuous married woman—'

'That was supposed to be *me*? They had a bet *on me*?' Francie was appalled.

'No, no! Michelle Pfeiffer!'

'Oh, don't joke about it, Robbie! I mean in *real life*!'

'Dave and Gabby had a bet on *you*? Forget it! They're not that clever, and you're not that virtuous.' He laughed. 'Or that married—'

'Shut up! What happened in the movie?'

'So, in the movie, Valmont falls in love with Madame . . . can't remember . . . Michelle Pfeiffer. And, come to think of it,' he said, sitting up again, 'you do look a bit Pfeiffer-ish.'

'Does she fall in love with him?' asked Francie, wide-eyed.

'Yup. And she is devastated when he leaves her. There's a line in there where Michelle says she can't help herself and someone says: *in such matters all advice is useless*. And Valmont says over and over again: *it's beyond my control*.'

'How do you know all this stuff?'

'Loved the soundtrack! Handel, Vivaldi, Gluck, Bach—bought it when I was a teenager. So . . .' Robbie sat up again and regarded Francie with a gimlet eye, 'is all advice *useless*? Is it *beyond your control*?'

In her particular version of this story Francie felt anything but an innocent. She was not Dave and Gabby's hapless victim.

'I haven't fallen in love with Dave, if that's what you want to know,' answered Francie, looking out to the garden and remembering it was her turn to dead-head the roses. 'And I've told Gabby what I think of her.'

'So, you win! Good for you! What else?'

'Of course I've taken *advice*. I look back on that night now and it was like an out-of-body experience. I don't know who that person was. I do know that will never happen to me again.'

Robbie laid one muscled arm across Francie's shoulders. 'You know, doll, there's one thing that people like you and me forget, and it's that we have something to look forward to that people in relationships reminisce about and wish for all the time.'

'What's that?'

'To experience falling in love. That's ahead of us. This amazing, exhilarating adventure! Love built the Taj Mahal, razed Troy. Why would we settle for any B-grade emotion not worthy of the name?'

'Is that why you're still celibate?'

Robbie reached his other arm around Francie. He looked out to the sun setting beyond the lilac tree, hemming each leaf with gold.

'Fuck, I hate that word! It's so pathetic because it implies there is an *absence* of something. I reckon that instead of living like something's missing, we should live like these are our final days of freedom. Blessed days. Days which will never come again. This is our last chance to be in love with ourselves without reservation. Before love obscures our true nature with lust— and then, inevitably, with duty and compromise.'

Robbie squeezed Francie until she surrendered her doubts to the descending darkness.

'Almost no-one's sure they're worthy of their *own* love, yet they're desperate for a *stranger* to love them. Isn't that odd? When you think about it?'

Francie had to agree that it was.

Twenty-Six

'Would you like to spend Christmas with us this year?' Amanda asked her two friends as she offered them a glass of wine. Francie and Olga shot a look at each other and both knew what the invitation meant—it would be a charity event.

A green plastic Christmas tree threaded with flashing lights stood in the front window of the flat. Francie noted the glass ornaments in the shape of baby booties and imagined the heart-warming scene as Amanda and Lachlan had hung them on the branches.

'Thanks, Amanda, that's really kind of you, but I'll probably be doing Hanukkah with my mum this year,' replied Olga.

'Same here. I promised Mum I would spend Christmas with her, thanks,' Francie lied.

Both Francie and Olga wanted to be spared the spectacle of Amanda and Lachlan playing happy families. The man of the house was out at a work function tonight, which was a blessing. There was so much to say that no-one knew quite where to start.

Francie took her glass of chardonnay and realised she would be drinking most of the bottle as Olga and Amanda poured themselves a mineral water each.

'How's it going without drinking?' she asked the two pregnant women.

'Actually, the thought of alcohol makes me feel really ill,' said Amanda.

Olga agreed. 'All you have to do is imagine this little foetus swimming in a bath of vodka and you just don't do it. It's a lot easier to give up than I thought.'

There were so many items on the agenda—faithless men, devoted husbands, morning sickness, maternity wear, baby names—that it was a good hour before they got around to the matter of Nick and Poppy's cohabitation.

'It's rebound bullshit, it can't be real,' said Amanda, and Francie was grateful for the sentiment.

'Although they're pretty well suited. I've seen worse relationships last,' added Olga.

Francie thought of the ring Nick had bought Poppy and how in the five years of living with him, she had never been presented with any jewellery. Maybe it was true. There was no such thing as a commitment phobic man. There were only men who hadn't met the right woman yet. She thought of Poppy on stage in *Stupid Cupid*, prancing around with a diamond on her left hand.

'Are they still going to do their show?' she asked.

'As far as I know it's supposed to be opening on Friday night. Are you coming?' Olga had asked this before and Francie still hadn't been invited, didn't expect to be.

Amanda was thoughtful. 'I wonder if what you wrote today will make any difference to their script? I thought it was a beautiful letter, Francie. I thought it took a lot of courage. Have you really quit the paper?'

'Yeah, it's fine. It was time for me to move on anyway. I just hope it was worth it. Johnno reckons she'll never forgive me.'

Olga was in no mood to forgive either. 'That can't be the reason you wrote it, surely. You can't expect to write a couple of hundred words in a newspaper and everything's put right.' Olga was in a dark place tonight.

'Well, you tell me, Olga, what should I do?' asked Francie. Olga's lack of support was irritating, but she supposed she'd have to put it down to hormones.

'Just get on with your life. It's out of your hands and no amount of wishing or conniving or diplomacy is going to make any difference.'

'But don't you think that showing I'm sorry, apologising, counts for something?'

'For you, maybe. But in the end it's only for you, and you can't expect anything in return. If you do, you're still being dishonest.'

They had driven up a conversational cul-de-sac. Francie was too tired to argue with Olga, too wrung out to explain or defend herself. She let it go.

'I see you got the wine off the wall,' said Olga. 'Sorry about that. I guess it was hormones . . . you know.'

'I wasn't in a much better state myself,' Francie replied.

'So how's it going with . . . ?' Amanda was caught out for a name and appealed to Francie with raised eyebrows.

'Dominic. Does he know about the baby? What did he say?' Francie caught the ball in safe hands.

Olga's fingers fluttered to her necklace.

'It's sort of why I wanted to talk to you both tonight. I want you to be my baby's aunts, like a family, because . . . I'm certainly not going to have one.'

Olga looked down at her lap and her long black hair fell like a curtain. Francie and Amanda could hear her gulping down tears from behind it. 'He just doesn't want to know. He said, "I can't offer you or the baby anything right now." It was so . . .' Olga couldn't find the words to continue.

'Oh my God!' said Amanda.

'Bastard,' spat Francie.

'I can't believe I fell for it. Can't believe I was so stupid.' Olga was rummaging in her little sequinned handbag for a tissue.

'Darling one, don't be hard on yourself.' Francie was instantly kneeling in front of Olga, sweeping hair from her face and tucking it behind her ear. Her own troubles were washed away by Olga's tears. 'After all,' she said, looking up at her friend, 'a husband, a baby, a family, it's got to be the least we can ask for, surely! It wasn't so many years ago it was every woman's birthright. Now it seems like it's something we have to fight for and only the deserving ones get. We go down so many blind alleys. Look at me, five years wasted and nothing to show for it.'

'We'll be your baby's family!' Amanda declared. 'Our babies will grow up like cousins. Between me and Lachlan, Francie, your mum, Johnno and Jessie, Nick and . . .' Amanda faltered. 'Well anyway, we will be a family and we can't wait for your baby and to see you as a mother. A mother! Doesn't that sound amazing, Olga? However it happens, in whatever circumstances, you have to see it as a blessing.'

'Amanda's right,' Francie added. 'It's one thing to imagine a baby swimming in vodka, but another to imagine it being pickled in a vat of regret.'

Olga and Amanda were startled at this image and both shot a look at Francie.

'What I mean is, they say the mental state of the mother has a lot to do with the temperament of the child. Is it true? I dunno. But you've got to keep your head up, for your baby's sake.'

Olga lifted her head. 'Thanks,' she said. 'I guess I always saw myself as a single mother, if I'm honest.'

Francie and Amanda opened their mouths to protest. Olga held up her hands.

'No. No, don't! I'm too difficult, I'm too odd. I just don't fit in. You know what I'm most afraid of?' Olga regarded her companions, her long eyelashes shiny wet. 'That my baby will feel the same. That one day my child will look at me and know why it hasn't got a father. It will see me as I really am.'

Both Francie and Amanda were appalled.

'Olga, that is *so* crazy. What you *really are* is an amazing woman,' said Amanda, taking her by the shoulders.

'She's right,' Francie added. 'You're an original, Olga. You're a one-off. Talented, beautiful. You're going to be an international success. Honestly, what would you change about yourself in the hope of attracting a man? Do you really think you can be anything less than you are? And why would you want to be? The one thing I do know is that losing this married man is the best thing that's happened to you. Unless you do that there'll never be a place for you to find a man who really wants to be with you.'

There was a knock at the front door. Amanda disappeared and then reappeared at the lounge room's double doors, her eyebrows arched with surprise.

'You won't believe this, *speak of the devil* and all that—it's Nick.'

Francie gripped the armrests of her chair as if she could see a giant pothole ahead and was about to motor into it. She recalled that her last words to Nick had been 'Goodbye, I hope you have a happy life,' and that was barely three weeks ago.

He walked into the room and she was jolted by the sight of him. Shocked because she noticed something she'd never seen before. Nick Jamieson wasn't tall, lanky and elegant, as she'd always thought. He was just plain old skinny. His shoulders were hunched over and the worried look on his face made you want to ask, 'What's wrong? Are you OK?'

Francie shook her head in surprise, trying to somehow match the man she saw before her with the image she had filed in her head. And then he spoke and everything fell into place. It was Nick, after all.

'Hi. Hope I'm not disturbing you gals.'

The sound of his voice was sweet and familiar to Francie and she could feel herself surrendering to it. Would she always?

Nick stood in the middle of the room, his hands thrust deep in the pockets of his jeans. 'Ah . . . look, I'll be honest. Olga told me you'd all be here tonight and I've ambushed you. Would it be OK if I had a moment with Francie?'

Francie was still rigid in her chair. Amanda and Olga fled from the room. Nick sat on the couch opposite Francie and she regarded his long legs which finished in a pair of scuffed black boots. He rearranged his leather jacket, crossed and uncrossed his feet. He spoke to the floor.

'Uh . . . thanks for today. It meant a great deal to me, and to Poppy, that you had the guts, the grace, to write that. I'll be honest. This last week is nothing we ever wanted or imagined but I, at least, want to believe that this whole episode has been a comedy of errors, a farce, more than anything else. I'm trying to convince Poppy of that. It's true, isn't it?'

Francie was horrified that she was having to face Nick over all this. Again. She was guilty of more than he would ever know. Wishing him and Poppy dead, in her mind, a million times over.

'It's true. I'm not sure where to begin . . .' Francie's voice trailed away.

She wanted to begin by laying her head in Nick's lap and having him stroke her hair. She could smell him from where she was sitting, and every nerve ending in her body was alive and aching for the touch of him.

'You probably heard that Poppy and I are moving in together,' he mumbled. Francie focused on a very nice pink cushion with green embroidery and a matching silky fringe.

'Johnno told me. And I believe there's a ring. Congratulations.'

Nick coughed. 'It's just an early Christmas present.'

Francie didn't believe him and Nick knew she didn't. But then, Francie reminded herself, he had never been honest when it came to Poppy.

'The point is, I want to make peace with you. So we can both get on with our lives. We're going to have to be here for Olga, Amanda, Lachlan and their kids, so . . .'

It all sounded so easy. As if their little group could somehow just pick up where it had left off. Breaking bread with Poppy at the table here in Amanda's flat. A simple rearrangement of the chairs. Francie could not imagine it and didn't think Nick could be serious.

'So we should smooth things over, Nick? So you can feel good about yourself?'

Nick lay back against the couch. He covered his face with his hands. 'Oh God, don't start this again!'

'It's not as simple as you—'

Nick sat up and raised his voice to her. 'Listen! You've had your pound of flesh. You've punished me hard. Let's just get together, pronounce the last rites on this fucking thing and give it a decent burial.'

His harsh tone lit the fuse of Francie's anger. 'And should I buy front row seats for the funeral, night after night, on stage? How am I supposed to get through that? I know I haven't behaved well, but—'

'We're not doing it. It's cancelled. It's cost us a bloody fortune, everyone's disappointed. The band's devastated.'

Francie was silenced.

'It's what you wanted, isn't it? You've punished Poppy too. She's willing to just let it go. Move on. So let's just say we're all even now and make an end to it.'

He was right. There had to be an end to it. She'd seen at her mother's place what it meant when there was war without end. A cold war which went on and on until it froze everyone's hearts solid.

'Olga says you're doing some kind of therapy, and maybe I should come with you. I thought if we could talk about a few things . . . you know, salvage some kind of friendship at least. It will be Christmas soon, after all.'

Christmas! The season of goodwill to ex boyfriends and their fiancées.

Francie nodded her agreement and, after making an arrangement to meet on Wednesday night, Nick hurried away.

When they heard the front door slam Amanda and Olga peeped around the door.

'So, how was that?' Amanda was doing some weird, cheery Martha Stewart hostess impersonation. The only thing missing was a tray of chocolate muffins from the oven.

Francie almost laughed to see her. *And here's a Happy Ever After platter I prepared earlier!*

'They've cancelled their show,' Francie said, trying to keep the relief out of her voice. As if it really hadn't mattered to her that much anyway.

'Good!' declared Olga. 'I told Poppy—'

'You talked to her?'

'Yeah. I could see what it was doing to you. There will be other starring performances for Poppy. This whole thing in the media has knocked her around. I think she's grateful in the long run to just lie low for a bit.'

Francie thought, now that Poppy was real and apparently staying and not just a product of her heartbroken imaginings, that she could ask, without sounding too tragic: 'Do you like her, Olga?'

Olga was thoughtful as she twirled the shell buttons on her cardigan.

'She's, I dunno, friendly enough, but self-contained. I can't imagine getting to know her all that well. She's not really a woman's woman, if you know what I mean. I can't imagine designing any jewellery for her. I've thought about it and all I can see is fake pearls.'

'Lachlan thinks she's a wanker,' Amanda piped up.

Francie smiled. Lachlan was suddenly her new best friend.

'She's invited us over to her place on Christmas night, but Lachlan doesn't want to go.'

'Don't blame you,' said Olga quickly. 'She'd be a fucker to try and beat at charades.'

Twenty-Seven

It was about 6.30 pm on Monday evening when Francie stood on the footpath outside the front door of the Shelling Gallery in Toorak Road, Toorak. She hitched up the straps of her silky top, tightened the belt of her black satin trousers and inspected her flat silver sandals. All in order. She checked her reflection in a car window. She looked pretty and, for the first times in ages, felt it too. She might even have gone so far as to say she felt a tad irresistible.

Stepping through the doorway and scanning the room for anyone she knew, Francie saw a crowd standing in small groups of three or four. Clutching drinks, they were deep in murmured conversation. It was an interesting gathering—some local 'it' girls in strappy sequinned dresses and high heels, a few boho types in tatty jeans and T-shirts, and a smattering of older art lovers decked out in expensive suits and impressive pearls.

And then there were the photographers—Francie could tell which ones they were from the way they stood. Their legs were planted firmly apart and arms folded manfully across their chests, nursing bottles of beer. Confident and sexy. Happily, Francie didn't recognise a single person.

She looked at the image on her invitation—a newborn baby in the arms of an anonymous camouflaged soldier—and still thought she'd like to get to know the man who'd taken this photograph.

Here was her chance. Karl Johansson appeared from the crowd, smiling and holding out his hand in greeting. Once again Francie was impressed at the sight of him. He was tall, broad-chested, with a tanned face and shiny mid-brown hair. His eyes sparkled like dark opals set in a sandy cliff. She took his hand and was even more thrilled to feel its warm firmness.

'Hey, hey, hey, Francie! Glad you could come.' Karl beamed at her, and she remembered that whenever he did that she felt her face get hot, as if he was turning on an intense spotlight.

'I didn't think you'd remember. I've been away shooting a story on some islands off Tasmania for a couple of weeks and only got back this morning.'

Francie couldn't believe her good luck. He couldn't possibly know of her reputation as a crazed undie-slasher! She turned her charm dial up to maximum.

'Hello, Karl! Of course I remembered. I've had this invitation pinned to my wall. I wanted to see what else you've been up to.' She smiled winningly and then thought to take her hand back.

Karl fetched drinks for them both and steered Francie around the room with his large hand in the small of her back. The photographs were a bloody scrapbook from the world's war zones—Iraq, Afghanistan, Eritrea, the Congo, East Timor. They were a matter-of-fact record of horrifying carnage. Windows on an unimaginable world of deprivation, poverty and desolation where military might levelled even the most humble of human endeavours.

Francie was stunned. There were a few images which allowed her to claw back some vestige of hope for humankind. Glimpses of undimmed personal pride to be found in the corner of a marketplace or around a campfire. Places where the flames of love and kindness were rekindled from the merest scraps of dignity.

Karl spoke about each one. He had been here and there, seen this and that, and all the while he talked Francie could feel nothing but shame for herself and her pathetic preoccupations.

It's a battlefield out there, baby! Hah!

She escaped the chatter of the room and sat outside the gallery on a concrete planter box by the side of the road, nursing a glass of wine and watching the traffic. She could feel her emotional landscape moving. Shifting like tectonic plates. New islands thrown up. Old continents submerged. She knew the navigation of this unfamiliar place would be a challenge, yet she was keen to set sail for the journey.

Karl sat down next to her and rested his hand on her back. Cars and taxis whizzed by. People hurried past laden with Christmas shopping. It was the usual pre-holiday scene, but Francie could see Karl was taking it all in appreciatively.

'It's good to be home,' he said. 'You go away to these hellholes and you get caught up in the drama, but the old familiar banalities of sending out Christmas cards . . . that's what you dream of while you're away. Funnily enough, you come home and you have to fight your way back to be a part of even the most mundane happenings. You realise you're not the same person you were before you went away, but you can't actually put your finger on how you've changed. Hopefully, you're wiser. God knows, you're older.'

He rested a heavy hand on Francie's thigh for a moment. Squeezed playfully.

'So come and meet some of my favourite mundane friends,' he whispered.

Karl took Francie firmly by the elbow and steered her through the crowd.

'Francie, I'd like you to meet Adam, my ex brother-in-law.'

'Do brothers-in-law become exes too, along with the wife?' Adam raised his eyebrows.

'Well yes, unless I marry your other sister.'

'No way! I'm not being groomsman at another one of your ill-fated weddings. Once was enough!' Adam teased.

So, that was that mystery solved at least. After a couple more hours of chatting with people who had no idea who she was, Francie was feeling buoyant. She was looking into the future. Seeing the person she would be when she could finally shake off her past. She liked this new confident and relaxed Francis Sheila McKenzie, and hoped she would see more of her.

And she also hoped she would be viewing more of Karl. By the way he was shepherding her through the evening, he was obviously feeling the same. When his hand wasn't on her back it was grazing her arm or lightly touching her elbow. As the crowd thinned out there didn't seem to be any doubt that Francie would be staying.

When at last there were only about half a dozen people in the room, a venue for dinner was discussed. And, before Francie knew it, she had Karl in her car—his head was nudging the roof—and she was heading for a restaurant across the Yarra River.

For the first time since she and Nick broke up, Francie drove past their old street in Richmond and didn't even notice. But she did reflect that the last time she'd had a man in her car it was Dave and they'd both reeked of vomit. The smell had lingered, and she'd scrubbed the floor and sprayed half a pump pack of vanilla-scented fridge cleaner on it. Surely Karl couldn't smell it now? Could he? She drove faster so he wouldn't notice. Which was obviously a stupid idea when she thought about it some more, so she slowed and wound down the windows instead. Then she wound the windows up again. She wanted to smell Karl. Aaarrgh! The scent of him was driving her crazy.

They were at some cute ethnic place which was all funky lamps and blackboards and mismatched chairs. Dinner went by in a hormonal haze. She was sitting beside Karl and could feel the heat coming off his thigh next to hers under the table. His friends were an interesting bunch—writers, photographers, artists. Thankfully no-one she knew from the *Press* was there, at least no-one who recognised her. What did they talk about? She scarcely noticed. What did Francie eat? No idea. She shovelled in some kind of sustenance and chatted amiably, but could not take her eyes off Karl. It was as if her mind was in neutral but her sexometer was flat out. Red-lining.

It was inevitable they'd sleep together. From the moment she'd first seen Karl this evening Francie knew she would bed him. After all, he'd been a fantasy object for her for a long time and, as it transpired, he had been watching her as well. They'd already put in almost a year's worth of foreplay—even if half of it was when Francie was with Nick. But what Francie hadn't counted on was the conversation she would have to navigate before her head hit the pillow. By the time they were alone at the table, it was late.

'So . . . you know that my wife and I are going to be divorced,' he said.

Francie was surprised at this—after all, it was breaking the cardinal rule she had been informed of by her single friends: 'Never, ever, EVER talk about your past relationships on a first date!'

'But why not?'

'YOU DO NOT WANT A SYMPATHY FUCK!' they had emphasised in capital letters.

But again, Francie thought *why not*? If two heartbroken individuals came together to find solace through sublime sex, surely that should be a blessing?

'I'm on the rebound too,' she ventured. 'Come on, you first. What happened?'

Karl sat back and took his time to relate his story. Francie could tell that this was some new policy of his—to lay all his cards on the table and see if she was scared off.

'We were married for about six years. We started out great, obviously. Jen supported me financially while I was trying to make a living from my art photography. Which was wonderful of her, I know that. But, to be honest, that was part of the deal we had. As soon as I was on my feet it was going to be her turn. Then I got the job at the *Press* and things were easier.'

Francie nodded. It was not unlike her scenario with Nick.

'The thing was that the more independent and successful I became, the more she couldn't handle it. It was like the more confidence I got, the more she lost hers. Then I had the chance to go away on assignment. I know I was away a lot and that it was hard for her, but to be honest? I think the things I was experiencing were always a part of my destiny. And while I didn't expect they were part of hers, I thought she would see that, for me, it was inevitable one day I would travel this path.

'Then it was like she started to sabotage me. She wouldn't push herself at work—she's a graphic designer—and instead started this whole domestic routine. Making elaborate dinners on nights when she knew I had to pack my stuff to leave. Booking holidays she knew I couldn't go on.'

Francie was listening to this intently and knew she was hearing her own story from a new perspective.

'She started talking about having kids all the time. Which was, you know, fine, but her timing was off. We'd always agreed it would happen later. It was weird.

'And I tried to tell her I needed more space—I know, that old cliché—but she just thought I didn't love her anymore. She just kept asking "Do you love me? Do you love me? Do you love me?" to the point where one day I just thought: "No, I don't". And I honestly don't know how that happened. I did love Jen, very much. But she was a different person somehow . . . I don't know why I'm telling you all this.'

Francie didn't need to ask what happened next because she could guess. He had started to have affairs.

'So I . . . and this is the bit I'm not proud of, not proud of at all . . . I started to have affairs. I'm sure Gabby told you. It was the coward's way out, but every time I thought about telling Jen I wanted to leave I could see it would kill her. Like every man ever on the face of the earth, I would rather have set myself on fire than tell her I wanted to leave. So . . .'

Francie filled in the next bit. 'So you just left.'

Karl looked at her. 'Yeah. Pathetic, isn't it? Emotionally retarded.'

'Uh-huh.' Francie toyed with her empty coffee cup.

'The thing is,' Karl continued, 'I still really love her, I always will, but I have learned something. And that's that the next time I get involved it will be with a woman who's more independent. Who has her own path and is passionate about it. I don't want to be worshipped like I'm some kind of religion. I've seen what religion does to people.

'Not that I'm in a hurry, I've got a bit of sorting out to do. So that's me, at the age of thirty-four, just learning to be "me", I guess, just finding out . . .' He shrugged. 'Ah, shit! Who knows . . . ?'

Francie realised that Karl's speech was the one she would never hear from Nick. But the bit about him learning to be by himself? That was a speech Poppy would never hear from Nick either.

'So . . . how about you?'

There didn't seem to be any point in going through the whole situation, since Karl had already said it all. But there were perhaps a couple of things worth saying.

'Same sort of stuff.' She waved her hand casually. 'Too young to get involved and we grew out of each other. I suppose I have to learn to be independent too. Learn to love myself. Which is a ridiculous thing to learn at my age. It seems that a lot of people of our generation are trying to learn the same thing, but we still want to be in a relationship—to be *in love*, all that—so it's not easy. Do you think our parents had to learn this stuff?'

'Like I said, who knows?' Karl shrugged. 'Maybe it's something you have to work on your whole life and maybe, in the end, being independent is totally overrated.'

'It could be. It could be absolutely overrated.' Francie fell silent.

'So, do you think we could learn to be by ourselves by being together at my place tonight?' Karl leaned forward and smiled one of his devastating smiles.

Francie smiled back. 'Hmm. I think a little bit of togetherness could be just what we need . . . in a totally non co-dependent way, of course.'

'Oh yeah, totally.'

'It could be something we just did for ourselves—together.'

'Absolutely!'

Francie and Karl threw some money on the table and left.

�֍

His flat was barely furnished: the dead giveaway of the newly single man. His television was on the floor in the main room. He had a two-seater sofa, a kitchen table, no chairs, and a bookcase made from stolen milk crates and a plank of wood stacked with expensive art books. His bedroom was equally sparse. Just a mattress on the floor covered with pristine white sheets. Dozens of framed photographs and piles of camera equipment leaned against one wall. His clothes were still in a suitcase on the floor.

In the end it was just as well there was nothing hanging on the walls because Francie spent a good part of the night bouncing off them. Karl was a phenomenon in the bedroom. And the kitchen. And the bathroom.

They went for it. Karl was monosyllabic. 'Come here. Sit down. Yes, now. Very good. Once more. Bend over. Like that. More please. That's great. Oh, yes!' He didn't seem to have any brain cells left over to form coherent sentences. His whole mind and body were dedicated to the task of taking Francie right over the edge. Everything Francie wanted was on offer, lots more she hadn't ever thought of, and as much of it as she could stand.

There was no way back to fantasies about Nick's silent ministrations after this. As for Dave? Francie was having trouble bringing him into focus as well. She knew that every time she thought about sex from now on, the image of Karl's muscled chest, his smooth back and his perfect, hard, urgent dick would be in her face. Like it was now. She reached out for him and did exactly as she was told.

Licked and fucked, caressed and kissed, bitten and bruised, sated and exhausted, Francie eventually slid into sleep at about 3 am, only to have another of Karl's huge erections nudge her awake a couple of hours later.

This time his performance brought the house down. If Francie hadn't been so weak in the knees she would have stood and applauded.

Twenty-Eight

'First, I have to say that it's quite surprising you've come here together. On paper your separation doesn't look too messy. You're young. You have no property together and no children. There's nothing to divide.'

Nothing but my heart.

'But you are both obviously stuck and looking for some answers from each other. Before we go on, I want to warn you that you shouldn't expect to get them tonight. This is just one session. You're both here, as you've told me, looking for some kind of completion and peace. So, let's start by asking what you want to hear from each other. Perhaps you could go first, Nick, because, as Francie told me, you're the one who thought this could be a good idea.'

Nick was studying Faith's walls and shifting uneasily. He caught Francie looking at him and gave her a tight smile. No doubt he was reflecting on exactly what madness had led him to be here tonight. Everything about the room—the soft light, the lavender aromatherapy candle, the box of tissues on the table—spoke of intimacy. This would not be pleasant.

He crossed his legs, folded his arms over his chest, coughed and sat forward as though he was wearing horse blinkers. As though Francie wasn't in the room.

'I'm only here because I want to make sure Francie is OK. I'm worried about her. I don't want to feel that I'm responsible for her happiness in the future. I've never wanted that. I never want to be responsible for anyone's happiness . . . or otherwise.'

Faith nodded. 'Al . . . ri . . . ght,' she drew the word out slowly. 'That's very clear. I will say I think there are some problems with that attitude, but you're not here for therapy with me. So, Francie, what do you want to hear from Nick?'

Francie had been sneaking glances at Nick's profile against the light of the amber shaded lamp. She had loved looking at that profile. She'd always thought of his fine, straight nose and full mouth as being poetic. Profoundly and perfectly composed. His long hands were lyrical and expressive of the emotion he kept inside. That's the story she'd invented for him anyway. Tonight, though, and it might only have been a trick of the half-light, he seemed to be a small boy, diminished somehow. She was once more torn between love and punishment.

'I want to hear from Nick why he stopped loving me. He's never told me. He's never told me anything. In fact, looking back, I'm not even sure I know why he loved me in the first place—'

Faith held her hand up in an attempt to interrupt. Francie was admonished by the loud clanking of Indian clay bangles, but she persisted.

'Doesn't the fact that I gave up so much for him, worked so hard to make him a home, mean anything?'

'Francie, stop!' Faith's voice was sharp. 'We are not here to go over old ground with Nick. This is not about looking back, it's about going forward, and—'

'No! I want to answer that!' Nick exclaimed. 'I never asked her to give up anything for me. She's the one who always gave up everything. I know I came before everything—her friends, her family, career. She always told me that. But I didn't want to be the person she gave up everything for. I never asked for it. I always thought she was waiting for me to turn into someone who would make all the sacrifice worthwhile. I don't know if I can ever be that person.

'She wanted too much. I always felt that whatever I did was never quite right, or not enough, or . . . she could never let things just *be*.'

Faith had given in, taken the attitude of Buddha, sitting back, letting the argument roll. Francie was indignant. What Nick was saying was unfair! She had to defend herself. She shook her head, trying to comprehend. She shifted to the front of her chair.

'Just *be*? What do you mean just *BE*? Our relationship wasn't one of your dumb trust exercises at the theatre, Nick! It wasn't acting. It was real!'

Now Nick turned to Francie. His voice was thin and ragged at the edges. 'Come on! There was a point when we both knew it wasn't going to work, but you didn't want to talk. You kept on booking holidays, organising dinner parties, bringing home fucking . . . sorry . . . furniture . . .' Nick hesitated, looked at Faith, and Francie saw her chance.

'I only did all that stuff because I knew *you* wouldn't. You never took the initiative. Ever!'

'And why would I? Because I knew it would never be up to the standard of perfection you wanted. I watched you rearrange every plate I put on a shelf, every flower I ever put into a vase, every bit of furniture, all the paintings on the walls. You even remade the bed after I made it! I knew that whatever I did, it would never be good enough. You're like my mother. Demanding, smothering, rescuing. What did you see in me? What did you *want*?'

This was too much for Francie. *She was like his mother?* He would be accusing her of sewing name tags in the back of his jumpers next! He wouldn't have the last word in front of Faith. Francie was paying for this session, after all. Faith was on her side, not Nick's.

'Well, you've ended up being like *my* father. Just fucking off with no explanation and leaving me to pick up the pieces!'

So there it was. They were actor and writer, both reliving some B-grade script written in childhood. They sat in silence, breathing deeply. Faith held up her hands, as if to call them to prayer. A moment to reflect. Francie let the ribbon of years unravel.

There was a warm early summer afternoon once—somewhere in the country—when they had parked their car on the side of the road and waded through a wheat field. The supple stalks supporting pregnant pearly heads of grain bent and slapped at their thighs as they pushed through a ripening tide. They had thrown themselves on the ground and, surrounded by a fortress of green, lain hand in hand looking up at a blue sky appliquéd with white clouds.

It was just him and her in that small space which would never again be made on the face of the earth. Safe from the past. Cast in a future they had both long dreamed of. She had a fanciful notion they were Adam and Eve that day, remaking the world from nothing but grass and sky and clouds and love.

Francie remembered the colours of him—tanned skin, brown eyes—against the green-stemmed walls. He had lifted her cotton top and kissed her warm skin from neck to breast to navel.

'I love you, Francie,' he had murmured. 'I love you with all my heart and soul. There will never be anyone for me but you.'

'I love you too, Nick. I've wished for you my whole life. It's as if I wished you true. I will never stop loving you.'

She had wrapped her legs around him and pulled him into her. Their bodies made a rainbow of pleasure, arching from rich dry earth to endless sky and back to earth again.

And then Francie was there sitting stiffly in the blue chair in the front room of Faith and John-Pierre Treloar, Relationship Counsellors, contemplating the bitter harvest of that wheat field.

Faith just let them think about it all, until she finally spoke in the calm, professional tone familiar to Francie. All emotion gone, just pure reason.

'You know, so many of us who have been abandoned, rejected, unloved or over-controlled as children, choose a partner who is like a ghost from our past. And then we set out to relive everything we know.'

Francie and Nick fidgeted in their chairs as if they were in front of the headmistress.

'When you came together, you recognised something in each other, you didn't know what exactly, but something which spoke to the other. I really believe you are both loving people and came together not to hurt each other, but to heal each other.

'But truly, Francie, Nick, the healing has to be done within your own hearts. This break-up? It actually is an opportunity— don't you say a word, Francie! It is a chance to rewrite your personal scripts. To look back and see the way your family life shaped you, so that next time you go into a relationship you can do it better and find lasting happiness. So, instead of blaming each other for what happened during the past five years, and punishing each other for the way it ended, why don't you thank each other for the time you had together?'

Nick looked at the ceiling. Francie checked out the carpet.

'Say *thank you* for being allowed to make mistakes. *Thank you* for being able to discover what you need to know so you don't have to make the same mistakes again.'

Faith turned to Nick.

'I asked you before what you wanted to hear from Francie. Instead, let's try it the other way. What would you like to *say* to Francie?'

Francie heard the creaking of Nick's leather jacket as he tugged at it. She heard him cough and inhale.

'Francie . . .' he began, still looking at Faith.

'She's just there, Nick. In the chair next to you.'

Francie turned to meet his eyes. The ones she had loved to see across the pillow every morning. The eyes she had secretly congratulated herself for capturing and holding fast for so long.

He reached out his hands. Francie took them and felt them slim and hard in hers, the warmth gone. She understood they belonged to someone else now.

'I'd like to say . . . First, that I'm sorry for the way this ended up. I didn't mean it to happen like it did. You have to believe me, there was no way I—'

'Keep going forward, Nick,' Faith steered him back on course.

'Second, I really, really did love you. I mean, I still do. I think about you so much. You probably think I've forgotten everything, but I haven't. Sometimes I wake up in the night and wonder where you are. And then I remember and I go back to sleep and you're there in my dreams.

'I was always so proud of being with you. Whenever we went anywhere I was never disappointed that I was with you. You were my girl.

'We learned a lot together and I will never, ever forget you. Thank you for everything you did for me. Thank you for . . . letting me go.'

Nick's chin dropped to his chest. 'Oh God, Francie! I really miss you.' And then he cried.

Francie had to let go of his hands because she was crying too. The tears were streaming down her face, her neck and splashing into her cleavage. But this time the tears didn't feel like the others she'd shed in Faith's room. Those had been hot, sour, acidic and had scoured her cheeks. This time her tears felt cool and clean, like spring water. She was bathing in them. Francie wiped her eyes with the backs of her hands. She flapped the moisture from her fingers, sniffed, wiped some more and the tears kept coming.

'Oh God! Oh God! Nick! Bloody hell! Hah! I'll stop, I'll stop, because I want to say something that . . . something you'll remember. Aaargh! Stop!'

She tore a handful of tissues from the box on the table and pushed them into her eyes. She sniffed, dried her neck and chest and sat up straight.

'Phew! Oh God! This is the hardest thing. It really is so, so hard! I just want to say . . .'

Nick raised his head and Francie could hear his breath catching in his chest, which was shuddering like a child's. She couldn't remember ever seeing him cry like this. Every instinct told her she should hold him to her breast. Smooth the hair from his forehead, dry his tears and make the hurt stop. She should cradle him. Croon *there, there* and *there, there* again. But she could see now that that's what she had always done, and it wasn't how she wanted to take her leave.

On a resolute outward breath she began. 'Nick. You are such a fine and sweet and good man. I wish I could have said goodbye gracefully. I wish . . . I wish that with all my heart.

'I can see now that our love was never going to last the distance, not the way it was. But honestly, I wouldn't have missed a minute of it for the world. You have been my darling, darling love.

'And you're wrong, you know, because I'm not letting you go. Not all of you. I'm keeping a part of you no-one will ever have. It's mine, for always.

'That time in our lives will never come again. I'm glad I shared it with you. I'll miss you too. Thank you for loving me, Nicky. Thank you for allowing me to love you. Be happy. I love you too.'

Francie and Nick both stood. They walked into each other's arms. She knew this was the last time they would hold each other like this. She rested her head on that familiar place—her ear on his heart. And in turn Nick posed in his lover's embrace, his chin on her blonde head. His arm—both arms tonight—were around her. She wished her dearest love a silent farewell.

✵

That night Francie dreamed she was Alice in Wonderland. She was crammed into a tiny gingerbread house. Its roof tiles were traced with snowy icing and studded with brightly coloured sweets.

Francie had one leg sticking out through the front door and one arm up the chimney. She tried to wriggle free but found she was stuck fast. How had she got inside, she wondered.

Through a tiny window just at eye level she could see into another room, where a long table was set with a tempting afternoon tea of fairy cakes with pink icing and a tall jug of lemonade.

Nick and Poppy walked into the room in their party clothes and sat down at two small chairs tied with balloons. She watched as they giggled together, shared their feast and chased each other around the table. They were happy and carefree and she smiled to see them. She couldn't help but feel she had stumbled into the wrong fairytale.

Then she looked into the room on the other side of her and could see an enchanted mirror. *Tell me what you see, Francie. Tell me why you love you?*

'I'm beautiful,' Francie replied, shifting her body to ease the cramp in her legs. 'I'm happy and I have nice hair.'

Sometime in the middle of the night Francie woke with a start. She was feeling thirsty and groped for the glass of water on the bedside table.

Her first thought was that it was almost Christmas and she should make an appointment with her hairdresser. Her second thought was that she was too big to fit in the Nick and Poppy fairytale house anymore.

Next morning Francie got out of bed and walked, completely unaided, down the hallway towards a bright light, the smell of buttered toast and the sound of laughter.

Acknowledgements

I can't quite believe I've been given the opportunity to write a second novel.

My eternal thanks again to my two best cheerleaders—publisher Richard Walsh and my agent Hilary Linstead. A writer couldn't wish for better encouragement, constructive criticism, enthusiasm and support.

Thanks too to my dearest little mascots, Marley and Maeve, who give Mum all the love she needs to feel happy and secure in this life.

The team at Allen & Unwin have again come through for me magnificently and I offer my heartfelt gratitude to Annette Barlow, Christa Munns and Jo Jarrah for their attention to detail and unfailing professionalism.

To all my friends who have embraced my literary endeavours with such open-hearted goodwill, I am in your debt. And, to Patrick C, a special thanks for being there and watching me grow up. You are still in my heart and dreams.

Finally, to the 'uncarved block', my husband Brendan, I am loving writing the Big Story with you day after day.